THE LINCOLN MOON

The Lincoln Moon

BASED ON CHARACTERS AND EVENTS FROM THE PEOPLE V. ARMSTRONG

MICHAEL PRICE NELSON

ISBN 978-1-7350297-1-9 (E-Book Edition)
ISBN 978-1-7350297-0-2 (Paperback Edition)

Publisher's Cataloging-in-Publication Data
Provided by Five Rainbows Cataloging Service

Names: Nelson, Michael Price, 1950- author.
Title: The Lincoln moon / Michael Price Nelson.
Description: Long Beach, CA : Michael Price Nelson, 2020.
Identifiers: LCCN 2020912806 (print) | ISBN 978-1-7350297-0-2 (paperback) | ISBN 978-1-7350297-1-9 (ebook)
Subjects: LCSH: Farm life—Fiction. | Murder—Fiction. | Lincoln, Abraham, 1809-1865—Fiction. | Farm life—Fiction. | Illinois—Fiction. | BISAC: FICTION / Historical / General. | FICTION / Small Town & Rural. | GSAFD: Historical fiction.
Classification: LCC PS3614.E47 L56 2020 (print) | LCC PS3614.E47 (ebook) | DDC 813/.6—dc23.

Library of Congress Control Number: 2020912806
Nelson, Michael Price
The Lincoln Moon by Michael Price Nelson

Front cover image by: Think, Create, Connect
Book design by: Deliberate Page

Printed and bound in the United States of America
First printing September 2020

Published by Six Swans Press
For permission to reproduce or record any part of this book, contact:
nelson.artsmarketing@gmail.com

Visit www.michaelpricenelson.com

This one's for Dale

If you wish to be a lawyer, attach no consequence to the place you are in, or the person you are with; but get books, sit down anywhere, and go to reading for yourself. That will make a lawyer of you quicker than any other way.

– A. Lincoln, 1858

Prologue

THERE PROBABLY ISN'T A FAMILY in the world without a story to tell. Often, we keep our stories to ourselves, recounting them only at family gatherings, passing them along like our own personal folklore from generation to generation. After all, who among us doesn't like to hear about the time Uncle Nate was bushwhacked by outlaws, or how Grandma met Grandpa at the county fair, or of Aunt Pamela's notorious adventures on the vaudeville stage?

Other family stories, the more significant ones, are those that make a difference not only in our own lives but in the lives of others. These are the ones we share with outsiders, a wider circle of friends, and even the public. Stories, after all, help define us, which is why we tell them in the first place, I suppose.

My family story is about the murder of James Preston Metzker and his accused murderer, William "Duff" Armstrong, who was my brother. Duff was the only suspect in the crime, and to most folks at the time, that was enough to hang him. But my Ma and Pa knew he was innocent, and proving that in court became a matter of life-and-death for our family.

In the years since, the case has become famous, largely because our defense attorney was Abraham Lincoln in the years when he was still practicing law. It was during Duff's trial in 1858 that Mr. Lincoln established a legal precedent which forever changed the rule of law.

Mr. Lincoln adored my mother and father. He knew them fresh out of Kentucky when he was just nineteen years old, and was newly arrived in the tiny frontier settlement of New Salem, Illinois. He was without a home when they took him in, but they made him part of their family, and he grew to love them like his own kin. Thirty years later, when they needed him most, he literally rode to their rescue.

The world of 1858 was quite different from the one in which we live today. There was no electricity, no horseless carriage, no radio. But there was slavery, and it was the scourge of the nation.

When the Dred Scott Decision in 1857 denied the rights of the Constitution to enslaved Negroes, the festering anger surrounding slavery was like a boil that had finally been lanced.

Arguments over its morality, that had primarily been voiced in legislatures, oozed forth into the public square, spilling over into homes, and finally onto blood-soaked battlefields.

As a child, I knew little of slavery. I had never met a Negro slave, nor did I know anyone who enslaved them. I didn't quite understand what slavery, as an institution, was. I just knew that it made folks mad. Still, slavery seeped in to my life, and became part of the fabric of my existence in ways I could not fathom nor foresee, and it is now part of my story.

While the history of Preston Metzker's murder has been reported accurately by historians, certain facts were known only to my family and we chose to keep these to ourselves. But since most of the key participants, including my dear brother Duff, have long since returned to their Maker, and because my own time here grows shorter, it seems a fitting time to finally tell my family's story.

Although I was but nine years old at the time of the trial, in this account I have tried to tell things truthfully and to the best of my recollection in the hope that it honors the memory of all who lived it.

Truman J. Armstrong, Esq.
Chicago, Illinois
January 1915

One

DUFF WAS MY HERO, SIMPLE as that. His real name was William Duff Armstrong, but for as long as I can remember, everybody called him Duff. Ma told me he was a sweet baby but a rambunctious toddler, always giving her the frights, as she called them. But from an early age, he knew my parents would forgive his mishaps once he flashed his winning smile at them. When he was old enough, he labored alongside Pa in the fields, eventually assuming a full share of the farm's burdens. My father said he didn't know what he'd ever do without him.

Duff was ten years older than me. When I finally came along, our mother explained it as God's will. She called me her "little prize."

"Yeah, the booby prize," Duff used to say.

We lived with our parents, Jack and Hannah Armstrong, on a little farm located in central Illinois. The tract of land had been awarded to my great grandfather, Frederick Joshua Armstrong, for his military service in the War of 1812. At the time he took possession, it was in still-unsettled Illinois Territory.

It was beautiful country with rich black soil and green grassy meadows, perfect for farming, with plenty of leafy green forests to allow for hunting and trapping. The land's virgin beauty was enough to feed a man's soul as well as his family, and soon little farms dotted the landscape and a community took root. They called it Cass County after one of the original settlers.

Our cozy little farmhouse and barn were built right alongside the creek that ran through our land because, for farmers especially, a good water source could mean all the difference between sustenance and starvation. In the spring, the water would surge to the top of its banks. In summer, it was liable to slow, depending on the heat or how much rainfall we had. Sometimes, it would become a mere trickle, leaving many farmers somewhere between life and death, which is why they called it Purgatory Creek.

Ever since Pa had taken the farm over from his father, he had planted corn and other crops, and raised just enough livestock to feed us. It wasn't a huge money-making concern, our farm, but it was my father's little piece of heaven.

Duff was everything I wasn't. He knew how to ride bareback, sink a fence post, shimmy up a tree, and balance bales of hay over his head with just one arm. Tall and muscular, he earned his golden tan and sinewy build from hours of plowing fields, splitting logs, and tending livestock. He had inherited our Ma's large blue eyes and Pa's devil-may-care grin, and his blond hair stubbornly insisted on tumbling over his brow. "Like a sheepdog," Ma bemoaned. She was always after him to comb it back, but it seemed to have a mind of its own.

I was small for my age, with curly red hair. I could scarcely lift Suzy, my large golden farm mutt, let alone a bale of hay. I had pale skin that burned easily in the sun and freckles sprinkled across my nose like a bad case of measles. Ma called them sun drops. Pa said they were more like polka dots. But as in most things, I tended to believe Duff, who teased me that they were just plain ugly.

"Aw, don't fret 'em," Duff told me when he saw my face fall. "All the gals will go nuts for 'em!"

I was not yet at an age to like girls, but I did like animals. Chickens especially, and our white laying hen Marianne in particular, probably because I had raised her myself from a fluffy yellow chick. Having watched her grow, I was unusually over-protective of her, which led to problems.

My folks, you see, saw livestock as an important part of their livelihood. I, however, saw them as pets. I named every last one, talked to them on a regular basis, and took it to heart when one of them had to be given up for dinner or sold at market. I would cry at their loss, and this flustered Pa. Thinking I'd be a farmer like him, he kept trying to drill the sensibilities of farm life into my young brain.

"They're just critters, dumb livestock," he would tell me over and over and over. "They don't have feelings like you or me. They're beasts of burden and meant to be slaughtered."

But it was no use. The tears came just the same. I was loyal to my pets and Pa just couldn't understand it.

After my daily chores were done, Ma was teaching me to read, as her father had taught her. There was no organized schoolhouse in the county yet, and she was determined that her children would not be illiterate. I learned quickly, too, much faster than Duff, she told me. Like most homes in those days, however, we didn't have many books, only the Bible, a few worn-out McGuffey's Readers, and *The Old Farmer's Almanac.* As for the "Good Book," as Pa called it, I didn't understand much other than the few stories Ma read to me. But the almanac thoroughly captured my imagination. I had never seen an ocean, but I tried to picture the tides going in and out on faraway sandy shores, as the almanac described. I prized its many tables that listed phases of the moon, solstices, first frosts, and spring rains. I relished the book's practical advice (*Potatoes are best planted during the full moon on Good Fridays*) and delighted in its humor (*'Put an egg in your shoe and beat it,' said the baker to the traveling salesman*). I read the almanac from cover to cover and when done, I'd start over, often discovering something new that I had overlooked in my previous trip through its pages.

My mother fed my interest in reading by bringing home dime novels purchased from the General Store. I loved them. She bought me mostly fairy tales, so I learned of giants and elves and knights and their fair ladies and I relished reading them over and over again.

My love of reading, of course, provided another chance for Duff to unmercifully tease me. He said if I wasn't careful, I'd soon be wearing glasses and the gals wouldn't like that, and then I'd end up alone and miserable. In all seriousness, I informed him I didn't care because any gal I liked would have to like books as well, and if she didn't, she "might as well go flyin' off a cliff."

"Just wait," he warned me. "That'll change one of these days, Scrump!"

Scrump. That was my nickname. I was actually baptized Truman Joshua, after a distant relative who had fought in the American Revolution, and I never much cared for the name. But Duff took care of that. He used to sneak into the neighbor's orchard with other boys to pilfer apples, which folks called "scrumping apples."

On the day I was born, Duff said my wrinkled red face and bright orange hair made me look like a "scrumped apple." The name stuck, and from then on, everybody called me Scrump.

Duff was my best friend. In the winters, he taught me how to sled, throw a snowball, and make angels in the snow. On spring days, when the planting schedule allowed, he took me into the woods and taught me to climb trees. And in summertime, we'd spend lazy afternoons on a nearby lake, where he taught me to swim and fish.

A real prankster, Duff was always getting into something. Like on the day Pa asked him to climb the roof of our barn to install the weathervane. Pa had purchased it from the General Store. As Duff, who was born with the agility of a monkey, rushed to climb the barn roof and install it, we all gathered to watch the spectacle.

My mother was holding me by the hand, I recall, while Duff skillfully shimmied up the rainspout and hoisted himself atop the roof. With an impish grin, he ran to the peak and walked precariously along it, wielding the weathervane like a circus performer uses a pole on a tightrope. More than once he pretended to be on the verge of losing his balance, causing Ma to scream so loudly that he did it again and again just to elicit more screams.

"Get to work, ya big ham!" Pa yelled up at him, shaking his head with disgust.

Duff grabbed a hammer and screwdriver from his overalls, twirled them like six-shooters, and deftly mounted the weathervane to the peak of the barn. Then, sliding down the sloping roof by the seat of his britches, he propelled himself off the eave with a mighty leap and sailed gracefully into the air before landing safe and sound in a fluffy haystack. That was the day I knew I wanted to be just like Duff.

"That was the day I got my first grey hair," Ma said in later years.

As the almanac had accurately predicted, the spring of 1857 arrived right on schedule and the morning of the equinox was bathed in warm sun as I awoke to the proud crowing of One-Eyed Phineas. Phineas was our rooster, my father's prized show cock whose tail plumage shimmered in dark blues, greens, and reds. With his beady black eye glaring out from under a floppy red comb and his sharp hooked beak, he always looked like he was scowling. In fact, I think he always was.

He was the meanest bird in the state of Illinois, and Pa had hoped to capitalize on him by entering him in cockfights. He won a couple of fat purses, too, but his fighting career came to an abrupt end when Pa brought him home one day all beaten and battered and missing one eye. His formerly proud and erect red comb was now broken and flopped sadly to one side. My mother was disgusted.

"Yeah, but you should've seen the other bird," Pa laughed, and after that our rooster was forever dubbed One-Eyed Phineas.

Phineas's crowing made me stumble sleepy-eyed out of my bed. I dressed and headed down to tend the chickens with Suzy behind me, merrily swinging her tail as usual. That was my job, you see, to feed them, clean the chicken coop, and gather the eggs. After collecting the eggs into my basket, I unexpectedly came upon One-Eyed Phineas, who was intent on doing what a rooster is wont to do, mounting a hen. Too young to realize this, however, I mistakenly assumed he was attacking my beloved pet Marianne and I rushed to rescue her.

Incensed, I grabbed a stick and chased Phineas all about the coop, his wings flapping wildly. But just as I had him cornered, his single black eye locked in on my two green ones, and he angrily shook the wattles under his beak at me. Before I knew what was happening, he flew right into me, his sharp spurs piercing my denim overalls all the way through to my flesh. I let loose a blood curdling howl and Suzy barked wildly. The other fowl furiously fussed and flapped, causing a torrent of dust and feathers to swirl about like a tornado. I wasn't done yet, however. I took my stick and was about to get one good whack at that wicked devil when a pair of powerful arms grabbed me from behind and pulled me out the door of the coop.

"What the Sam Hill are you doing?"

It was Duff, red-faced and angry.

"How many times do I have to tell you? Stay away from that crazy rooster. He's mean! You're going to get hurt!"

Angrily, I explained that One-Eyed Phineas had been attacking Marianne.

"What a dope! He weren't attacking her, Scrump. He was mounting her."

I stared blankly at him.

"Come on, little brother. You seen animals breed before. Where do you think chickens come from, anyway?"

"They just pop out of eggs, I figure."

He rolled his eyes. "I'll explain it to you later. Better get inside. Ma's waiting breakfast for us."

The kitchen greeted us with the skillet smells of sizzling bacon and fried eggs. Pa sat impatiently drubbing his fingers on the table.

"Sorry we're late," announced Duff.

Duff and I went to slip into our usual chairs.

"Scrump," said Ma, "I think you should give us the blessing this morning."

"Me? I ain't never said no blessing before."

"Just say what's in your heart. Give it a try."

I sighed. I hated when she sprang things like this on me. I bowed my head and struggled for words, any words to come out of my mouth, let alone my heart.

"Dear God... Thanks for grub. A-men!"

"That ain't much of a blessing," groused Duff.

"I stuck a 'a-men' on it!"

"That'll do," said Pa. "Nice prayer, son. Short. Now eat up."

Eagerly, he took a generous stack of fluffy warm biscuits from the platter before him and, after pouring on a pool of gravy, served himself portions of bacon and eggs, making sure to pass everything along before he commenced downing his meal with gusto. Pa had an appetite that matched his oversized frame and always counted on a large spread to start his workday. Thanks to Ma's cooking, he never set off hungry.

My mother, Hannah Armstrong, was not only an exceptional cook, she was beautiful, too. Her raven black hair was increasingly streaked with more and more grey, which she continued to blame on Duff, and her milky white skin and sparkling blue eyes gave her a look younger than her years. Even when she smiled, which was often, you could barely see a wrinkle. Pa always said he was lucky to land her. He wasn't what you'd call handsome, but he had just enough manly charm to finally win her hand. They were the perfect match.

"Hey, Pa. Did you hear? Old man McDougal's winter wheat got a blight. He may lose his crop," began Duff.

"What kind of blight?" asked Pa.

"Some kind of yellow spot on the leaves."

"Wheat rust. Sorry to hear that."

"What's wheat rust?" I asked.

"Well, it's kind of like a pox that gets on the underside of the leaves. Makes the plants sick and kills 'em. Look it up in your almanac. There must be something in there about it."

"Aw, he's always got his nose in a book anyways, Pa," Duff said. "Don't give him no more excuses."

Ma set another platter of warm biscuits onto the table and sat. There was a moment of silence, but Duff broke it with a question.

"Say, Pa?" he said with reticence. "There's a barn dance this coming Saturday night. I was hoping to take the buggy. If you and Ma don't mind, I mean."

"Oh? Who you takin'?" Pa asked, as if he didn't know the answer.

"Sarah May Metzker," I answered for him. "He's sweet on her," I teased, and puckered my lips to make kissy noises.

Duff flicked his napkin at me, and I yelped like an injured pup.

"Settle down!" ordered Pa.

"Seems to me you're seeing quite a lot of Sarah May Metzker these days," commented Ma.

"Yeah. I guess so."

Pa grinned at him. "Of course, you can take the buggy, son. I'm glad you two are getting along. But you see you get Sarah May home at a decent hour. I don't want her pa coming round to complain to me."

"Thanks, Pa."

Another silence. Then I remembered something.

"Hey, Pa, I heard somethin'. Tubby Wilson says they found a dead body hanging from a rope out at Old Man Spiner's place."

"Truman J. Armstrong," scolded Ma. "That's not a fit subject for the table. Eat your breakfast."

"But Scrump's right, Ma," Duff chimed in. "Jasper Tompkins told me the same thing. Sheriff thinks it was a runaway slave from down South."

"If you ask me, somebody needs to talk to that sheriff," said Pa, his tone rising in anger. "Whoever's behind these lynchings ought to be—"

"Merciful heavens, what is wrong with you menfolk? Didn't you all hear what I just said?"

"But Ma, Tubby Wilson said —"

"I don't care what Tubby Wilson said! You are *not* allowed to discuss this at the table."

The rest of the meal was finished in silence.

Following breakfast, Pa headed for the field and Ma washed dishes while she dictated to Duff a list of supplies she needed him to fetch from town.

"Can I go with him, Ma? Please?"

"If it's all right with Duff."

"I reckon. If you don't pester me none," said Duff.

He headed to the door, but seeing that her back was turned, he went to take an apple out of a bowl on the sideboard.

"Put it back. Those are for a pie I'm baking today," she ordered, without so much as looking at him. Duff sighed and returned the apple to the bowl.

As we walked to the barn to hitch our filly, Paintbox, to the wagon, Ma poked her head out the door and yelled after us, "You look after your brother now! See that he stays out of trouble!"

"Okay, I will!" Duff hollered back over his shoulder.

"I was talking to Scrump!"

Two

DUFF AND I ROLLED ALONG the dusty lane headed for Beardstown, a growing center of trade and commerce, on the banks of the Illinois River. The yawning branches of sleepy sycamores stretched over us and dappled our faces with morning sunlight. With the steady squeaking of the wagon wheels and the clippety-clop of Paintbox's hooves, I was just beginning to drift off to sleep when the thunderous approach of a galloping horse startled me wide awake.

I looked back and saw a fine red buggy pulled by a powerful black gelding. The driver whipped furiously at the horse, and the buggy caught up to us, revealing the driver and his passenger—Preston Metzker and his sister, Sarah May.

Preston was the youngest of the three Metzker sons and Sarah May was his only sister. John Metzker, their father, was a hugely successful rancher who owned more land than anyone else in Cass County and, of course, Preston never let anybody forget that.

He wore his father's wealth like a showy badge. His boots were always shiny, he sported wide-brimmed felt hats, and he was quick to flash his cash around, as if to remind the rest of us that we didn't have any. Even though he had the frame of a brawny ranch hand, it was hard to believe Preston had ever done a day's work. He was always running a fidgety hand through his wavy brown hair, especially when gals were around, I noticed. He loved showboating for them, but I suspected they liked his money better than they liked him.

Preston and Duff never got along. Preston envied Duff's agility and good looks, his easy-going manner, his natural affinity for people, his popularity with the girls. Most everybody liked Duff and Duff liked most everybody. Except for Preston.

Preston, you see, thought he was better than Duff and was always trying his temper. He would poke fun at Duff's clothes, laugh at his moppy hair, or taunt him about the size of our farmland. Sometimes Preston would get a rise out of him and Duff would sneer, clench his fists at his sides and quietly seethe. He surely could have whupped Preston if he'd wanted to, but somehow he managed to control himself, if only for the sake of Sarah May.

Duff had long been sweet on her, but only in the last few months had they officially started courting. It was plain to me, if not the entire county, that he was head-over-heels for her. But who could blame him? She was a stunner. She had silken chestnut hair, luscious red lips, and dark green eyes, which she kept exclusively for Duff.

"Hello there, Duff!" Sarah May cried out gaily as their buggy paced alongside us. "I'm looking forward to Saturday night."

Duff's lips curled into a dopey grin the moment she spoke, and his hair fell forward into his eyes, eyes which he couldn't keep off her. The wagon veered left.

"Duff, the road!" I yelled.

He pulled the reins to right us. Sarah May sat next to her brother, her hair flowing out from under a stylish spring bonnet as she tilted her head coyly at Duff.

"Hey there, Armstrong!" shouted Preston. "Hello, Skunk!"

"The name is Scrump!" I bellowed back.

"Ain't no difference to me."

"Don't be picking on my little brother, Metzker."

"Aw, where's your sense of humor, Armstrong? Hey, that's some worn-out old nag you got there. Haven't I seen her picture on a bottle of glue?"

Sarah May rolled her eyes while Preston guffawed loudly at his own joke.

Duff and I loved Paintbox, our spirited pinto, a brown-and-white filly. Pa had paid near fifty dollars for her, and up until that time she was the finest horse we'd ever owned. Duff was real proud of her, and when Preston mocked her, I could literally feel him fume.

"I'll put Paintbox up against that old plug of yours any day of the week, Metzker!"

Which was just what Preston wanted to hear, of course. His horse was a strapping black stallion with muscular haunches and a cold, steely gaze. I wasn't at all sure Paintbox could take him on.

"Oh yeah? Name where and when. I'll be there."

"No time like the present!" replied Duff, taking up the challenge.

"Okay. We'll race you to town. All the way to the end of Main Street! See ya there, slowpoke!"

In the very next instant, Pres cracked his whip and the red buggy lurched forward. Sarah May grabbed onto her hat as they shot away in a cloud of dust.

Duff snapped the reins, and Paintbox lifted her head, breaking forth in a feisty gallop.

"Hold tight, little brother!"

With nothing to grab but the wagon seat, I held on for dear life as the filly took flight, her mane jetting out behind her, and the sound of hooves drubbing my ears. We gained quickly on them, but Pres whipped his horse harder, and it sped ahead.

Paintbox would not be outrun. With each stride of her young legs, she moved valiantly forward, gaining on the Metzker buggy.

"That's it, Paintbox, that's it," Duff urged her.

Stride by stride, we pulled even, and I saw the angry look on Pres's face and then the shock in Sarah's eyes as he cruelly whipped his horse to spur it onward.

"H'yaw! H'yaw!"

Clouds of dust rose about us. Sarah May coughed and pulled a handkerchief from her pocket to cover her nose and mouth. We pulled a full length ahead, then another, and it looked as though we had outpaced them.

Duff whooped and hollered, taking his eyes off the road to look back at them, and that's when I saw it.

"Duff! Up ahead!"

There, in the lane before us, a hay wagon loped lazily along, and we were on a direct collision course!

Duff swerved right, barely averting disaster, but we lost some ground. Metzker came barreling through behind us and clumsily veered too close to the hay wagon, forcing it into the ditch. Sarah May screamed at the near miss, but Preston didn't care, so the red buggy surged on.

The two beasts ran neck-and-neck for an instant, and it felt as if the buggy might pass us by. But like a Roman charioteer driving his team, Duff slowly stood up in the driver's box to command the filly. Paintbox responded magnificently, her powerful legs propelling us once more to the fore.

The Metzkers' buggy receded behind us and I let out a cheer! "Woo hoo! C'mon Duff, you can do it!"

Duff, the charioteer, led us onward to certain victory. Beardstown loomed ahead, and we were a juggernaut.

As we approached the city limits, however, we could see pedestrians casually crossing the road, and they suddenly heard the raucous rumbling of the horses' hooves. Moments later, folks started jumping left and right to avoid being mowed down as in a game of ten pins.

The road had seemingly cleared for us, but then a familiar middle-aged couple stepped off the wooden sidewalk and directly into our path.

"Duff, dead ahead! The Wellmans!"

At the sight of us, Mrs. Wellman bleated like a baby lamb. But Mr. Wellman, carrying a tower of parcels, had no view of us, and no idea that we were rocketing his way. Miraculously, Duff careened around them, but the boxes sailed skyward and poor Mr. Wellman stumbled face first onto the dusty street.

Duff slowed to a halt, hugging the side of the street, and I watched dejectedly as Pres zoomed by, howled with laughter at our mishap, and raced on ahead. We had lost.

Jumping from the wagon, Duff ran back to help Mr. Wellman. We both knew if he ever told Pa about this, we'd be in for a good whupping.

Mr. Wellman and his wife, you see, were our nearest neighbors. They and their two sons, Matthew and Luke, tended the land next to ours. They were Quakers, and good farmers, who had always been there for us over the years. After I was born, they had even pitched in to help Pa build the second story to our farmhouse. It was a relationship born not only of geography, but of mutual respect and lasting friendship. We helped each other with the harvest every year as well.

As a rule, Mr. Wellman was soft-spoken and polite. But not this time.

"Duff Armstrong! Have thee taken all leave of thy senses?"

"I'm so sorry, sir," Duff said.

We scrambled to gather the parcels that littered the road.

Meanwhile, Mrs. Wellman, a plump and gentle soul, tended to her husband, brushing the dirt from his dark suit. I retrieved his broad-brimmed hat, which had gone sailing in the near collision, and ran it back to him. He snatched it angrily from me.

"I've a good mind to buggy whip the both of thee!"

He clapped the hat on his head and grabbed at the parcels Duff held out to him.

"Thomas, thy tongue!" chastised Mrs. Wellman.

Mr. Wellman muttered something, then heaved a submissive sigh.

"Duff Armstrong. Thy father taught thee better, I know."

"Yessir."

"And thy mother," Mrs. Wellman said, "what would she think to see thee setting such a poor example for thy young brother?"

Duff lowered his eyes, too ashamed to answer. Mrs. Wellman shook her head. "Thee need be more careful. May God be with thee. Come along, Thomas."

"Thank you," Duff mumbled as we watched them continue on their way.

"Whew, that was close!"

"Think they'll tell Pa and Ma?"

"Hope not," Duff grimaced. "C'mon."

We finally pulled slowly into town and hitched the wagon at the end of Main Street.

"Better luck next time, Armstrong," smirked a voice. Of course, Pres and Sarah May were waiting for us.

"Don't gloat, Preston," ordered Sarah May. "At least *he* stopped to help the Wellmans. Thank you, Duff, for being such a gentleman."

Duff's face flushed beet red when she spoke his name.

"Preston Metzker! Duff Armstrong!" boomed a bass voice.

It was Sheriff Jim Dick, the town's bowlegged lawman who sported a tin star on his chest and a six-shooter on his belt.

"You boys got no business racing through my streets like you done! I've a good mind to lock you both up."

"My father wouldn't care for that none, Sheriff," smirked Preston.

"Your father may own half this county, Preston Metzker, but he don't own me," huffed the lawman. "I don't allow no racin' in my town."

"Sorry, Sheriff," offered Duff.

"I'm surprised at you, Duff."

"We were just having fun, Sheriff," continued Preston.

"Your idea of fun is gonna get someone killed one of these days. Maybe even yourself," cautioned Sheriff Dick.

"Unless I kill him first!" spouted Duff angrily. It was an unusual flash of temper in front of Sarah May, but I could tell he'd had more than his fill of Preston for one morning.

"You fellers get on with your business and go back to your homes," he ordered, and then swaggered off.

"What a windbag," sneered Preston when the lawman was far enough from earshot. "Come on, Sarah May."

Metzker led his sister off down the wooden sidewalk as she threw Duff a longing glance over her shoulder. He smiled back at her, but it faded as soon as she was out of sight. Then, without a word, he stalked off to the store and I hurried to keep up with him.

My stomach was in knots every step of the way. Here I'd been told by Ma to keep him out of trouble and I'd failed miserably. The race, the near miss with the Wellmans, and now the sheriff. And I had even egged him on! If word ever got back to Pa, we'd sure be up for a time in the woodshed.

Duff walked so quickly I could scarcely keep pace with him. He brushed briskly past anyone in his way, then pushed through a crowd of farmers who buzzed over something posted in the window of the newspaper office. But this caught my attention, so I stopped.

The penny press, so called because it could be cheaply produced and sold for only a penny, had just come to Beardstown, and the editor often posted the front page with blaring black headlines in a front window, hoping to gin up sales. Pushing my way through the crowd, I stood on tiptoe and read:

DECISION OF SUPREME COURT
IN DRED SCOTT CASE!

My eye scanned the page, but I hardly understood a word. My instincts told me that something big had happened, but I didn't know exactly what.

"Dang it, Scrump! Get over here, or I'm going on without you!"

I caught up with him just as he entered the General Store with the list of things Ma needed, but I waited outside so I could listen to the bunch of farmers talking about this headline.

When he'd finished up at the store, Duff took me back to the wagon. We were loading in Ma's supplies when we suddenly heard a loud angry voice, and there was no mistaking whose it was.

"Damn you! You stay away from my sister, you understand me, boy?"

Preston Metzker had seized a small Negro feller by the shirt and pressed him against a wall, threatening to beat him within an inch of his life. Sarah May was horrified, and the man's poor wife watched on helplessly.

"Preston! He didn't mean anything by it. Leave him be!" pleaded Sarah May.

"Please, sir! Don't hurt my husband!" begged the man's wife, frozen with fright. "I beg you, sir!"

The red-hot anger in Preston's face was chilling. "Well, boy? What's you got to say for yourself? Do I have to teach you a lesson, boy?"

"No, sir, no! Oh, please, let me be, sir! I'm sorry for anything I done wrong!"

Preston balled his fist and was about to strike the poor feller when Duff raced in and yanked him off.

"What the hell's wrong with you, Preston? Stop acting crazy!"

"This here fool tipped his hat to Sarah May, all nice and fancy like, giving her the eye."

"Preston!" yelled Sarah May. "He was just being polite. He did nothing wrong. Why are you behavin' this way?"

"Better get going, folks," Duff told the accused man and his wife, and they hurried away down the street.

Preston sneered as he called hatefully after them, "Niggers!"

Up to this point, I had spent most my time with my family on the farm, and this was a word I'd never heard before. In fact, I could never recall it being used by anyone in our home. I'd have to ask Pa about that, I decided.

Sarah May shook her head. "Thank you, Duff."

"What are you thanking him for? He's the one who should've been standing up for you! Your precious beau here!"

"Preston, can we just go now? I've had enough for one day," she scolded, and pulled him toward their buggy.

"How'd a gal as nice as her ever end up with a nasty mean brother like him?" Duff mused aloud. "Come on, Scrump. Let's get out of here."

With the supplies loaded, we started back home. To Duff's dismay, I peppered him with questions.

"Duff, what do you suppose makes Preston Metzker so mean?"

"Danged if I know. He sure hates Negro folks, though."

"Duff, who's Dred Scott?"

"Some slave feller, I believe."

"What's a slave?"

Duff struggled to explain as best he could that slaves were people who had to obey their masters, no matter what.

"Like we have to obey Pa?"

"In a way, but worse."

"Worse how?"

"Well, I hear they get treated like horses or cattle. They get whupped real bad if they don't do as they're told."

This explanation horrified me, but it explained a lot about slavery. I had more questions, of course, but I could tell Duff's patience with me was wearing thin, so I decided to wait till I could talk to Pa.

When we arrived home, we found Pa working in the barn. After we'd unloaded the supplies, he sent Duff off to mend a fence by the cornfield. Then Pa asked how things were in town and I told him all about the headline in the paper and the feller named Dred Scott. I repeated what Duff had said, that he was a slave who was no better off than a horse or a cow.

"I reckon that's so," said Pa.

He continued to listen patiently as I chattered on, telling him how Preston Metzker picked on a feller for no good reason. Then I asked the question that had been nagging at me since our encounter with Preston that morning.

"Hey Pa, what's a…nigger?"

He stopped dead in his tracks and stared down at me. "Why are you asking me that? Where'd you hear that word?"

"That's what Preston Metzker called the feller in the street this morning."

He sighed, pushing his hat off his sweaty brow as he considered his answer.

"Well, son, there's lot of white folks who use that as another word for Negroes. I can't help what they say, but I don't want to hear you using it."

"Why not, Pa? Is it a cuss word?"

"Well, no. But don't it sound hateful? Isn't that how it sounded when Preston used it?"

"Yeah."

"So you see, there's a bad feeling that goes along with it. Your ma and me, we don't use that word, and we don't want you using it either. You be respectful to everyone you meet. Understand?"

"Okay, Pa."

I have thought of this exchange with my father often over the years and continue to marvel at it. Here was a frontiersman and a dirt farmer who bore no ill will to anyone, even folks who were hated by other farmers or townsfolk. He got along with most everyone, and when it came to race, he understood that the names we use for each other are just as important as how we treat one another.

It was a lesson I never forgot.

THREE

THE HEAVY WORK OF PLANTING and tending the crop was done by my father and brother, but one particular chore was reserved just for me. Walking corn.

Once the crop was in the ground, it was my job to patrol for weeds. Clover was the worst, a relentless foe with creeping tentacles, silently choking tender young shoots. By midsummer, and especially as the corn plants matured, I would wield a corn knife to whack at stalks of milkweed and cocklebur that popped up. If we'd had a fair amount of rain, the work could be muddy, but then it was easier to pull the weeds out, roots and all, from the damp earth.

It was a cloudless, humid afternoon in late July when a dark shadow passed over us. Suzy stopped in her tracks, ears pricked, one paw raised, eyes fixed intently skyward. Squinting against the glare of the harsh sun, I watched a hawk glide ominously through the blue sky with a hungry eye. Rodents, squirrels, or...chickens!

My heart pounded in my chest. My mind raced. *Were the hens roaming freely about the coop? Had I locked the hen-house door?* I couldn't remember.

When I finally arrived to the coop, I was out of breath and the hens were indeed roaming. I shooed them furiously inside, kicking at One-Eyed Phineas till he angrily followed suit. Then I slammed the door of the henhouse and heaved a sigh of relief. But I knew it was just a matter of time. The hawk would be back.

That night at supper, I told everyone of my encounter.

"Well, you just need to keep a watch on our hens from now on," advised Pa.

"I could scare it away with your rifle," I offered eagerly.

"You'll do nothing of the sort, Truman Armstrong," scolded Ma. "I don't want you anywhere near your Pa's rifle. Tell him, Jack."

"Your mother's right. Never touch a rifle, boy, until I say you're old enough to learn how to use it. Now eat your supper," he said, passing me the potatoes. "You keep a close eye out for the hawk and when you see it, you tell me or Duff. Any shooting needs to be done, we'll do it. Understood?"

"Yessir," I said, as my hopes of shooting at the hawk myself flew away.

He continued. "Hannah, did I tell you I run into William Witherspoon last week in town?"

"Will from Clary's Grove? How was he?"

"Just fine. He told me he saw Abe a few weeks back. According to Will, Abe is thinking of running again."

"Running for what?"

"Whatever's coming up next. Damned if I can keep up with him."

We'd heard a lot about Abe Lincoln in my family. My folks and he used to share a house together and they'd known him since, as my father put it, "he was a poor know-nothing hillbilly." In the little river settlement of

New Salem where they'd all lived, they'd shared a lot together, each other's joys and sorrows, hopes and hardships. Some of those friends from those years had died, and most others, like my folks, had moved on. These days, Lincoln and the others were separated not only by distance, but by the passage of years.

As they got to reminiscing, Pa said he was especially grateful that he'd found a home in New Salem, because that's where he'd met Ma.

"Pa? I thought you was born right here on the farm, like me."

"I was."

"Remind me why you went off to New Salem. I forget."

"Well, son, my life was different from yours here," he said, reaching for his pipe. "You boys got it easy, seems to me."

He told us his own pa—our grandfather—had inherited the land from his father. But Pa's father was a bully and a lazy farmer who spent all his money on drink. When Pa was just six years old, his father had him out clearing fields, harvesting corn, and chopping wood.

"My years as a young'un was durn mis'rable, that's for sure."

When Pa was a little older, his brutish father sent him out to earn his keep. Most of his days were spent laboring for other farmers, and he never saw a dime of his wages. What little he earned went right to paying for his father's liquor. If Pa ever complained, he'd get a licking.

"My childhood taught me one thing, though, and that's how slaves must feel, 'cause I sure felt like one myself."

When he was eighteen, he told us, he returned from a hard day's labor with pay in hand. But this time, when his drunken father grabbed at it, Pa snatched it back. In his anger, he lashed out violently at his pa and gave him such a thrashing that his mother had to pull him off. For once in his life, he'd stood up for himself, and he knew then that he couldn't stay on the farm any longer.

That night, with just the clothes on his back, he left home, resolved to find a new start far away from his troubles. He hopped onto his horse and rode straight away toward the Sangamon River, figuring he'd find a place to camp. What he found instead was the tiny frontier settlement of New Salem.

"It weren't much more than just a row of little log cabins that sprung up 'round a grist mill, but I figgered I could find work there," he recalled. "Sweet little spot, it was."

Here, Pa stopped to light his pipe.

"But there's more to the story, ain't there, Pa?"

"Too much more," complained Duff, dipping a biscuit into the gravy boat.

Pa gave Duff a look as he blew a puff of smoke and continued his tale.

"Anyways, there was an old feller who ran a kind of a general store and trading post on the edge of the little settlement. His name was Denton Orfutt. Old Mr. Orfutt knew everybody, and everybody knew him. He said he liked to help newcomers, so he pointed me toward Clary's Grove, a little ways downstream. He thought I might find a place to sleep there. That's when I took up with the Clary's Grove Boys."

The Boys worked hard for their living, he explained, mostly by hunting and trapping. They usually went to New Salem to trade their pelts—and also to bet on wrestling matches. With his burly build, Pa soon enough became a contender, and he turned out to be one of the best, too, often winning a lucrative purse for himself and the Boys.

"Get to the part where you met Ma," I insisted.

"Well, your Ma sewed quilts and such, and she brought them into the store to trade for goods. Lucky for me, I happened to be at the post one day when your Ma came in with a new quilt. My, she was as dark-haired a beauty as she is today, and I reckon I fell in love with her on the spot."

"Oh, Jack..." Ma said humbly.

One spring day, he continued, a delivery for Old Man Orfutt arrived by flatboat. The young boatman somehow got it hung up on the riverbank. He was trying to free it with his pole, yelling for help. Soon a crowd gathered and man after man waded into the river and tried to push the flatboat free. Even when Pa, known to be one of the strongest fellers around, joined in, it still wouldn't budge.

Finally, the boat's lanky pilot left his pole and jumped into the water himself.

"He was the tallest feller any of us had ever seen," recounted Pa. "Kind of funny lookin', with a mop of bushy brown hair, kind of gangly, but muscular enough, I guess. Anyway, we all stood in the shallows and watched this beanpole splash his long legs into that river and place both his arms on the edge of that flatboat as if to push it free. I wanted to laugh out loud 'cause I thought he just couldn't be as strong as me! But don't you know, he heaved with all his might and actually got the dang boat to floating free? Old Mr. Orfutt was mighty impressed.

" 'What's your name, young feller?' asked Orfutt. 'I'm Abe Lincoln,' says he, and right then and there, Orfutt offers him a job as a clerk in his store. He figgered Abe could do all his heavy lifting for him, I reckon."

Pa told us that Lincoln said no to the job. But when Mr. Orfutt said he could sleep in the store for free, Lincoln figured that working as a store clerk was a right step up from working on the river, so he took the job.

"Of course, next time your Ma brought her sewing into the post, she met up with him and she, well, took an interest in him, you might say. Made me hoppin' jealous."

"I took a *sisterly* interest is all," she interjected. "That poor boy was so shy, and he certainly needed someone to mend his tatty britches and knit him some socks for those big feet of his. Every now and then I'd slip a hint about bathing, or even using tonic to tame that wild hair of his. He wasn't too bad looking when he tried."

"You sure you weren't sweet on him, Ma?" teased Duff, and she shushed him so Pa could continue.

One afternoon, Pa said, he'd overheard Mr. Orfutt bragging to a customer that his new clerk was not only strong as an ox, but a crackerjack wrestler, to boot.

"Well, that's all I needed to hear," explained Pa with a glint in his eye. "Before the sun set that very day, I challenged that beanpole to a match, just to show him up in front of your Ma. I don't like to brag, but any match with Jack Armstrong meant big business at Orfutt's.

Whenever I rassled, his clerk sold a slew of whiskey, chewing tobacco, and rock candy."

This was my favorite part of the story. When the big day arrived, word had spread, and the villagers journeyed to Orfutt's to place their wagers on the match. It was the biggest event ever seen in those parts. For old Mr. Orfutt, it was a silver bonanza as the coins clinked in his coffer. He kept track of the wagers, too. Turns out the Clary's Grove Boys and most other folks bet on me. All except for one, that is.

"Yeah, we know. Ma bet against you," said Duff.

Pa took a puff of his pipe and leaned back, grinning at Ma.

"Well, it wasn't so much betting against your Pa as it was feeling sorry for Abe. Someone had to be on his side."

As the story goes, Orfutt cleared space for the match right in front of his store, and soon the two opponents, Abe and my Pa, faced off, ready for battle. With the wave of a red bandana, Orfutt shouted "Go!" and the match was on.

Like two angry bears in a wood, Pa and the young clerk warily circled each other. Pa finally made his move, rushing Abe, and they grappled, they twisted, they rolled, each applying his might against the other. The crowd whooped and hollered, urging them on, expecting an easy victory for my Pa. But the minutes passed, and to everyone's amazement, the skinny clerk held Pa off. An hour into it, everyone was amazed that the upstart, the flatboat newcomer, the beanpole-of-a-clerk, had so far held Jack Armstrong completely at bay.

"They couldn't believe their own eyes," continued Pa. "Why, Abe kept dodging my grasp for the entire time! Most fellers wouldn't last an hour agin me, but finally I thought I had him. I was about to move in, to flip him to the ground, when out of the blue, whoosh! He rushes me like lightning. Boom! One quick lunge and I'm suddenly in a headlock. Another quick move and he throws me right to the ground, and piles on top of me. I tried every move I knew, but danged if I wasn't pinned!"

Mr. Orfutt counted to three and then he reached down, raised the clerk's arm, and announced the previously unthinkable.

"The winner and new *champeen*!"

Now there should have been cheers at this point. Instead, a tense uncertainty hung in the air. Folks stood silently, fearful of what would happen next. The Clary's Grove Boys had never lost a bet before. Not on Jack Armstrong, anyway.

"Somethin' ain't right here," Tom, the eldest, finally says to Mr. Orfutt. "Seems like your man here cost us quite a pile of money. We put us down some big bets."

"And they began closing in on Abe," Pa continued. "They pushed him up right against the wall of the store, threatening him until I stepped forward. 'Boys,' I told 'em, 'Abe here beat me fair and square. You better be backing away now, or you'll have to fight us both.' That was enough to make 'em back off."

"Hooray!" I yelled.

Duff yawned loudly.

"And don't forget," added Ma, "my winnings were a tidy sum. Your Pa just wanted to marry me for my money, you know."

Pa laughed. "Well, not a year later we were husband and wife. But then old Orfutt closed up shop and poor Abe was out on his ear. So, what could we do but take him in to live with us till he was on his feet? He had nowhere else to go. That's when he become one of the family. Used to babysit Duff, you know."

"You remember that, Duff?" I asked.

"Of course not."

"From then on, Abe took odd jobs, saved his money, found a business partner, and opened hisself a store in town to take the place of Orfutt's. He was a square dealer, though. You know that he once short-changed a feller three cents and when he figgered it out, he walked two miles just to make it right? After that, we called him Honest Abe, yessir. He was with us in New Salem for six years. Of course, this was before he got all mixed up in politics. Did I ever tell you boys how he came to be a U.S. Congressman all the way up in Washington, D.C.?"

"Yes, Pa. A million times," complained Duff.

"Okay, I'll spare you. But I will say, losing that wrestling match to old Abe was one of the best things that ever happened to me. Orfutt made a lot of money that day, but it was me who hit the jackpot. When I stood up for Abe after the fight, Scrump, that's what won me your Ma's hand."

Four

IT WAS MA'S MOST PRIZED possession. She had always dreamed of having one, so Pa secretly saved for two years and surprised her with it on their tenth anniversary, the year I was born. A grandfather clock.

Its seven-foot walnut cabinet was ornately carved with flowers, leaves, and two merry birds perched above its gleaming golden face. Elegant Roman numerals encircled its delicate hands that pointed to the time of day, while below, a large brass pendulum perpetually swung to and fro. At the top of every hour, its deep chimes sounded sonorously. When I was small, I would press my face against the glass, trying to find the feller who played the chimes, and was forever scolded for leaving handprints and nose prints behind.

Ma carried the brass key which wound it in her apron pocket. Many a morning, I watched as she carefully opened the great glass door, stood on tiptoe to insert the key in its face and slowly cranked it. Then she would gingerly close it back up, step away to admire it, and pat her pocket once the key was back where it belonged. It was a daily ritual and she performed it with an almost prayerful attitude.

The clock was woven into the fabric of our lives. It told us when to sleep and when to rise and when to eat. Its ticking filled the silences that fell between us, especially in the evenings when we would gather after supper in the parlor by lamplight. Ma would often sit in her rocker and sew, Duff and I would sit on the floor playing Pitch, Pa would puff at his pipe, and Suzy would snooze away in a corner.

It was one such evening, a few minutes after the clock had chimed eight, we were startled by a sharp rap at the door. Suzy barked. Nighttime visitors were practically unheard of in the country, and we looked at each other quizzically.

Pa opened the door part way and saw a tall, rough-looking cowboy.

"What can I do for you, mister?" I heard Pa say.

"Sorry to be botherin' you folks, just need some help. Lookin' for somebody mighta been seen 'round these parts. Mind if I come in?"

Pa opened the door a little further and the big feller barged right into the parlor. He wore a rumpled cowboy hat and had a wiry mustache that curled up at the ends. He was covered with trail dust and his duds were worn and dirty. Smelly, too.

He took off his hat when he saw Ma. He explained he was a slave hunter on the trail of a runaway from down south. I immediately noticed the jangly spurs on his boots. Polished and shiny, they caught the glint of the lamplight, and their reflection darted like knives around the parlor.

From the pocket of his plaid flannel shirt he pulled out a wrinkled flyer and passed it to Pa.

FIVE HUNDRED DOLLAR

REWARD

ISAAC, RUNAWAY SLAVE.

DANGEROUS.

USE EXTREME CAUTION.

"You seen anyone like this? Anything suspicious?"

"No, sir," said Pa with distaste and handed the flyer back to him.

The stranger eyed him silently and glanced over at Ma. Then his look shot past them to me and Duff.

"What about you boys?"

He passed us the flyer. We studied it and shook our heads.

Then he said, "I see you got a barn out there by the crick. He mighta slipped in there without you knowin' it. I'll jes' have a quick look."

"You can look on your way out," Pa scowled.

Before he put on his hat, he said, "Well, if'n you should see anything suspicious, y'all just tell the sheriff. He'll know how to find me."

We watched from the door as he went to the barn, peered in, and then galloped away into the night.

"That man gives me the willies," Ma said, and Pa put a comforting arm about her shoulder.

"Don't fret, Hannah. We won't hear from him again."

"What's he mean by 'slave hunter'?" I asked.

"He's a feller who goes after folks that broke the law, and if he catches them, he turns 'em over to the sheriff for a reward," explained Pa.

"Did this feller Isaac break the law?"

"Well, son, the law says he did. You see, that feller's a slave, runnin' from down South. His crime is runnin' away from his owner."

"Owner? That don't sound fair to me."

"You may be right, Scrump, old man. But the law's the law. That's the way things are."

• • •

It happened on a brisk morning in mid-November. As usual, I woke to the crowing of One-Eyed Phineas. I rose, slipped sleepily into my clothes and tramped outside. The hens squawked and spilled into their yard when I opened the hen house door. Fluttering about, they were eager for their feed. Marianne, like always, hugged my feet as I started scattering chicken feed.

Suddenly, I heard the rustling of strong wings, followed by an unearthly screech. I whirled about and saw the great hawk swooping down toward the yard. When Suzy barked, the hawk flew up, but then circled again for another attack.

I had rehearsed this moment in my mind a hundred times, just in case, and now it was here! I knew exactly what I was going to do. Dropping my seed bucket, I ran straight to the house where Pa's rifle sat in its corner of the kitchen. I grabbed it and ran back out the door, right past Ma as she carried in a water pail from the well. As

I whizzed by, she fought to hold onto her pail, even as the water splashed up on her dress.

"Scrump? Scrump, what are you doing? Come back here right now!"

I reached the chickens just in time to see the hawk grabbing for One-Eye Phineas in his sharp talons. Just as I'd planned, I raised the rifle, took aim, and pulled the trigger. But I didn't anticipate the recoil. It knocked me backwards hard onto the ground. Of course, I had missed my mark by a mile. Scrambling to my feet, I watched the hawk recede into the distance carrying off poor old Phineas.

Duff appeared out of nowhere. "What the hell are you doing?" he demanded.

"The goldurn hawk, Duff! It got One-Eyed Phineas! I almost hit him." I raised the rifle and Duff wrenched it from my hands.

"You coulda got yourself killed!" he yelled at me.

Then I felt a sting to my right cheek.

In all the years I'd known him, he'd never raised a hand to me. Suddenly, nothing mattered any more. Not the hawk, not the rifle, not the chickens. My eyes watered as I ran through the yard, past Ma, and into the house.

Up in our room, I had thrown myself across my bed, lost in my tears and the shock of having my hero strike me. Things would never be the same.

The door quietly opened.

"Scrump?"

"Go away!"

"No. I'm staying put right here," he said, sitting next to me.

"I don't want to talk to you ever again!"

"Can't say that I blame you much for that. Scrump, I'm sorry. But you got no idea how to handle a firearm." He touched my shoulder and I flinched. "I was scared."

"Of what?"

"Of you, Scrump."

"What do you mean?" I sniffled, finally looking at him.

"You never pick up a rifle unless you know what you're doing. Something bad could happen."

"You never hit me before, Duff."

"I know, little brother. But you gotta promise not to touch Pa's rifle again."

I nodded.

Unexpectedly, his strong arms wrapped about me and hugged me tight. It was the first time he'd shown such affection and it repaired the breach that had opened between us.

"Now, you got to reckon with Pa."

When he came in from the field, Pa whupped me but good. I crawled into bed that night with a sore backside and an empty stomach. I'd gotten no supper.

Several nights later, I had almost fallen asleep when I heard Pa's voice from downstairs, and it woke me up. Duff was sleeping soundly in the bed next to mine. Quietly, I threw back the covers and tiptoed to the top of the stairs to listen. I couldn't hear everything, but managed to get just enough.

"What brings you out this late, Thomas?" asked Pa. "Family well?"

"Yes, I thank thee," our neighbor Mr. Wellman said. "I have come to speak to thee about the Dred Scott decision."

"I know about that."

"Then thee know it is unjust. 'Once a slave, always a slave!' That's what the court has said. They dare to tell the Negro, *a man*, he has no right to be free."

"It's the law, Thomas. Not much we can do about it, whether we like it or not."

"Surely thee do not agree with this?"

"No, 'course not."

"As any good Christian would not. A conspiracy is what it is."

"Conspiracy? By who?"

"Slave masters, of course. Lawmakers dance to their wicked tunes, the government enforces their unjust laws, and now this—from the highest court. A conspiracy to be sure."

Now Mr. Wellman spoke in hushed tones. I struggled to make out his words.

"I've taken measures of my own against this abomination."

"Thomas, what are you getting at?"

"There is a brave Negro man, name of Isaac. He brings runaway slaves to me to hide in my barn until he can get them to freedom."

"We don't want no trouble, Thomas."

"It's desperate times for these people, Friend Jack. The slave hunters are making inquiries."

Slave hunters! My mind flashed back to the silver-spurred cowboy.

"Yep, one of them stopped by here the other night. I sent him packin'."

"God bless thee."

"What do you expect me to do?" Pa asked him.

"Purgatory Creek runs all the way from my land to thine, then clear out of the county. The runaways heading north tread the creek by night...no tracks, no scent for dogs. If thee would but consent to shelter them in thy barn by day, it would be yet another safe harbor for these hungry and desperate pilgrims. Isaac will help them continue their escape along the creek after dark."

"Thomas, there are laws, we abide by them. I don't want to risk my family and my farm by getting involved in this. We could both lose our farms, maybe even get ourselves arrested."

"And what does it profit a man to gain the world if he loses his soul? It is our Christian duty to help these unfortunates."

"That may be so. But I'm sorry, I won't put my family in harm's way. We'll keep your secret, but we can't help you. It's too risky."

He sighed. "I thank thee for hearing me out. I know I can trust in thy confidence."

After he left, I tiptoed quietly back to my room and climbed under the quilt. I'd certainly heard more than I bargained for.

The very next morning as I sat at the table, Ma set a plate of flapjacks before me and asked how I'd slept. She looked worried. No doubt Pa had told her about Mr. Wellman's visit last night. Duff and Pa were talking about what chores needed doing, but I was only half listening.

"Scrump, you hear me, son?" Pa said. "You got to groom Paintbox."

"Uh...yes, Pa."

"Get your head outta the clouds, old man. There's work to do."

I nodded, but my mind was on slave hunters and Mr. Wellman's secret.

As things turned out, it wouldn't be a secret for long.

FIVE

THE FIRST SNOWFALL OF THE year came in early December, just as I expected. The almanac was right again. It was Sunday, so nobody was up early, as it was a day of rest. Even Suzy was still asleep.

Of all the sights in my childhood, there are few more thrilling than an expanse of fluffy white snow covering our front yard. It beckoned to me through a frosty window. Careful not to wake Duff, I slipped into my winter clothes, including a stocking cap Ma had knitted the winter before. I tiptoed down the stairs to the kitchen, then put on my boots and snuck out the door.

There, I hurled myself off the stoop into the fresh powder, landing with a muffled clomp, then laid down in it, waving my arms till I'd given birth to a snow angel. I rose to survey my handiwork, then brushed the snow off and stood for a moment in the silence. Then I heard a creak. The door of the hen house was swinging wide open. I ran over and checked the hens, and they were all on their nests except for Marianne. She was missing. I stumbled back out and panicked when I saw paw prints and traces of blood leading out to the woods. It looked like a fox had snatched her away.

Mad as hops, I resolved to capture that critter and wring its neck with my bare hands! I followed the tracks to a nearby copse of birches. The further I tracked, the deeper I headed into the woods—farther from safety, farther from help, farther from home. A jay shrieked in the distance.

The prints led me from the copse to the edge of a field, then further into a secluded grove of mighty oaks that my father planned to clear-cut the following spring. Then I heard the slow creaking of a branch overhead. I looked up. Something was swaying above me.

It was the body of a Negro man, twisting slowly from a rope in the frigid cold of winter. A noose was tight about his neck, his hands bound at the wrists. His tongue was extended, swollen and purple, his countenance contorted and lifeless. His shirtless torso was marked with bloody stripes and blood trickled from one corner of his mouth. His blank brown eyes stared down at me as he twisted at the end of the rope.

Eyes wide and mouth agape with horror, I stumbled backwards onto the snowy forest floor. Scrambling to my feet, I hightailed it out of there, my heart pounding fiercely as my home came into view. The rest of the way, I sprinted as fast as my young legs would propel me until I burst into the house, panting, breathless. The loud bang of the door behind me shook everyone from their slumber, and like me, they awoke into a nightmare.

"Scrump, what in the name of Pete are you doing up so early on a Sunday morning, raising holy hell?"

"Pa, there…there's a dead man hanging from a tree in the forest."

Pa threw on his coat and boots and grabbed his rifle. "Show me, son."

I led him into the woods, all the way to the grove and to the tree where the body hung.

We rounded a corner, and then I pointed out the tree.

His body stiffened when he saw it. He stared in disbelief and finally spoke. "I was hoping you'd made this up. Come on, son," he said quietly. "We gotta get back and notify the sheriff." Then he swooped me up in his arms and carried me all the way home.

Ma and Duff met us at the door.

"What is it, Jack? What's happened?" asked Ma.

"Later, Hannah. Duff, saddle up Paintbox and fetch the sheriff out here."

"Pa?"

"Now, Duff."

About an hour later, Sheriff Jim Dick rode up with Duff and stepped into our parlor.

"What's the matter here, Jack? It better be important. You know I don't work on Sundays 'less there's an emergency," groused the sheriff.

"There's been a lynching in our woods over yonder."

His irritable demeanor instantly melted away. "Any idea who done it?"

Pa shook his head. "My boy found the unfortunate, hanging from a tree this morning."

"Lead the way."

Duff and I started to put on our coats.

"I want you boys to stay with me," Ma said.

"But Pa—"

"Mind your Ma," Pa ordered.

"Yes, Pa," we said, feeling dejected as they took off.

Meanwhile, Ma put on a pot of coffee and we waited. When Pa and the sheriff returned, they wore grim expressions.

"You menfolk come in out of the cold and have some coffee," Ma said, greeting them at the door.

"Much obliged," replied the sheriff gratefully as he sat down at the kitchen table. "Helluva thing," the sheriff started in, after taking a sip. "Can't figure what he was doing running in the cold like that. Where'd he come from?"

Pa looked at Ma. "Don't make much sense, somebody tracking a man at night during a storm," he said.

"Seeing as there was no footprints but your boy's here under the body, I reckon it happened just before the storm. New snow covered their tracks."

"Who would do such a horrible thing?" asked Ma.

"We've had 'em before, but ever since that dang Dred Scott decision, things have gotten nothin' but worse. This is the fourth lynchin' in Cass County in just two months. Hard to believe our local folks would do this, but…some folks just downright hate the Negroes."

"This happened on our land. Is my family safe, Sheriff?"

Sheriff Dick nodded. "Whoever done this, Mr. Armstrong, is not a threat to white folks, I promise you that. I'll come back with my deputy to cut the body down later today."

"What will happen to him?" I asked.

"We got a pauper's field outside of town for buryin' nameless souls like this. Race don't make much difference there. We're all equal in the end." The sheriff stood. "Much obliged for the coffee, Miz Armstrong."

After he left, we remained huddled around our little kitchen table. Ma placed a plate of muffins before us, but they went untouched. Our appetites had fled.

"Damn shame," Pa muttered as he lifted his cup to sip. "Ain't nothin' we can do about it now, though."

Ma stared hard at him before she finally spoke. "So, fugitives run for their lives through our land and we just go on like nothin' happened?"

"Hannah?" He could hear the tension in her voice, and it disturbed him.

"It's not right, Jack. Think about when we came back to these parts after your father died. There was an old Indian couple livin' in a little shack just a ways down Purgatory Creek."

"Yep. They were from the Sauk tribe, as I recall. Nice old folks, too. Couldn't speak much English."

Ma nodded. "Neighbors wanted to run them off just 'cause they were Indians, remember? But you said 'no,' and you stood firm. You said to just let them be, and folks backed off."

Pa put his cup down and was silent for a long while before speaking. "This is different. These folks are strangers. Runaways. They're breaking the law."

"Jack, they're people just like you and me. All they want is to be free. Don't you see? There's an evil lapping at our doorstep, and we need to do something."

Pa took her hand in his. "All right, Hannah. The Good Lord will show us the way."

"Seems to me like He already done so." She looked directly into his eyes and I knew right then she was talking about Mr. Wellman's proposition.

"Let me think on it some more," Pa said softly.

We carried on with the rest of our day, trying to resume our normal routine, but try as we might, things didn't seem normal to any of us. Midafternoon, the sheriff and deputy showed up with a wagon to take the dead man away. Ma kept Duff and me in the house until they were gone.

My sleep that night was fitful. Every time I closed my eyes, I kept seeing that man swinging in the tree. I looked over at Duff in his bed.

"Duff? Duff, you awake?"

He stirred slowly, rolling over to face me.

"Am now. Somethin' wrong, Scrump?"

"I can't sleep."

"Come on, get in."

I scrambled in next to him. As I settled in under his covers, he pushed his pillow over to share with me. The light of the winter moon streamed through the window and we laid silently side by side till he spoke.

"Guess this is one day we'll never forget."

"Who do you suppose he was, that dead feller?"

"Somebody looking for a better life, I reckon."

"You think his folks will miss him?"

"If he's got any."

"Think that was the runaway the slave hunter was lookin' for?"

"Maybe."

"Think he'll be back?"

"Who?"

"The slave hunter."

"Nah. You worry too much. You best try to sleep now."

Sleep finally came to me, lying next to Duff, where I felt safest in all the world.

Six

THE FOLLOWING MORNING, A BITTER chill gripped our farmhouse. Duff set a fire in the fireplace and before long, the crackling logs had the parlor feeling warm as toast. Pa had left just after breakfast, but he didn't say where he was headed.

"Where's Pa goin'?" I asked.

"He has some business to tend to. You best quit asking questions and do your chores now."

"Yes, Ma."

Pa returned in time for dinner. Ma met him eagerly as he hung his hat and coat on a wooden peg by the door. "Any news?"

He nodded. "We can talk about it at dinner."

Duff and I were already at the table waiting to say grace for our midday meal when Ma and Pa sat down.

"Scrump, you may ask the Lord's blessing," said Ma, and for once, I think Duff was glad my table blessings were so short. Like me, he must have been wondering what Pa was going to say to us.

After Ma dished out the meal, Pa finally spoke up.

"Boys," Pa began, "that man hung on our property yesterday was a runaway slave."

"We know that, Pa," volunteered Duff.

"There are a lot of runaways like him trying to get to the territories, so they can live free. They're desperate folks, and they need help. Your Ma and me, we discussed it and we feel it's our duty, our Christian duty, to lend a hand."

"That's agin the law, ain't it, Pa?" asked Duff. "I mean, helpin' runaways."

"True enough. But slavery ain't right and no law makes it so. We got to follow a higher law."

"You mean like in the Bible?"

Ma nodded.

"But Pa, couldn't they put you in jail and take the farm away if they found us out?" Duff asked.

"What your father's trying to say is," Ma interjected, "we think all people have a God-given right to live free. It makes no difference the color of their skin. We are all obliged to aid our brothers on their journey, if we can."

"How we gonna do that?" I asked Pa.

"Well," he began, looking nervously at Ma before he continued, "if they should come here, we'll hide them in our barn until they can move on," Pa explained.

Duff whistled, something he did when he was surprised by something.

"And whenever they're with us," Pa continued, "all of us will go about our business as usual. Do our chores, work the fields, take our meals like always. We won't tell a soul what we're up to. We can't rouse no suspicion. You boys understand?"

"Yes, Pa," we said together.

"Now, let's eat. We got work to do getting the barn ready. I hear we might have visitors soon."

"Heard from who?" asked Duff.

"Never you mind, son."

"You are a good man, Jack Armstrong," Ma said, putting her hand over Pa's.

After supper, we prepared the barn to receive the runaways. We cleared a spot in the corner that couldn't be seen from the main door, laying down straw for makeshift bedding. We stacked a pile of blankets nearby, and Duff helped Pa load in hay bales, too, so folks could sit around on them if they wanted, and we covered both the side door and the baling loft door with wood and burlap to keep out the cold, not to mention prying eyes. All things considered, by the time we were done, it looked pretty homey for a barn.

That evening, Duff and I played Pitch, Ma stitched her needlepoint, Pa relaxed with his pipe, and Suzy made herself at home by the fire. The grandfather clock ticked away, and we all pretended that nothing momentous was about to happen.

Just before nine, we heard rustling in the front yard. Suzy growled, but I hushed her.

A rough and raspy voice called out from the blackness.

"Mister Armstrong? Mister Armstrong?"

"You all stay here," Pa said to us. "I'll tend to them."

He put on his coat and hat, grabbed his rifle and held the lantern to illumine his way, moving carefully through the inky darkness.

Watching from the window, we saw Pa meet up with a group of black folks.

"They must be awful cold," I said. "They got no coats on."

Pa took them into the barn, then walked back to the house.

"Let's get them something to eat, Hannah. Boys, bring a lamp."

Doing as he ordered, we headed to the barn.

There were five of them altogether of various heights, all shivering with cold and hunger. They had wrapped themselves in blankets and were sitting on the hay bales we'd put out. The littlest feller, who was their leader, thanked us for our hospitality. I gave them a jug of fresh water and Ma arrived with a basket of warm cornbread muffins and bacon.

"Welcome, gentlemen," she said. "This isn't much, but I think it will tide you over."

"Much obliged, ma'am," one man said to her. "We ain't had nothin' to eat for days."

Pa introduced us all as they ate hungrily. "My name's Jack Armstrong. This here's my wife, Hannah. My sons Duff and Truman."

"Only folks call me Scrump," I piped up.

"Scrump? Like scrumpin' apples? Now ain't that a funny name," laughed the little feller with a raspy voice.

"I give it to him, and it kinda just stuck." Duff added.

"Glad to meet you all." Then the little feller introduced his companions as Jeb, Juniper, Pete, and Solomon. "And me, they just calls me Isaac."

"Nice to meet you, Mr. Isaac," I said.

His dark face was marked by a deep scar above his left eye.

"Where you from?" I asked.

"Down south a-ways. We been travelin' a long while. But we jus' passin' through."

Pa poured hot coffee into cups and Ma passed them around. Warming their hands on the cups, they drank eagerly.

"Where you headed?" asked Duff.

"Can't rightly tell you that. Jus' as far away from them massas on the plantations as we can."

Pa nodded. "Well, you're safe here. Get some rest and we'll see you in the morning."

"Yes, sir. Thank you, sir, and God bless you folks."

At noon the next day, Duff and I carried food out to them. The barn door creaked when we entered with our trays of food. Inside, we looked about. No one was there.

Duff yelled into the empty barn. "We brought food for you!"

Then we heard a noise and Isaac rose from a crouch behind a hay bale. The others came forth from various corners of the barn, under a pile of straw, or between feed bags stacked in a corner. In the light of day, their faces were tired and fearful, and I could see they were ready to bolt at the first hint of trouble, if need be.

Duff set a pot of hot coffee and a tray of sandwiches before them. I carried one of Ma's apple pies along with cups, forks, and plates.

"You folks sure is kind," said Isaac, delicately plucking a sandwich from the platter. The others murmured their thanks as well.

As Duff turned to leave, a fork fell to the floor.

"Uh oh!" said Isaac, picking it up. "Fork falls, lady calls. You be gettin' a call today from a lady visitor, Mr. Duff!"

"Nah, I don't believe in that stuff. Thanks just the same."

"Believin' in it got nothin' to do with it. You'll see," he said with a wink.

Later that day, someone came knocking at our door. We froze. Instinctively, we all realized this was a test for our current situation, a trial to be met with resolve and nonchalance. Nothing we did could appear out of the ordinary. Everything depended on it.

"Just act natural," Pa cautioned.

He rose and peered out the kitchen window. "Well, I'll be!"

"Who is it?" asked Ma.

"Sarah May Metzker."

We all looked to Duff. He blushed.

Ma smiled and went to open the door.

"Well, hello, dear! Step inside out of that cold."

Sarah May moved inside. She was dressed in a green wool coat trimmed in white rabbit fur that complimented her silky brown hair, and over one arm hung a food hamper. She smiled brightly when she saw Duff, who entered fastening his top collar button.

"Sarah May!"

"Hello, Duff!"

"Um…nice to see you."

There was an awkward pause between them till Ma finally spoke.

"Duff, why don't you invite Sarah May into the parlor while I put up a pot of tea?"

"Thank you for asking, Mrs. Armstrong," answered Sarah May politely, "but I can't stay. Preston made me promise to come right back to the ranch. He needs the buggy."

"So what are you here for?" I blurted.

"Scrump. Manners," Ma cautioned.

"You see, I was baking pies today and thought to myself, 'Sarah May, you should drop one of these off for the Armstrongs to enjoy.' So...here I am!"

Ma smiled. "How thoughtful of you."

Sarah May removed a fresh-baked pie from her hamper and gave it to Duff.

"Mm, smells great," he said, taking it in.

Sarah May smiled. "Enjoy it. Well...I guess I'll be on my way now."

"Let me walk you to your buggy," Duff offered eagerly. He handed the pie off to me and I carried it back to the kitchen.

"Be sure to give my best to your folks," Ma said. "See you at church."

When Duff came back inside, Ma smiled at him.

"That girl is mighty sweet on you, son," said Pa.

He blushed again. "I reckon."

That evening at supper, Pa said, "You all did mighty fine, not letting on about our visitors when Sarah May was here."

But before he could say anything, I asked Pa, "Can me and Duff go out to the barn and see how they're doin'?"

But when we got there, I was surprised to see they were gone.

"They didn't even say goodbye," I said sadly.

"Well, I reckon we don't know 'nuff about how they travel, Scrump."

"I just hope they're safe."

"That feller Isaac sure seems to know his way around. I got a feelin' we might be seein' him again."

Seven

EVERY YEAR, CHRISTMAS OFFICIALLY BEGAN for us when Pa went searching for our tree. The Christmas tree was still a relatively new custom in America, and my family didn't begin the tradition till I was born in 1848. Finding "the right tree" became one of my father's great joys. He would scour our own land with a discerning eye, wander into the country, even ask neighbors if he could examine their trees. When he finally found one he liked, he would take Duff and me to see it, and if we approved, the three of us would chop it down, load it on the wagon, and drive it home to show Ma.

This particular year, 1857, he found a shapely, lush blue spruce. As we did each year, we trimmed it with strips of colorful cloth left over from Ma's quilting, paper ornaments, and strings of popcorn and cranberries. When we were done, Pa reached up and placed a lacy angel that Ma had crocheted at the very top.

On Christmas morning, Suzy and I were up first and we ran downstairs to discover the apples and peppermint sticks St. Nick had left in my stocking. Under the tree, packages wrapped in brown paper and tied with string awaited us.

Duff's package was larger, so he opened his first. His face lit up. "A new shotgun, all my own!"

"Well now, it ain't exactly new," explained Pa. "Joe Stevens was buying another, so he sold me this one. But I got her all cleaned up for you."

"Thanks, Pa, Ma."

"You be careful with that gun, Duff," Ma said.

"Yes, ma'am."

"Your turn, Scrump," Ma said, handing me my package.

Eagerly, I ripped into it. They had given me two dime novels, and my own copy of *The Old Farmer's Almanac for 1858.* I beamed when I saw it. For me, the almanac was the best gift ever.

"Anybody who reads that thing as much as you do, ought to have one of his own," Pa said. "Besides, now I won't have to fight you for my copy. Study up, old man. One day something will pop out of those pages that could change your life."

Pa's gift to Ma was a new sewing kit and she gave him a pouch of his favorite cherry tobacco.

While Pa sat down with his pipe, enjoying his present, Duff and I settled in to play checkers. Meantime, Ma worked all morning in the kitchen and the smells of her cooking made our mouths water. When we were finally called in at noon, she had set the table with my grandma's best lace tablecloth and fine linen napkins, used only for special occasions. She had set out boiled potatoes, onions in cream sauce, a plate of buttermilk biscuits, and a huge stuffed goose.

Impulsively, I reached for a biscuit, but Duff stopped me. Pa was about to give the blessing, and I bowed my head with the others.

"Dear God, we thank you for this meal and for us being together. Give us good health, good weather, and a good crop this year. And keep us strong enough to help them folks who have no home, no food, and no freedom. Amen."

"Amen," we all echoed, and commenced to eating our special meal. After we stuffed ourselves as full as the goose, Ma brought out slices of spice cake topped with egg custard. For Pa, she poured out a small glass of whiskey, which he only took on special occasions.

"I knew I married you for a reason," he joshed after his first sip, and we all laughed. "Merry Christmas, Hannah. Boys."

"Merry Christmas!" we all replied.

The following afternoon, Mr. Wellman and his family joined us for supper. Being Quakers, they didn't celebrate Christmas, so the folks usually invited them the day after. Over the years, it had become something of a tradition.

The Wellman boys, Matthew and Luke, were closer to Duff's age, so he at least had some fellers to enjoy. I, on the other hand, knew I would be saddled with their little daughter Rebecca, a year younger than me. She was a pretty girl with flowing blond locks and cornflower blue eyes. They mesmerized me, those eyes, in a way I couldn't explain, but I found her girlish ways rather annoying.

They arrived as the clock chimed five and were greeted at the door by Ma and Pa with laughter and pleasantries. Mrs. Wellman, a wonderful cook in her own right, brought a huge plate of sugar cookies. She chatted cheerily as she followed Ma into the kitchen. Matthew and Luke, both trying to grow Quaker beards like their father's without much success, shook hands with Duff. Before they hung up their coats, Duff said he wanted to show them his new shotgun. Pa suggested he take them out back for that, and they headed off. As for me, I was left alone with Rebecca, and all I could muster for her was a glum "Hello." I plopped myself down on the steps, and she ran my way holding a rag doll with red yarn hair and button eyes.

"Look, I brought my Dolly," she cheerfully announced.

"Hmm. What do you call her?"

"But I just told thee. Dolly! That's her name, Dolly!" she insisted, staring at me like I was the dumbest kid in the county.

Trying to think of something to restore my wounded dignity, I said, "That there's our Christmas tree."

"It's so beautiful."

"Thanks," I said. Then, just to make small talk, asked her, "So…how big is your tree?"

"Oh, no, we don't have one. A Christmas tree wouldn't be right for us, because we believe every day is holy, not just some days."

"Oh, yeah. I forgot. Don't this make you want one, though?"

"No," she said, matter-of-factly. "Father says if we were to have a special tree for Christmas, we'd have to have a tree for every day of the year. The angel on top is pretty, though."

So much for small talk.

Just then, Ma came into the living room. "Scrump, go fetch Duff and the other boys. Supper's ready."

"Sure, Ma," I said, happy to get away from Rebecca.

Everyone crowded around our little table, and Mr. Wellman offered the blessing. We all set in to savor not only Ma's cooking, but also the bonds of friendship, love, and laughter.

The meal was capped off with Mrs. Wellman's sugar cookies and a mulled cider that Pa had concocted from a recipe he'd learned back in New Salem.

As the women cleaned up in the kitchen, Duff took Matthew and Luke up to our room. As for me, I was bored as a toad with Rebecca, so I sat silently with her in the parlor while she played with her doll. Suzy was sitting next to me.

"Hey, want to see my Christmas present? It's a new *Farmer's Almanac*."

Rebecca looked up and smiled, "Oh, I love to read."

I fetched the book and surprisingly she was actually interested in it, especially all the charts explaining the constellations.

Nearby, Pa visited with Mr. Wellman and enjoyed a bowl of his new cherry tobacco. I listened secretly when I heard them speak of the runaways.

"Thomas, I've yet to ask you this. When did you get involved with these runaways?"

"A year ago last fall. We were at Meeting when the Spirit moved me to speak of the evils of slavery. I was quite impassioned. Later, one of the leaders of our little community came to our door. He confided that he was an organizer for what they call the Underground Railroad, so named because it moves people along and into freedom."

"Interesting."

"He said that my farm, being along Purgatory Creek, was a perfect route of escape. Moving through water, runaways can travel unseen and untracked. After much prayer, I agreed to be part of the Underground Railroad, and he conferred upon me the position of Station Master."

"Station Master?"

"Those who hide runaways are called Station Masters on the railroad. Men like Isaac, who guide them to freedom, are Conductors. The runaways themselves are called Passengers."

"Then I'm a Station Master too," mused Pa with a puff of his pipe. "How many of us are there, would you say?"

"Hundreds, I suspect."

Pa whistled softly, the same sort of whistle Duff used when he was surprised.

"So, the feller that brought 'em here, Isaac. We'll likely be seein' him again?"

"I expect thee will. He has been to our farm three times unannounced, so thee must always be prepared."

Just then, the women entered and sat and there was no more talk of the Railroad. Rebecca and I continued to pore over the almanac until her mother noticed snow falling outside the window.

"Oh, my! We'd best be going, Thomas," said Mrs. Wellman.

"Duff, our company is leaving," Ma called up to our room.

Soon as they had bundled up, they said their goodbyes and headed for home before the snow got worse.

A week later, the four of us counted down the chimes to midnight and raised glasses of eggnog to welcome the

New Year. It was now 1858 and our family had never been happier.

But two days later, our lives were changed in a heartbeat.

EIGHT

SUNDAY MORNING DAWNED COLD. I stayed in bed while Duff got up early to milk the cow. When I finally arose, I dressed and scurried down to the kitchen. Ma hummed to herself as she stirred the porridge for our breakfast, and Pa quietly sipped his coffee. After we ate, Duff headed back to our room, and I helped Ma in the kitchen. That's when she mentioned that a leg on one of the kitchen chairs was loose.

Pa didn't speak, but he rose somewhat slowly and ambled to the barn. I noticed he was breathing heavy when he got back with his toolbox. Then, as he kneeled down to make the repair, he keeled right over.

"Jack!" Ma yelled.

I jumped to his side and called out, "Pa? Pa!"

But he didn't stir. He lay with his eyes closed, not moving. Duff hurried down the stairs when he heard the commotion.

"Duff, it's your Pa. Go fetch the doctor. Now!" Ma ordered.

He threw on his coat, ran to the barn, and galloped off on Paintbox, riding bareback.

Ma knelt next to Pa and held his hand.

"Jack? Jack, honey, it's me. Can you hear me?"

He moaned.

"Praise be, he's alive."

Together, Ma and I managed to get him into a chair. His face was ashen, and he complained about pains in his chest. Ma soothed him, bathing his brow with a cool, damp cloth.

The clock in the parlor ticked away the minutes. It seemed like forever until Duff returned with Doc Parker.

Dr. Eli Parker was the town's only doctor. He was there when babies were born, when folks felt poorly, and when they had died. He always wore a stiff white collar and a meticulously tied cravat, though his jacket was rumpled because he took it off so often. His mustache hung over his upper lip, making him look somewhat like a friendly walrus.

When he asked Ma what had happened, she replied, "He just fell over, right there, and couldn't get up. He was silent till I roused him."

He nodded and took Pa's pulse.

We all stood quietly as he examined him. He opened his medical bag and put a stethoscope to Pa's chest. He listened intently.

Then Pa spoke. "What's all this tomfoolery?" he said, pushing the stethoscope away. "I'm just tired, is all."

Doc Parker looked at him. "I'm afraid it's more than that, Jack. You've had a heart attack."

Ma gasped.

"These things can happen when we reach a certain age. You got to take it easy for a while." He turned to Ma. "Hannah, he mustn't climb the stairs to his bed. Too much of a strain on his heart."

"Me and Scrump can bring my bed and mattress down for Pa," said Duff. "Us two can bunk together for a while."

"Sure, we can."

"Crazy old fool! I'm going upstairs to rest in my own bed," mumbled Pa, trying to lift himself off the chair.

"Jack Armstrong, you're staying put," Ma ordered, gently pushing him back down.

Pa leaned back and nodded, and then he pulled the pipe from his pocket.

The doctor snatched it away. "And no more of this for now."

"You're a quack, you know that?"

"Hannah," the doctor said, "your stubborn old mule of a husband here needs plenty of rest and quiet. See that he doesn't exert himself. No farm work, no heavy lifting. That and a simple diet of meat and vegetables, no spirits, and he just might live long enough to learn some manners." He snapped his bag shut. "I'll be back to check on him in a few days."

"Thank you, Doc. We'll make sure to keep him rested and well fed."

Duff and I walked the doctor to the door.

"Anything else we can do for our Pa, Doc?"

"Just see that he does as I said, Duff. Make sure he don't do no farm work. That'll be on you for the time being. Understood?"

"Yessir. Ain't much to do until spring, anyway. He'll be stronger then, right?"

"We'll see," he said, forcing a cheerful tone. But he didn't fool us. We both could see the worry on his face. "Good luck, boys."

• • •

Word spread of Pa's condition and the Wellmans were the first to stop by. Mr. Wellman offered his sons to help with chores, but we declined. Duff and I wanted to handle things ourselves. Still, neighbors kept us cheered with a steady supply of firewood and good wishes.

One winter afternoon a few weeks later, Matthew stopped by before supper and left us a couple of rabbits he'd hunted.

"That was mighty good eating," commented Pa after his meal that evening. But these days he always left food on his plate.

Two months after Pa's heart attack, he seemed to be recovering steadily, but he was still very weak. Going up and down stairs and taking short strolls outside the house were permitted now, but Ma still made sure he didn't smoke his pipe or lift too much weight. Doc's orders.

Duff, Ma, and I kept up with the farm as best we could. Duff mended fences, chopped wood and tended to the fields while Ma milked the cow, and I fed the livestock. They were long days, but somehow we kept things moving.

"Slow down!" Ma admonished Duff, as a shiny buttered biscuit disappeared into his wide-open mouth in one bite.

He sat across from me at the table, and tonight he was scrubbed from head to toe. He had clean nails, wet combed hair, and fresh-washed clothes. On this particular Saturday, he was not headed to the field, but to a camp meeting.

What we then called a "camp meeting" is along the lines of a church revival. This meeting was supposed to attract the young people of Cass County. It was to be held under a large tent pitched near Salt Creek, about four miles away.

Duff wasn't so big on religion, but I knew the real reason he wanted to go. "You pickin' up your *girlfriend* on the way?" I teased.

"You got one big trap, little brother, ya know that?"

"Scrump, don't make fun of your brother," Ma ordered. "He needs some time away from home for a change. He's earned it."

"You go along and enjoy yourself with Sarah May, son," Pa told him. "But I hear them meetings can get raucous. Mind yourself and Sarah May real well, and don't be out too late."

"No, sir, I won't."

Finished with his supper, Duff headed out to hitch Paintbox up to the buggy and then set off cheerfully. I spent the rest of the evening reading my almanac, while Pa studied his newspaper.

The clock chimed nine, and Ma looked up from her darning and asked, "Wonder if Duff's on his way home yet?"

At the chime of ten, she put away her sewing kit and again wondered aloud about him.

"Honestly, Hannah. You're acting like one of our mama hens. You know how those camp meetings go on. Duff'll be home in his own good time."

When I awoke early the next morning, I looked over to Duff's empty bed. It hadn't been slept in. I heard

Paintbox whinny out front, and figuring Duff was finally home, I ran down to the front door, planning to tease him mercilessly. Instead, I saw that our filly had returned alone, without the buggy and without Duff.

I ran to wake Ma and Pa. "Something's happened to Duff!" I told them that Paintbox had come home alone without the buggy.

Of course, Pa's first instinct was to go in search of Duff, but he wasn't near strong enough, and Ma wouldn't allow it.

"Scrump," Pa instructed, "hook Paintbox up to the wagon and go straight to the Wellman farm. Tell Mr. Wellman that Duff didn't come home last night. Tell him we need a search party for your brother."

"Yes, Pa."

When I got over to the neighbors and told them that Duff was missing, they jumped right in to help. Matthew and Luke saddled up for the search, and Mr. Wellman got into our hay wagon with me.

"Give the filly her head, boy. Tell her to take us to Duff. She'll do it for you."

"Okay," I said. "Paintbox, take us to Duff. You remember Duff, girl. Take us to him."

Paintbox seemed to understand. I loosened the reins as she started along the road and then took the fork leading to Salt Creek. She pulled us through a winding stretch of woods till we were alongside a ravine. Then her gait slowed, and she came to a complete halt. We peered down into the chasm.

Wheel tracks. Broken branches. Our buggy tipped on its side on the hill. And then—Duff. He was lying face down, awkwardly wrapped around a tree that must have stopped his fall.

"There he is!" I hollered, jumping out of the wagon and tripping my way down the hillside, with the Wellmans close behind.

"Duff! Duff," I cried, when I reached him and struggled to turn him over.

Oh, please, God, I prayed. *Please let him be alive.*

Mr. Wellman saw that Duff was still breathing, so he and his sons carefully carried him back up the hill and placed him into the wagon. We got back home as quickly as we could. Ma and Pa were anxiously waiting at the door.

Luke and Matthew carried Duff from the wagon upstairs to his bed, with Ma and Pa close on their heels. When they laid him down, he moaned for the first time.

"Duff? Duff, it's your Ma, son," she said.

Duff slowly opened his eyes.

"Ma? Where am I?"

"You're home now, honey. You had a bad accident. Do you remember?"

He weakly shook his head, then closed his eyes and drifted off.

Mr. Wellman sent Matthew to fetch the doctor.

Doc Parker came quickly. Duff had a large bump on his head, and a lot of bruises everywhere, but no broken bones. When the doctor questioned him, he remembered nothing of the accident and could recall few details from the night before.

"Where were you last night?"

"A church revival, up at Salt Creek."

"Salt Creek?" said the Doc. "The same one Preston Metzker went to?"

"Yeah. I remember going, but not much else. It's like I blacked out or something."

Doc explained that this was not uncommon after a blow to the head. He predicted his memory would return with the passage of time.

As Ma walked him to the door, she asked, "He'll be all right, won't he, Doc?"

"Yes, he'll be fine. Only..."

"Only what?"

"I was called to the Metzker ranch early this morning. Their boy, Preston came home with a bloody wound to his head. He didn't make it."

"Merciful heavens, no!"

"I probably shouldn't have told you. But Duff'll be just fine. Keep him quiet."

Soon as he left, I asked Ma if she was going to tell Duff about Preston.

"No, not right away. He needs his rest. And don't you say anything to him either. Your Pa and I will handle this."

The rest of the day, Ma nursed him with hot soup and warm tea. She bathed him with a cool cloth to keep him comfortable, and she let him sleep through the day and on into the night.

• • •

The following afternoon, Monday, Duff was finally awake enough to come down and sit with us in the kitchen. But just as he joined us, we heard someone ride up in the yard.

Pa went slowly to the door and we heard Sheriff Dick's voice.

"Hate to trouble you, Jack, but I need to see your son Duff."

Ma hurried to the parlor with me following close behind. "What's wrong, Sheriff? Duff's right here. He's been getting over a spill he took in the buggy."

"Well, I'm sorry to hear that, Miz Armstrong," continued the sheriff. "Mind if I come in and set a spell? I think we need to talk."

The sheriff removed his hat as he entered the parlor.

"You folks heard about the Metzker boy?" he began.

"Doc Parker mentioned it when he was here for Duff. We were shocked, Sheriff. What happened?"

"He was murdered."

"Murdered!" I cried."

"Folks, it pains me to tell you this, but I got two witnesses saying they seen your boy Duff do him in."

We were dumbstruck.

"No, not Duff. That can't be," insisted Ma. "They must be mistaken. In the condition he's in, he couldn't have hurt anyone. Someone tried to hurt him, more likely. He was run off the road! Why don't you go find who did that 'stead of picking on our boy?"

"Hannah, please. Sheriff, Duff was found near dead in a ravine on Sunday morning. What you're saying don't make any sense," Pa said.

"Well, sense or no, I still got a job to do, so I guess I better show you this."

He held out a piece of paper. Ma took it and studied it.

"An arrest warrant?" she asked.

"Duff, get on in here," Pa called, not even looking at the paper.

Duff stepped gingerly in from the kitchen. "Yeah, Pa? Oh, howdy, Sheriff Dick," he said.

"Son, the sheriff wants to know what happened up at that camp meeting Saturday night."

"Why? Somethin' wrong?"

"Duff," Ma interjected, "the sheriff says that Preston Metzker is dead."

Duff was dumbfounded. "What? Preston, dead?"

"Murdered is more like it, Duff. And there's two eyewitnesses that swear you done it."

"Well, they're lyin'!"

"And I hope that turns out to be the case, I really do," said the sheriff. "But in the meantime, Duff, I have to take you into custody."

"Pa, Ma...I ain't done nothin'," stammered Duff.

"Sheriff, please," Ma said sweetly. "Can't you at least give him the chance to explain it to you? I'm sure if you'd only listen—"

He cut her off sharply.

"Look, Miz Armstrong. He'll get his chance—in front of a judge, all legal and proper. I can promise you that. Aw, now don't worry, folks. I'll take good care of him. He'll have a warm bed and hot food till he gets his day in court. Till then, he'll be in jail, probably at least a few weeks."

"A few weeks?" cried Ma.

"You all can visit him as much as you like, Miz Armstrong. If this is a mistake like you say, it'll clear itself up. The law's fair. But right now, Duff, you got to come along with me. You're under arrest."

"No!" Duff shouted, pulling away as the sheriff reached for him.

"Best you go with him, son," Pa said to Duff. "It's just one big misunderstanding. We know that, your Ma and me. So we'll get to clearing things up and then you'll be home for good. I promise you."

"But Pa!"

I watched helplessly as the sheriff clapped hand irons onto Duff's wrists. Then he took him outside and gave him a leg up onto his horse. Pa wanted to follow them along in the wagon, but Ma convinced him he was too weak to make the trip to town. The sheriff again assured us Duff would be safe. Ma cried as the sheriff rode him away to jail.

Right after Duff was gone, Pa insisted he had to go see after him. But by now, he was so agitated, he was having trouble catching his breath. His face had blanched white.

"Jack, honey, you're just not up to it," she said, trying to calm him. "There's nothing you can do to help Duff right this minute, is there?"

He continued to argue with her, but then Ma announced that she herself would go directly to the jail and see after Duff. She had such a way with Pa that he reluctantly gave in, but only on the condition I take her into town in the wagon, because he didn't think she should go alone.

So Ma quickly dressed for town while I hitched up Paintbox. When Ma climbed in and sat next to me, I was nervous. For one thing, I was eager to visit Duff, but I dreaded seeing my hero behind bars. For another, it was the first time I would be driving all the way to town, not just riding along with Pa or Duff. I'd driven to the fields before, of course, that was one thing. This was entirely different.

The first time a boy drove into town was always considered a rite of passage in those days. It would have otherwise been a joyful occasion, but today it was a somber journey. We rolled along the main road toward town quietly, seldom speaking. My eyes were extra-attentive to the road. A farmer passed by in his wagon and scrutinized me. Ma nodded to him.

"You're doing just fine," she offered reassuringly.

Once into town, we pulled up before the Sheriff's Office, and I hitched Paintbox to the post out front. We entered a cramped space whose walls were lined with gun racks and 'Wanted' posters. Those grim notices about desperados and runaways stared out at me wherever I looked. The sheriff sat with his boots propped up on his desk, but he scrambled to his feet as soon as Ma appeared in the doorway.

"Afternoon, Sheriff. I'd like to see my son."

"Yes, ma'am. Let me take you to him. I'm sure sorry about all this, Miz Armstrong. Just doing what I got to do, you know."

He retrieved a small ring of jangling jail keys from inside his desk drawer and escorted us through a heavy wooden door off the corner of his office. We walked down a narrow hallway that led to three small cells. A drunk was passed out in the first, snoring loudly. No one occupied the middle one. Duff was in the last, lying on a cot with his back to us. Midway up the wall above, a lonely barred window provided the only view of the outside world.

"Sit up now, Duff. Your Ma's here."

Duff rolled over and bounded to his feet. His eyes and nose were red, and while he'd never admit it, I suspected he'd done some crying like we all had. I couldn't blame him.

"Ma! Scrump!"

The sheriff put a key in the iron lock, admitted us in, and then stepped out and locked it up again. "Call me when you're ready," he said, and disappeared from sight.

Duff clung to Ma and fought back tears.

"Now don't fret. We'll get you out of here."

"Why am I even here, Ma? I ain't done nothin' wrong."

"You know we believe you, don't ya?" I said.

"It's some big mix-up, that's what it is. I'm going to get us a lawyer to bring you home."

"But we can't afford no lawyer, Ma."

"Show some faith, Duff Armstrong! Just be patient. Do you remember what happened up at that meeting, son? Anything that might help you?"

"No, I... I keep trying, but it's all a blur. I just know that I couldn't have done what they say, Ma. I never would have!"

"Of course you wouldn't. Everybody in this town knows the good young man you've become. I'll talk to Sheriff Dick to see if we can find out what's what."

"How's Pa?"

"Taking this hard. Just not himself. We had to fight him something awful to keep him from coming here. You understand."

"Sure, Ma. Tell him I'm real sorry."

"Yes, dear." She eyed an empty tin plate on the bed. "They feedin' you?"

"Yes, ma'am."

When it was time to go, his spirits were cheered, but mine were conflicted. Seeing Duff caged like an animal made me angry and afraid for him all at once. Ma gave him a goodbye hug and I shook his hand.

"See you soon, Duff," I told him, trying to be brave.

We called for the sheriff who came and led us back to his desk. Ma immediately sat herself down in a chair. The sheriff sat also. I stood, leaning against the wall.

"I want to know exactly what's happened, Sheriff. Or what you *think* happened and what they're saying about my boy. And don't varnish the truth."

"I don't know if I can say it in front of the young'un here."

"He'll hear it sooner or later, Sheriff. Speak your piece."

"Well, near as I can figure, Duff and a few other fellers about his age got restless at the camp meeting and headed up Salt Creek a ways till they found a—"

He glanced my way and hesitated.

"A what, Sheriff?" Ma demanded.

"A whiskey camp."

"A whiskey camp! Gosh!" I blurted.

"Scrump, be still," ordered Ma. "Go on, Sheriff."

"Evidently he arrived there pretty angry and things got heated between him and young Metzker. Before you know it, they say your boy Duff grabbed a wagon hammer and hit him in the head."

Ma bit her lip.

"Duff'd never do that! They're makin' it up," I blurted.

Ma turned and gave me one of her looks. I knew to keep quiet from then on.

"How do you know all this?"

"From an eyewitness. Two of 'em, in fact."

"I see. But there must have been others around. How do we know what they saw?"

"That'll all come out in the trial. First the magistrate will report to the circuit judge, who will review the facts. Once the judge arrives in town, Duff will most likely be charged with murder."

"And if he's judged…guilty?"

"Well…sentencing would be up to the judge, ma'am. But…it ain't good." He cleared his throat. "Of course, Duff being young and all, it might go easier for him than for some."

Ma was silent a long moment before speaking.

"Thank you for your honesty, Sheriff," she said, and rose to leave. "I'll be back with food for my son tomorrow. I'll bring some for you, too."

"Thank you, ma'am. Oh, before you go, you might want this." He handed her a note he'd scribbled. "You're going to need a good lawyer to defend him, Miz Armstrong. There's a law office down the street, Walker & Mason. I already told Henry Walker all about Duff's case. I think you should talk to him."

Ma took the paper from him. "Appreciated. And don't you forget your promise. You keep my boy safe."

NINE

SHORTLY AFTER WE LEFT THE Sheriff's Office, I pulled us up in front of a small red brick building with a shingle announcing, "Walker & Mason, Attorneys at Law."

After securing the wagon to a post, I followed Ma through the large oaken door and into a small, dingy office that smelled of cigar smoke. An empty desk stood against one wall, fronted by a series of stacked compartments and shelves, all stuffed full of lawyerly detritus. Over these was a shelf displaying the owner's mementos—a feathered quill pen, a bundle of yellowed letters tied with a blue ribbon, a chipped pottery bowl, and a tiny green vase full of dead flowers. On the wall just above it hung a law diploma, and next to that was a portrait of George Washington.

Nearby, a second desk was shoved into a dark corner. A thick layer of dust covered its empty top.

The wall opposite the door was lined with a towering bookcase that rose from floor to ceiling, far outsizing the number of books. What few books there were appeared to be shelved in no particular order, a mishmash of sizes, many of them laying down instead of neatly organized like a proper law library.

"Hello there! Welcome, welcome," called a man's voice, piercing the quietude, as a door to a backroom opened. A squat, round man with a u-shape of grizzled hair about his bald pate walked in and closed the door behind him.

"Henry Walker of Walker & Mason, at your service, ma'am," announced the little feller and held out his hand. Ma shook it politely.

"Mr. Mason, my partner, is sadly dead these three years, so it's just me now," he sighed.

"Mason? Yes, I believe I knew his wife, Elvira," recalled Ma. "From church."

"A fine woman. I'm not much on church myself. Please have a seat."

He pulled the chair from his desk and offered it to Ma, and then pulled up another for himself from the empty desk in the corner. I stood behind Ma's chair and listened.

"Thank you. I'm Hannah Armstrong. My husband Jack and I own a farm a few miles outside of town. This is our youngest, Truman."

"Armstrong, Armstrong," he repeated. "Oh, of course. Armstrong! The lad who's currently incarcerated on the charge of murdering the Metzker boy."

I couldn't keep quiet. "He's innocent!" I blurted out.

"Of course he is, sonny. In this country, everyone is innocent until proven guilty."

Ma began by describing Duff's predicament, but quickly he cut her off, confessing that the sheriff had already filled him in on the details.

"He's in a very difficult spot, your son."

"But can you help him?"

He rubbed his stubbled chin, pulled his chair closer, and leaned toward her.

"Let me put it to you like this, Mrs. Armstrong. The law says it takes just one witness to prove a fact."

"I don't follow you."

"That's a problem with this case. They got two witnesses who say Duff did it, so the law is going to take a witness's word as fact. Even one single witness can prove a fact as well as the crime."

"But they're lying!" The words rushed out of me beyond control.

"Well, sonny, both witnesses are saying the same thing. Now we've got two people to prove the facts *and* the crime."

"Only if folks believe 'em," I insisted.

"Hush, now, Truman. So what can we do, Mr. Walker?"

"This is a tricky case, ma'am. All the cards are stacked against your son at this point. Your best bet might be for your son to plead guilty. You know, throw himself on the court's mercy and hope for a lighter sentence."

"My boy is innocent, Mr. Walker. Me and his pa want someone who'll fight for him."

"Yes, of course, but a long, drawn-out trial could wind up costing you folks a pretty penny."

"If you were to take my boy's case, you'd get paid, I assure you. You ask anyone in this town. We Armstrongs pay our bills."

"I didn't mean to suggest otherwise, ma'am. I'm just being realistic. Two eyewitnesses. It's open and shut."

"If you don't mind my saying so, Mr. Walker, it sounds an awful lot like you already made up your mind about Duff."

"Facts are facts in the eyes of the law. But I'll give him a good defense, if that's what you want."

She abruptly stood. "No, Mr. Walker. Duff needs a fighter who believes in him. Thank you for your time, but your services are not needed."

"As you wish, ma'am. I'm just being honest, based on my years of experience."

"Good day, sir."

Seizing my hand, she pulled me toward the door. "Come along, Truman."

When we headed home, the sun sat low in the sky and intermittently blinded us as we passed under the branches of the sycamores. Ma was lost in thought, same as me. And I'm sure we were both thinking the same thing—*What in the world are we going to do now?*

When we pulled up at the farmhouse, Pa was waiting on the porch and he hurried out to greet us. Although pale and gaunt, his step seemed to have found a new vigor.

"Jack! You promised you'd stay in bed!"

"Bah, I'm fine. How's our boy?"

"Scared. Jail is no place for a boy like him. Puts on a brave front, though," she said, stepping down from the rig.

"What did he say? When is Duff getting out?"

"It's bad, Jack. The sheriff says there's two witnesses who both say they seen Duff do it."

"That can't be!"

"And there's a judge coming to town in a few weeks, and there's going to be a trial. He'll be in jail until then."

"Trial? But Duff's innocent. Didn't you tell him that?"

She nodded. "He sent me to this lawyer feller about defending him. Mister Walker."

"Henry Walker?"

Ma's eyes watered and she brushed away a tear. "Even he thinks Duff is guilty based on the facts. He's no help. We got to save our boy," she said, starting to cry.

"Now, Hannah," said Pa, putting his arms around her. "You and I both know the Lord won't give us more than we can handle," he smiled. "But guess what, I got a plan. It came to me just as you left."

Pa began to cough, so Ma and I guided him gently back into the house, sat down with him at the kitchen table, and waited for him to catch his breath.

"Now what's this plan?" Ma asked him. "What are you talking about?"

"It ain't what, it's *who*. Abe Lincoln! He's a lawyer, ain't he? And a good one at that. 'Member all them books he studied at our house? Why, he knows his way around the law real good. He'll help Duff, I know he will."

"Oh, but Jack. He's in Springfield now. We haven't heard from him in years. You don't think he'd really..."

"Of course he would! Abe's a good man and a better friend. 'Sides, don't he owe us something for giving him a start? I'm going to write him right now. Scrump, fetch the writing desk."

"Yessir!"

To me, this was exciting beyond words. I was finally going to meet the hallowed Abraham Lincoln and he was going to get Duff free.

I watched over his shoulder as he slowly printed.

Dear Abe,

It is been a long time since New Salem. I am sorry to beg your help in such suden maner as this here letter. But our boy Duff is got in trouble with the law, and is in the jailhouse. They say he killed a feller, but he didn't.

Please Abe, make your way here soon as you are able. I woud be eternaly grateful. Hannah and my youngest boy Truman send regards.

Sincerely,
Jack Armstrong
Beardstown, Illinois

When he was done with the note, he folded it carefully and turned to me. "Scrump, old man, first thing tomorrow morning, you head right back into town and give this to the postmaster yourself. Tell him I said to put it in a strong envelope and send it out pronto to Mr. Abraham Lincoln, Law Office, Springfield, Illinois. Can you do this for me, son?"

"Sure I can, Pa." I put the letter in my shirt pocket.

"Good boy. Your brother's life depends on it."

He dug into his coin purse and fished out a nickel and a few pennies. "This here's for postage, and anything left over is yours."

"Thanks, Pa. But maybe we better keep the change to pay Mr. Lincoln."

He smiled. "Well, you decide."

I hadn't seen him full of this much life in weeks. Hope was a powerful remedy.

"It's in God's hands now, I suppose," Ma said. "You rest while I fix supper."

That night, I was waiting in the hallway after Ma had tucked Pa in.

"You think Mr. Lincoln can really help Duff, Ma?"

"Well, your Pa seems to think so. It's surely worth a letter to find out."

TEN

THE NEXT MORNING, I SADDLED up Paintbox right after breakfast and rode directly into town to post Pa's letter. The postmaster, Mr. Wade, said it would take a week or more to reach Springfield.

When I arrived back home, I found Ma ironing in the kitchen.

"Got it posted," I announced. "Where's Pa?"

"He's napping. You let him be. Here, wash up and put this on."

She held out a clean, pressed shirt to me.

"We goin' somewhere?"

"To church."

"But it ain't even Sunday," I complained. We weren't regular church-goers, but that was mainly 'cause our farm was farther out and Pa and Duff were always dog-tired on Sundays. Still, Ma liked to go whenever she could. "Why do we have to go today?"

"I need you to drive me there in the wagon. There's a funeral."

"Whose?"

"Preston Metzker's."

I gulped. "But Ma, them folks think…"

"We need to pay our respects, Scrump. Now get ready."

Sangamon Christian Church, our little white frame church with a bright red door, was situated on a hill a good hour's ride from our farm. The wooden steeple, which housed the church's bell, was crowned with a cross and could be seen for miles around. When we pulled up, there were all kinds of rigs and horses hitched out front. I parked the wagon and we went inside.

We took seats in a rear pew as Mrs. Hoffman, our white-haired organist, pumped away, playing a mournful tune.

Directly in front of us, I noticed the Hudgins family. One of their four children, Billy, was my age. Billy and I played together at church socials and such, so when he saw me, he turned to wave. But this caught Mr. Hudgins' eye, and he whispered to Billy, who turned away from me and glued his eyes to the front.

The Metzkers entered from a side door and filed past a wooden casket sitting before the altar. Baskets of flowers surrounded it. Mr. Metzker normally walked with great pride in being the most prominent rancher for miles around, but today his shoulders were stooped as he looked down on his son's lifeless body. He was of average height, and he wore a black suit and matching vest. Mrs. Metzker, a lovely woman about the same age as Ma, was in a simple black dress with a black bonnet and veil. She sobbed into a handkerchief as her two surviving sons and Sarah May led their parents to a front pew and sat.

Parson Akerson stood in the pulpit and offered words of consolation before calling on us to sing a hymn. Then we sat for Bible verses and a very long sermon. The parson memorialized Preston as a wonderful son, a faithful friend, and a model citizen who had lived a life full of good works. This sounded nothing like the Preston I knew, but of course, we were here to pay our respects, so I figured they had to make Preston sound respectable.

As the sermon concluded, we sang another hymn and rose to our feet when the coffin was carried out by several men of the congregation, followed by the grieving relatives. They passed by us and Ma reached out to touch Mrs. Metzker, but her husband steered her away. At the gravesite in the church cemetery, Ma and I hung back while the coffin was lowered and the final commendation was read.

Back at the wagon after the service, I took the reins and Ma noticed I was red-faced with consternation.

"You all right, son? Somethin' wrong?"

"It's the way all them church folk treated us. Like we had head lice or somethin'."

"They're grieving, Scrump. It's hard for them, especially on account of us being Duff's family. It's sad all around. We need to forgive them."

"Seems to me like they're blaming us for Preston's death. Don't they know Duff is innocent?"

"No, they don't, because it hasn't yet been proved. But think if it was turned around, and it was Duff's body in that casket. Just imagine how you would feel."

"Well..."

"Truman, it's your Christian duty to be forgiving. Jesus expects it of us."

It was always hard to disagree with Ma, especially when she dragged Our Lord into it. When she did, you knew you had lost for sure, so I kept quiet the rest of the way home.

Ma and I visited Duff as regularly as we could, with Ma carrying him baskets of home-cooked food, enough for him, the sheriff, and the deputy to gobble up. Duff asked repeatedly if we'd heard from Sarah May, but trying not to disappoint him, Ma would say something like, "Give her time, dear. Try not to think about it."

"Did you hear from Mr. Lincoln? Is he going to help, you think?"

"Still waiting on his letter, but your Pa is sure he'll come to our aid. It's the kind of thing Abe would do."

Our jailhouse visits with him always made Duff a littler cheerier, but as the days dragged on, it was harder to keep his spirits up.

Every day when we left the jail, we stopped to ask Mr. Wade at the Post Office if a letter had arrived for us. But every day we got the same answer. "Sorry, not yet. Maybe tomorrow."

On the way home, Ma would usually fall silent as a moonbeam. I could sense she was afraid for Duff's future. I sure hoped God had good plans for us, as she believed, but I couldn't see things getting better anytime soon.

"I just pray Abe gets your Pa's letter," she confided one day. "It's taking awfully long."

It was a good two weeks, and many a jailhouse visit later, when a letter finally arrived.

We were sitting in the parlor just after our dinner when Mr. Wade himself rode up to the house and knocked on the front door. Pa answered it.

"Afternoon, Jack. How you feeling?"

"I'm gettin' along. What brings you all the way out here?"

"I knew you folks were waiting on this, so I figured I'd bring it out myself."

He held up a letter. Pa froze, staring at it.

"Yes. Yes, thank you!" said Pa, taking it from him. "You want some coffee?"

"Appreciate the offer, but I best be getting back. I hope it's good news."

"Yes. I think it may be. Thank you very much."

Pa closed the door and turned to us, letter in hand. "It's from Abe," he said solemnly.

I ran to him. "Hurry and open it, Pa!"

He carefully ran his pocketknife along the top edge of the envelope. My heart pounded as he silently read.

Ma could wait no longer and finally burst out with, "Well? What does he say, Jack?"

He read aloud, "I can hardly believe Duff capable of the crime alleged against him. I am anxious that he should be given a fair trial, at any rate. My gratitude for your long, continued kindness to me in adverse circumstances prompts me to offer my humble services gratuitously on his behalf."

"Praise the Lord," Ma sighed, sinking into a chair with relief. "He's going to do it."

"I knew it all along," said Pa. "I knew he wouldn't let us down!" He grabbed Ma in his arms and hugged her.

"Pa, what's...gratoosly?"

"Gratuitously," corrected Ma. "It means he won't accept money from us. When's he coming, Jack?"

"He says as soon as he can. No more than a couple of weeks, he says. And he signed it, 'Your grateful friend, A. Lincoln.'" He handed the letter to Ma so she could read it herself.

"Pour me a glass of that whiskey from Christmas," said Pa.

"Now Jack, Doc said no spirits," she reminded him.

"Can we just forget that quack for one night? We got hope for the first time since this whole thing happened."

"All right, but a taste is all you get," Ma relented. "Scrump and I will toast, too, with cider."

That evening, the three of us were happier than we'd been in a long time. Pa laughed and told stories about Abe from the old days. And we all agreed that things were certainly looking up for the Armstrongs.

Next morning, as I was helping Ma put out breakfast on the table, she called cheerfully up to Pa. "Come and get it, sleepy head! Rise and shine!"

But there was no answer.

"Jack? Jack, honey?"

In the silence that followed, she looked at me. Her eyes widened with fear and I knew something was wrong.

"Jack! Jack!" she shouted as she raced up the stairs. I followed right behind her.

At the bedroom doorway, she stopped and stared. Pa lay unmoving under the covers. She approached him quietly and sat gently next to him, her eyes brimming with tears. She held his cold hand to her cheek. The curtain over the open window fluttered quietly in the breeze.

"Oh, Jack, Jack...my darling..."

She reached out to me, pulling me close.

"What's wrong, Ma? What is it?"

"Your Pa's gone, Scrump. He's...with the Lord now."

Ma kissed Pa's forehead and rose up off the bed. Taking my hand, she led me directly to the parlor where she opened the grandfather clock's glass door and stilled the great brass pendulum to mark the hour of Pa's death. The house fell eerily silent.

"When will you start it up again, Ma?" I asked, wiping away tears.

"Just as soon as Duff is back with us. I promise."

• • •

There are many things I remember from the time of Pa's death. The news spread like wildfire in the community where he'd spent most of his life, and folks from all over showed up at our home to bring food and offer condolences. I knew Ma was grateful, as she was so grief-stricken that she could scarcely move at all that first day.

But the next day, Ma and I had to go to the jail to tell Duff. I'm sure it was the hardest thing she'd ever done. As they stood there in the cell talking quietly, I saw the sorrow in Ma's eyes and the pain in Duff's. Those feelings were every bit as real in me as my heart ached for Pa.

When we'd finally left the cell, the sheriff said, "I'm surely sorry for your sorrow, Miz Armstrong. Your husband was a good man."

I remember when Parson Akerson came to help us plan the funeral. Though he hadn't seen Pa at church very often, he knew Pa to be a kind, generous, God-fearing man who loved his family very much.

When the day of the funeral came, our little church was full once again. I know Pa was well-liked, but I had an uneasy feeling that some folks came out of curiosity, wanting to get a look at Duff. Because of the penny papers, he was a local celebrity.

I saw a small woman who entered quietly and sat in the back. Like the other mourners, she wore black, but her veil completely hid her face. My heart skipped a beat when she lifted the veil ever so slightly to dab at her tears, and I realized it was Sarah May Metzker.

The crowd broke into a murmur when Duff arrived with the sheriff. His hand irons had been removed before he entered, so at least he'd been spared that indignity. Still, a lot of folks strained their necks for a glimpse of the accused murderer of Preston Metzker.

When Duff came to us at Pa's coffin, he took Ma in his arms and hugged her for a long time, and then bent over and lifted me up, holding me close as I nestled into his shoulder.

After our embrace, Sheriff Dick stepped up to Ma and said, "Duff can stay with you today as long as you want."

"Thank you, Sheriff," said Ma as she wiped her tears. She wore her black mourning dress and her topaz brooch, a beautiful yellow gem set in filigreed gold. It was Pa's wedding gift to her, a treasure passed down through generations of his family.

There were stirring eulogies from Parson Akerson and others. The parson called Pa "a tall tree" and spoke of his strong roots, his sheltering arms, and his towering presence in the community.

Mr. Wellman talked about Pa's love for family and friends and his willingness to help the stranger in need.

Mr. Schultz, a neighboring farmer, recalled Pa working to rebuild his barn after a fire.

Neighbor after neighbor shared stories such as these, attesting to Pa's faithfulness, how he was always there for them anytime they needed help.

After the final hymn, the church bell rang solemnly as Pa's coffin was carried out to our wagon. A long procession followed us back to his final resting place, a plot next to our ancestors' graves on our farm.

As the coffin was lowered into the hole, the parson said, "ashes to ashes, dust to dust," and each of the three of us sprinkled a small handful of dirt onto the lonely wood box lying in its grave.

Our closest neighbors returned to the house, bringing hampers filled with fresh bread, boiled eggs, ham, apple cobbler, and gooseberry pie. A few of us children sat on the stairs with plates on our laps, listening to stories of Pa punctuated by the sounds of clinking silverware and, occasionally, laughter. My mother, trying hard to be a good hostess, fought back tears every moment.

I remember how empty the house felt after everyone had left and the sheriff took Duff back to the jail. That's when I realized for the first time how different our lives would be without Pa. The future loomed before us like a dark, deep cavern. My mother was a widow, my brother was about to go on trial for murder, and our farm was now in the hands of Ma and me alone. I couldn't imagine how we could get through this, but I knew that now more than ever, I had to be strong for Ma.

ELEVEN

FIVE DAYS AFTER THE FUNERAL, I was resting my chin on the windowsill when I saw a tall, erect figure riding up into our yard on a distinguished chestnut horse. He deftly dismounted his steed and strode with purpose up the front steps, rapping energetically at the door. Suzy barked and scurried down the stairs and I quickly followed. I recognized him from Pa's stories as the "tall skinny beanpole."

"Ma, Ma!" I hollered. "It's him! He's here, Ma!"

Eagerly opening the door, I was met by the tallest feller I'd ever seen. My gaze traveled up a length of rumpled pinstripe trousers to a dark frock coat hanging just above his knees, then to a white cotton shirt with a deep blue cravat. His tall black felt hat made him look like a giant. I looked up to his face, dumbfounded and speechless.

"Hello there, young'un," he greeted me. A wide grin spread across his hollow cheeks. His clean-shaven face was weathered by sun and etched with creases like a dry hillside. His kindly eyes crinkled at the corners when he spoke to me. "I'm Abe Lincoln, a friend of your Ma and Pa's. I'm guessing you must be Truman. Your Pa told me about you."

He bent forward and offered his hand.

"Pleased to meet you," I said. "Only most folks call me Scrump."

"Abe? Abe Lincoln, is that you?" called Ma.

Mr. Lincoln came into the parlor as Ma rushed from the kitchen. Her step was lighter and her eyes were brighter than I'd seen them in quite some time.

"Hannah Armstrong! My, you're looking lovely as ever. Where's that husband of yours?"

Her lower lip trembled. It was still hard for her to speak of it aloud, and she put a hand on my shoulder to brace herself.

"Abe, we lost Jack two weeks ago. His heart."

"Oh, Hannah, no," he said taking her hand. I could see he was thunderstruck by the news. "I am so sorry for you, for you both. Jack was a wonderful friend. I shall never forget our happy times together."

"Thank you, Abe." She choked back tears. "And thank you for coming. I'm so...well, we're just so glad you're here."

While Ma composed herself, I said, "I like your hat, Mr. Lincoln. You keep anything under it?"

"See for yourself."

He handed it to me, and I fingered it curiously, studying the fine hand-stitching of its black ribbon brim, and there, snugged inside the inner band, I recognized Pa's letter.

"My, my. Where in the world did you get all that red hair?" he said, looking down on me.

"I reckon it came with the head," I shrugged, and he let out a laugh that trickled like a refreshing stream.

"But, Abe, you must be hungry and tired after your trip. Come on into the kitchen and I'll fix you something to eat."

"Just a cool drink of water would do fine."

As I went to return his hat, he plopped it onto my head.

"I have a boy just about your age and he likes to ride piggyback. Want to give it a try?"

"Sure!" I said. He stooped low to let me hop on, and then we were off on a race to the kitchen.

"Abe, it's wonderful to see you. How long has it been?"

"Oh, way before Mary and I were wed," he answered.

As he bent down to let me off, he said, "It's a horrible misfortune, Hannah. Losing Jack on top of young Duff's troubles. How are you holding up?"

Her brave exterior faded and her face saddened again at the mention of my father. "Well, I'll confess, I honestly don't think I'd have been able to go on if it wasn't for Scrump here. But we keep each other goin'. He's cheerful 'most all the time, and he's the reason I get out of bed every morning."

"Children give us purpose, that's the truth. Mine certainly do," observed Mr. Lincoln. "So you see, Truman, you are small but mighty."

Turning to Ma, he asked, "And the farm?"

She told him how the Wellman boys took turns helping out since Duff's arrest and Pa's passing, and Mr. Lincoln remarked how friends like that are hard to come by.

"You were one such friend to me in New Salem," he told Ma. "I don't recall if I ever told you, but when I left home in '28, I was grief stricken."

"We knew you were sad, but we didn't know why."

"My only sister, Sarah, had just died in childbirth. I had known sorrow and loss as a child when my mother passed, but I didn't understand the depths of despair I felt until I lost Sarah. She was my best friend, and I feared I'd never find anyone to fill that hole in my heart. That's when I wandered into New Salem. I met you and Jack, and when you took me in, it began to feel like I had a family again."

Ma smiled. "You just say that 'cause I mended your britches and forced you to bathe?"

He chuckled. "Yes, I was a might rough in those days. And your sewing was remarkable. I often tell Mary that, until her, you were the only woman to know my latitude *and* my longitude. My, those were fine times. Life was simpler."

She poured his coffee as they continued trading stories of their days in New Salem, speaking of people she and Pa had never mentioned. Then the conversation moved to him and his interest in politics. He told Ma he was planning a run for the Senate.

"You are a very busy man these days, it seems," Ma said. "I can't tell you how much I appreciate..." Her voice trembled with emotion. She covered her eyes.

"There, there. You go right ahead, Hannah." He offered his handkerchief, adding, "You know I can't bring Jack back, but I will do everything in my power to bring Duff home. If there's a way, I'll find it. I promise you that."

He talked of his three sons and Mrs. Lincoln, passing her thanks to Ma for "making him into a gentleman." He told us about his law practice, the people he'd met on his travels. He even invited us to visit him in Springfield. He never grew tired of talking and we never grew tired of listening.

Finally, finishing the last of his coffee, he stood. "I'd like to meet with Duff and the sheriff as soon as I can."

"All right, but I'll need a few minutes to change into something else if we're going to town. Scrump, you show Mr. Lincoln where Pa is buried, then meet me with the wagon out front."

She went upstairs and I led Mr. Lincoln out to the plot of green grass that sat under a shade tree not too far from the house. Inside a small white picket fence stood five headstones. My grandparents and great grandparents had been laid to rest there, and now Pa rested alongside them.

Looking down at the grave, he was silent. Then he took something from his pocket and fingered it.

"What's that?" I asked.

"Just a nickel. When your pa and me were last together, we shared a meal at a place in town. We planned to split the cost of the meal, but I didn't have the last nickel to pay for my portion. Your Pa paid the five cents for me. We agreed that I would pay him back whenever we should meet again. I was planning on finally giving it to him. Guess he'd want you to have it now," dropping the coin into my little palm.

Stunned by the story, and happy to have a nickel, all I could think to say was "Thank you." But I sensed that the friendship between us would be something special.

"He was a good man, your Pa. Strong as a Russian bear, too. He ever tell you about our wrestling match?"

"Oh, yes," I replied, remarking that it was one of my favorite stories.

"Then remind me to tell you *my* version someday. You can tell me if it's any different from the one your pa told."

We had only just met, but his easy-going manner had made me feel like I'd known him my whole life. I would have trusted him with my life, too, and I was certainly ready to trust him with Duff's.

Heading toward town, Ma and I rolled along in the wagon while Mr. Lincoln trotted alongside on his horse, Old Bob.

Old Bob was a beautiful specimen of horseflesh. He was a sturdy, reddish brown steed with a silky mane and a steady, intelligent gaze. Mr. Lincoln told us he'd ridden him around the legal circuit for eight years, and he had come to think of him as more of a traveling companion than a horse.

"We've covered a lot of miles, Old Bob and me."

"How'd you come to give him that name?" I asked.

"Well, the feller I bought him from called him Robin. But over time I got the feeling he didn't much care for that. Must be embarrassing for a horse to be named after a bird, I figured. So I started calling him Old Bob and he seems to like it fine." Old Bob snorted his approval.

Along the way, I pointed out our wheat field, full of young sprouts, and he asked me questions about farming.

When we arrived to the jail, we secured the horses, then went inside.

"Afternoon, Hannah, Scrump," Sheriff Dick said. Looking up, he asked, "And who might this gent be?"

"Abraham Lincoln, attorney at law and friend of this family." They shook hands as Sheriff Dick introduced himself.

"I'm here to meet with Duff. I'll be taking full charge of his defense," Mr. Lincoln explained.

"Well, I wish you luck, sir. You sure got your work cut out for you. C'mon, I'll take you back to see him," said the sheriff, reaching for the keys.

At the cell, the sheriff locked us in and left us alone with Duff. Ma hugged Duff tightly, and then introduced him to Mr. Lincoln.

"Thank you for coming all this way, sir. I'm sorry I was too young to remember you from New Salem, but Pa was always talkin' about you. He loved tellin' his rasslin' story. Me and Scrump must've heard it a million times."

"So you're that homely baby I used to dance on my knee," joshed Lincoln, shaking Duff's hand. "But you've grown into a fine-looking young man. I imagine the gals are chasing you all over."

"Not lately, they're not," replied Duff, dolefully hanging his head, his spirits as low as I'd ever seen. "Mr. Lincoln, I didn't do what they're accusing me of. I swear it. You gotta believe me."

"Of course I believe you, Duff," he told him, clapping a hand on his shoulder. "And I am going to do everything I can to get you out of here. You'll be home where you belong soon enough, I promise you that. Tell you what. I need some time to settle in, but then I'll come back and we'll have ourselves a talk. I need to hear your side of the story."

"Yessir. I'll tell you all I can, which ain't much after the accident. A lot of things are missing."

Ma told Abe about Duff's injury at the ravine.

"Sounds like quite a spill. Lucky you didn't break your neck."

"Yes," answered Ma. "When Scrump and the Wellmans brought him home, we fetched Doc Parker right away. He said he had a...what was it...a concush..."

"Concussion. Affects the memory."

Duff nodded. "Doc said I might recall more after the swelling in my head went down, but so far nothin's comin' to me."

"Well, never mind for now. Try not to worry. I'll be back."

Ma called for the sheriff to let us out. We returned to the office, and Mr. Lincoln asked Sheriff Dick what evidence he'd gathered against Duff.

"The boy went to a holy roller revival meeting with Preston Metzker and two other fellers, Jim Norris and Charlie Allen. Jim and Charlie said the four of 'em got bored, so they slipped off to a whiskey camp and got themselves rip roarin' drunk."

"Slow down a bit there, Sheriff," said Lincoln as he jotted down some notes.

Sheriff Dick continued, "There was a fight between Duff and young Metzker, and the witnesses say Duff attacked him with a wagon hammer. Metzker made it home to his folks, but he died early next morning. I found the hammer at the murder site, just like the witnesses said."

"And what did you say their names were?"

"Charlie Allen and Jim Norris."

"Had they been drinking as well?"

"Well, that's the only reason I know that fellers go to a whiskey camp. But they apparently weren't so drunk that they couldn't remember what happened, and they swear they seen Duff do it. Their stories match up."

"You talk to anyone else?"

"Yes, sir. There's the preacher who ran the tent meeting, the old-timer who ran the whiskey camp, Doc Parker, of course, and Mr. Metzker. Him being the richest rancher around, I figured he might know someone else who'd been there. But no. Only Jim and Charlie say they actually saw it happen. They come right in and reported it to me."

"Good Samaritans, eh? They came to you that same night, did they?"

"Oh no, not till the next day."

"After they'd sobered up."

"After they'd heard Preston had died."

"Thank you, Sheriff. You've been very thorough. I'll be back tomorrow."

We left the office, and Ma asked, "Abe, you give any thought to where you'll be staying?"

"Can't say as I have."

"You could sleep in Duff's bed, but I'm afraid it wouldn't be very comfortable for you."

"Don't fret. I'm sure I can find some accommodations in this fine town." Then Ma smiled. "I know just the place."

Our next stop was Jenkins' Boarding House.

Ma knocked at the front door of the large wood frame house. The door opened, and there stood Mrs. Jenkins, a plump, grandmotherly lady with a white bun on the very top of her head.

"Why, Hannah Armstrong!" she said, sweetly surprised. "How are you these days?"

"Good as can be expected, Thelma, thank you."

"What brings you to my door?"

"Got a boarder for you, Thelma. This here's Mr. Abe Lincoln. He's going to be Duff's lawyer."

"Nice to meet you, Mr. Lincoln. I guess you'll be staying a while."

"Yes, ma'am, I suspect I will."

"Got just the room for you. Follow me."

She led us up a long, creaking staircase and down a narrow hallway to the rear of the house. There, she opened a door onto a room where sunlight filtered through white lace curtains and onto rose-patterned wallpaper. The furnishings, chairs and tables, were what you might expect, except for the extra-large four poster that stood in the center of the room.

"I don't think I've ever had a guest as tall as you, sir, but this here bed is more than adequate for a man of your size," said Mrs. Jenkins proudly.

"Indeed, it is," Lincoln told her, sitting on the bed and testing the feel of it.

"How much?" Ma asked.

"Two dollars a week, with breakfast and supper included."

"Sounds more than fair, thank you," said Abe. "I'll take it."

After we unloaded his things into his new lodging, Lincoln wondered if Ma might know where he could find an office space. He explained it would be better if he had a desk where he could spread out his papers as the trial progressed.

That's when I recalled the dusty desk in the corner at Mr. Walker's. Ma, however, was not keen on the suggestion.

She explained her prior meeting with Mr. Walker. His attitude about Duff's innocence still angered her.

"What do you say we go see him, anyway?" said Lincoln.

"Why on earth?" said Ma, clearly surprised.

"Tell you what. Give me five minutes with him, Hannah. If it doesn't work out, we'll look elsewhere."

Heading back across town, the three of us found ourselves standing in the musty law office of Walker & Mason.

"Welcome, Mrs. Armstrong. Didn't think I'd be seeing you again. And who might you be, sir?"

"Abraham Lincoln, sir, of Lincoln & Herndon, Springfield."

"Are you now? Henry Walker of Walker & Mason at your service, sir."

"An honor to meet you, Mr. Walker. The firm of Walker & Mason is known all the way to Springfield, you know."

"It is?"

"Oh, indeed. And as I'm sure you realize, reputation is everything in our profession."

"How right you are. How can I help you, Mr. Lincoln?"

"Well, since I'll be representing the Armstrong boy, I'm in need of professional space to do the proper legal work. I was told you might have a desk available."

Walker grimaced. "Well, yes, I do. But speaking lawyer to lawyer, I fear you've come all this way for a case that has little prospect of success."

Ma glared daggers at him, but Mr. Lincoln responded, "Then again, every man is entitled to his day in court."

"Of course, but...well, seeing as you're a colleague and all, I'm sure we can work out something for a reasonable price."

"I appreciate that, Mr. Walker, and when I return to the capital, I will tell everyone how *the* Henry Walker of Walker & Mason offered his resources to aid a poor, bereaved widow and her fatherless son. When I get the chance, Mr. Walker, I'll even mention it to Governor Bissell himself. The governor is a friend from my days when I sat in the legislature. He's known to make referrals of important clients to men he respects."

"Oh, he does?" Mr. Walker considered this a moment. "In that case, Lincoln, I think I can make accommodation for you while you're here in our fair town."

"*Pro bono*, then?"

"Certainly," mumbled Walker, who was just realizing that Mr. Lincoln had talked him into a corner.

And with a handshake, Abe Lincoln secured a desk in the law office of Walker & Mason. It had taken less than the five minutes Ma had allowed him.

"Mr. Lincoln, what's...'pro bono' mean?" I asked once we were outside.

"It comes from the Latin, son. *Pro bono publico*, which means 'for the public good.' To us lawyers, it means offering services for no charge."

"You mean Mr. Walker is just *giving* you an office? For free?"

"That's right."

"Wow, gratoosly." I exclaimed.

At the end of our first day together, I was left with many impressions of Mr. Lincoln, not the least of which was this: Honest Abe was sly as a fox.

Twelve

SINCE PA'S DEATH, WHEN IT was just the two of us, my mother and I developed our own evening ritual. After supper, we'd wash dishes, play a hand of cards, and then I would go upstairs to read until she came in to turn down my lamp before turning in herself.

But this night, at the end of our first day with Mr. Lincoln, she sat on my bed, took the almanac from my hand, and asked a question.

"Something troubling you? You were awfully quiet at supper."

"I'm fine. It's just..." I stopped mid-sentence.

"Just?"

"Something Mr. Lincoln said today at Mr. Walker's. He said I was fatherless."

"I'm afraid it's true, Scrump."

"I just never thought of it that way. I really miss Pa."

"I know, we all do. But you'll always have your memories of him, wonderful memories. Pa will always be with you."

Then I asked her the question that haunted me, "You're not going to die, are you, Ma?"

"No, Scrump. Not for a long, long time. Don't be worrying about that," she said softly, pushing my hair back and kissing my forehead.

I yawned. "I sure like Mr. Lincoln."

"He likes you, too. You know, he's asked if I'd let you help him tomorrow. He wants to talk to some folks, but he needs someone to show him around town. Would you want to do that?"

"Will it help Duff?"

"I think that's the idea."

"Then 'course I want to."

"Okay, then. Get a good night's sleep, and right after breakfast, you go into town and meet him at the Sheriff's Office." She leaned over to kiss me goodnight, but then stopped short. "Oh, and Scrump, remember what Pa told you about sheltering runaways in our barn? He said never tell anyone. That includes Abe."

"You think he wouldn't like it?"

"He might not. I don't know for certain."

"I won't say nothin' about it, Ma. Promise."

"All right, then. Good night." Now she kissed me on the forehead and dowsed my lamp.

The next morning, I rode back into town, and after hitching Paintbox to the post out front, I entered the Sheriff's Office. Sheriff Dick was busy at his file cabinet, shuffling paper folders, but then he looked up and saw me standing there alone.

"Where's your ma?"

"Back home. I'm supposed to meet Mr. Lincoln here."

"He's with your brother," he explained, turning back to his filing.

I made a beeline toward the door leading to the cells.

"Whoa there, partner!" He grabbed my collar and pulled me back. "You can't go in there. You got to wait here. Sit in that chair over there and keep quiet till he's done."

He pointed me to a chair against the wall. I wasn't too keen on waiting, but while I sat with folded arms, I studied the 'Wanted' posters tacked to the wall opposite me. What would happen to all these fellers, I wondered. How did their names end up here? Then again, Duff was in jail and he was no criminal, so maybe some of them were innocent too.

Then one poster in particular jumped out at me because of the large words. *Slave Runner*. I squinted to get a closer look.

Reward

$500

WANTED ALIVE

SLAVE RUNNER

NAME OF ISAAC.
SCAR ABOVE LEFT EYE.
WANTED FOR CRIME OF
LEADING RUNAWAY SLAVES
TO THE TERRITORIES

My heart quickened as I read the name of this slave-running outlaw—the very same Isaac who had stayed in our barn.

Just then, Mr. Lincoln called from Duff's cell. The sheriff grabbed his jail keys and went to him, leaving me alone. Moving fast, I went over, reached up, and tore the poster from the wall. Folding it into my pocket, I quietly hurried back to sit on my chair just before they returned.

"Good morning, Truman!" Lincoln greeted cheerfully. "Glad you could join me today."

Lincoln turned to Sheriff Dick, who by now had removed a pouch of tobacco and a pack of cigarette papers from his desk.

"Sheriff, according to the report you gave me, you say there are witnesses to the crime my client is accused of." He looked at the paper in his hand. "Charlie Allen and Jim Norris?"

"That's right," said the sheriff, who showed more interest in rolling his cigarette than helping Duff's lawyer.

"Where can I find these men?"

"You'll likely find Charlie over at Mulgrave's Stable where he works. Jim Norris is a trapper. Lives in a little shack off Old Potawatomi Trail. He'll be harder to find."

Mr. Lincoln looked to me. "You know these places?"

"I know how to find 'em!" I replied.

"You're just wasting your time, Lincoln. Their stories are solid. It's not that I don't like the Armstrong family. I even like Duff hisself. But...facts are facts."

"Much obliged, Sheriff." Lincoln ushered me out, shutting the door on Sheriff Dick and his opinions.

Leaving Paintbox and the rig behind, Mr. Lincoln hoisted me onto Old Bob, then lifted himself into the saddle behind me, and we headed off toward Mulgrave's.

"Sounds like these fellers got nothing good to say about Duff. Why are we goin' to see 'em?"

"Because I need to know what happened the night Preston Metzker was killed. Your brother can't remember because of his concussion. Mainly I want to find out just what kind of characters Charlie Allen and Jim Norris really are."

We arrived at Mulgrave's, a sprawling wooden stable painted as red as our barn, trimmed in white. We were greeted by Henry, one of the Mulgrave brothers, who brushed a gleaming black mare with long, steady strokes.

"Hey, Mr. Mulgrave," I called, as Mr. Lincoln let me down from his horse. "You seen Charlie Allen today?"

"Hey, Scrump. Sure, try the forge at the far side of the stable."

"Thanks."

"Ever seen a horseshoe made before, son?" Lincoln asked as we passed by the smithy. "He's making one right now," he explained. "See that iron bar he holds in his tongs and the way it's glowing red hot over the fire? Well, in a moment, he'll dip the ends in water to cool them down. That leaves just the center hot, so it'll stay pliable. Then he uses a hammer and anvil to turn it into a horseshoe for the farrier."

"What's a farrier?"

"It's a fancy name for a feller who shoes horses."

I watched attentively as the smithy skillfully worked with the metal, exactly as Mr. Lincoln described. When he had pounded it into a U-shape, he held it up for us to see.

"Nice work," complimented Lincoln. "You're not Charlie Allen, are you?"

"Nope," he said, and pointed us to a stall behind the forge. There we saw a pudgy, young feller about Duff's age. He was shoeing a beautiful palomino. As we neared his stall, we saw him brace the horse's rear fetlock between his knees and then nailed a horseshoe onto its hoof.

"Beautiful animal," Lincoln said, as he was done. He ran a hand along the palomino's muscular haunch, stroking her admiringly.

"Thanks. Just bought her."

"Must have cost a pretty penny, a horse like this."

The farrier didn't answer.

"Are you Charlie Allen?" Mr. Lincoln asked.

"Who wants to know?"

"I'm Duff Armstrong's lawyer, Abe Lincoln. This is his younger brother, Truman."

"Yeah, I know Scrump. What's on your mind, mister? I'm busy."

"The sheriff tells me you were there the night Preston Metzker was killed."

"That's right. Seen the whole thing."

"I'd like to hear about it."

"I already done told the sheriff everything."

"Yes, but I'd like to hear it for myself, if you don't mind."

"I mind."

"You can either tell me now, Charlie, or wait till you're in the witness box. That's up to you."

Charlie put down the hoof, stood up, and pushed back his greasy hair. "Well, we was at the tent meeting, Duff, Preston, me, and Jim Norris. By nightfall, we had our fill with all the prayin' and carryin' on like they do, so we decided to head out to this whiskey camp we done heard about."

"Whose idea was it to head up there?"

Waiting for an answer, Lincoln's piercing grey gaze locked on him.

Charlie sighed, put down his hammer and began his tale. "Look, it was Duff who came up with the idea to go there," he began. "Once we got to the whiskey wagon, we got some pours. Then Jim Norris and me split off and talked to some other fellers. But after a spell, we heard them arguing. They was pretty loud."

"Anybody besides you two hear this?"

"Maybe old Mr. Watkins. He's the feller who pours the whiskies. Anyways, we followed the sound of their voices and found them facing off against each other, in a clearing. We got there in time to see Duff take the first swing."

"How do you know it was the first swing?"

"'Cause it was."

"Go on."

"Duff was hoppin' mad at Pres. He kept goin' at him, yellin' at him till he finally pulls something out and hits him with it. You could hear it hit Pres's skull. That's when he fell to the ground."

"Did you see what struck Preston?"

"No, but I reckon it was the bloody hammer the sheriff found the next mornin'."

"And how about Duff? Was he hurt?"

"Not a scratch on him. He cleared out of there but fast! He knew what he done, all right. That feller's got a mean temper."

"Don't you talk about my—"

Lincoln reached down and squeezed my shoulder, a signal to keep quiet.

"And what about Preston Metzker, did you help him?"

"Tried to, but he kept sayin' he just wanted to get home. So we brung him to his buggy, and he drove hisself off. Wasn't till later that we heard he died. Went straight to the Sheriff's Office then."

"Very admirable. Tell me, had they been drinking, too, Pres and Duff?"

"It was a whiskey camp. What do you think? They was plenty drunk, 'specially Duff."

"What about you, Charlie? Were you drunk?"

"I know what I saw, if that's what you're gettin' at."

"Just trying to get the facts straight, is all."

Lincoln picked up a shoe from the ground.

"Interesting. This shoe has cleats on either end and an iron bar across the toe."

Charlie snatched the shoe back. "Yeah, it gives the horse more traction. I make 'em special fer a few of my friends."

"Tell me, did you hear what Duff and Pres were arguing about?"

"Couldn't say."

"Couldn't or won't?"

"Didn't hear."

"Seems a bit strange as you were so close by." Lincoln fell silent and waited.

"I don't know why you're asking me all these questions, mister. I ain't the one in jail."

"Like I say. Just trying to figure what happened that night."

"Yeah, well, you got it." He picked up the palomino's hoof and went back to work.

"Thanks for your help," said Mr. Lincoln as we left him.

"Why'd you let him say all them things about Duff?" I complained. "You didn't do nothin'! You just stood there."

"Well, Truman, right now we're in a game of cat-and-mouse."

"How do you mean?"

"I think Charlie knows more than he's telling. At trial, he'll have to tell the truth or go to jail himself, and that's where we'll get him. So don't you fret none. His time is coming."

We were moving toward the open stable door where Old Bob was hitched to a post and waiting for us. But a stranger passed, and I stopped cold. His boots had shiny silver spurs.

"Mr. Lincoln! See that feller there?" I pointed after him. "He's a slave hunter! He came to our farm lookin' for runaway slaves."

"Yes, unfortunately the law allows such men to ply their ugly trade."

"They're low-down-dirty skunks, if you ask me. Them slaves is running 'cause they're wantin' to be free. What's wrong with that?"

He stopped and looked down at me. "My, for one so young, you certainly have strong feelings about this."

I didn't reply.

The sky clouded over and the warm afternoon sun disappeared as we left Mulgrave's Stable and rode east out of town to Old Potawatomi Trail in search of Jim Norris. It made for a cooler ride, but it also heralded that rain was coming. We both hoped we wouldn't be caught in a downpour.

Old Potawatomi Trail was a footpath that had been used by the Potawatomi tribe for decades. These days it was just a rocky track that led upward to a wooded high ground, a strip of forest that stretched several miles westward. The early settlers used it after the U.S. government removed the tribe to Nebraska in the thirties. But by this time, the trail had fallen further and further into disuse. Hardly anyone traversed it anymore.

Years ago, this area had been popular with trappers, but a lot of the forest had either been cut down or lost to forest fire, so in that regard Jim Norris was something of a hold-out. He most likely earned a meager living off the few animals left to trap.

Fortunately, I found the trailhead, but Mr. Lincoln feared the terrain was too unstable for a horse, especially one carrying two riders. He hitched Old Bob to a tree, and we made our way up the trail on foot. I worried aloud about snakes, but Mr. Lincoln, an old woodsman, said if we saw one, to just hold still until it was gone.

I clambered quickly up the rocky trail, but Mr. Lincoln struggled behind me. When I turned to look back at him, he had shed his coat and hat and loosened his cravat. Sweat poured under his white cotton shirt, and he huffed mightily as we neared the top, berating himself for not bringing a canteen along.

He took a few minutes to catch his breath before we began the search for Jim Norris's shack in the woods. I led the way through a high brush and into a leafy glen, where we found a shack so worn and rickety that a good gust of wind would have finished it off.

Tall weeds had sprouted all around, but someone had worn clear a path to the front door, which wasn't really a door at all, but an animal hide hung over the entry. Lincoln knocked hard on the wall.

"Anybody home? Mr. Norris?"

No answer.

Pulling aside the old hide that served as a door, he ducked low to avoid hitting his head and stepped over the threshold into the cramped dwelling. I followed behind. Inside, the air was thick and stale. A cot sat on the dirt floor and next to it, a potbellied stove and a rickety wooden table with a single wooden chair. An open whiskey bottle and empty glass sat on the tabletop. Lincoln picked the glass up and sniffed, twisting his face as if he'd just inhaled a skunk's scent.

"Let's see if he's around back."

Exploring the rear of the shack, we found a yard with several racks used to stretch hides, as well as a pile of rabbit pelts stacked nearby. Lincoln commented that it seemed likely Norris had gone off to check his traps.

That's when I spotted fresh horse tracks in the dirt and pointed them out to Mr. Lincoln. There was a bar on them, too, a cleat like the horseshoes Charlie Allen made. He squatted to study them.

"You've got a good eye, Truman. These tracks are fresh all right," he agreed.

We followed the tracks into the woods, but lost them when they disappeared along a leafy trail. Suddenly, a branch snapped up ahead. Lincoln froze and ducked low behind a bush, signaling me to follow.

"Hello? Anyone there?" called Lincoln.

Silence. Then something rustled up ahead in the brush.

We started to move back onto the trail when a gunshot rang out and a bullet whizzed past.

"Run!" he yelled, protectively putting me ahead of him. We ran back toward the shack, but he was out of breath and clearly rattled.

"Think they was shooting at us?" I huffed.

"Let's not stay around to find out."

We hurried back down the trail and by the time we got to Old Bob, the sound of thunder rumbled in the distance. A storm was gathering.

We hopped into the saddle and hightailed it straight back to the Sheriff's Office.

"Truman, you've been a big help today. Thank your mother for me, for allowing you to be my guide."

"I will," I said, feeling a might proud to be considered his guide.

Paintbox took me quickly home, and we arrived just as the first drops of rain began to fall.

I rushed in to tell Ma all about my exciting day. When she heard about the gunshot, however, her brow furrowed, and she looked alarmed.

"Thank God you're both all right. But I think your sleuthing days are over, young man. I believe you've helped Abe quite enough. Let's leave things to him from now on, shall we?"

Soon, rain was pattering on the roof and we enjoyed a hearty bowl of beef and potato soup before a hand of Whist, and finally I headed to my bed to read. After a while, Ma slipped in to say goodnight. That's when she noticed the 'Wanted' poster lying on the table by my bed.

"Where did you get this?"

"Well…I took it off the wall at the Sheriff's Office."

"That was a risky thing to do, Scrump."

"I know, Ma. But I couldn't just leave it there and have somebody catch up with Isaac. We're supposed to be helping him, ain't we?"

"Yes, we are. Just…be careful."

"Ma, do you think we'll ever see Isaac again?"

"Not for a long while, honey."

The steady patter of raindrops pelting my window sent me into a deep slumber. Soon I was dreaming of Isaac holding aloft a great rod to part Purgatory Creek for thousands of slaves to cross into freedom. And there, on the other side, Pa was waiting to greet them.

THIRTEEN

RAIN BUCKETED DOWN THROUGHOUT THE night and into the next day. We couldn't go see Duff because the wagon-rutted roads made it impossible to get to town, so we stayed home and tried not to worry about Duff's fate. I missed the tick of the grandfather clock measuring our day.

Ma allowed me to go out to feed the chickens and gather eggs, while she occupied herself with baking bread and knitting. Back inside, I leafed through my almanac. We were engulfed by the sound of rain pelting our rooftop. An intense awareness of time, the heaviness of the unknown, weighed upon us like a deathwatch.

By evening, the storm had grown violent. I left Suzy upstairs trembling under my bed and found Ma knitting by lamplight in the parlor. Suddenly, a bright flash burst into the room, followed by a ferocious crash of thunder. Hurrying to the window, we stared with disbelief as another blinding bolt of lightning struck a big oak in our yard, ripping its trunk in two with a dreadful explosion. Sparks flew and smoke filled the air as half the tree fell toward the creek, and the other half collapsed onto our little chicken coop. The smell of singed wood drifted into the house and hung ominously in the air.

When the smoke cleared, we saw that the tree had ripped a hole in the roof of the henhouse. I thought of One-Eyed Phineas and my beloved Marianne being carried away by predators, and I knew we couldn't afford to lose any more chickens. They had to be saved, if at all possible, before they were drenched, or worse, drowned.

Ma knew we had to go out to save our brood. We waited until the thunder and lightning receded in the distance. The rain continued to fall at a fierce pace as I put on my slicker and Ma donned her hooded raincoat.

"Once you're inside the barn, set up a dry place for the hens to nest," she ordered. "I'll go to the coop and bring 'em in one-by-one to you. But you're to stay put in the barn, understood? I don't want you out in this downpour. Understand me?"

"Yes, Ma."

The wind blew brutally against us as we went into the yard, where the rain seemed to pelt the earth like bullets in a battle. I stumbled on the way to the barn, but Ma caught me before I fell. Safe inside, I prepared a place for the chickens, blanketing one corner with straw and pushing hay bales into place to form a pen away from the other animals.

Ma fought her way to the henhouse, where she found rainwater pouring in through the gaping hole in the roof. She grabbed the first of the hens, tucked it securely inside her coat, and strained against the driving rain to bring it safely into the barn. Struggling from henhouse to barn and back again, she delivered the soaking birds to me, one by one, and I gently set them in the enclosure I had prepared.

"Only one more to go," she finally said, shivering with cold. "Wait for me."

But she didn't return. I waited till I could stand it no longer. Then I went to the barn door and looked out. She was nowhere to be seen.

What could have happened to her? What if she's fallen? What if she's in trouble and needs my help?

My imagination went wild, and I could feel my heart racing.

"Ma! Ma!" I yelled. But there was no answer and I couldn't see her anywhere near the coop. If I was to find her, to save her, I would have to disobey her orders and leave the barn.

I stepped out into the downpour and that's when I saw that the other half of the fallen tree had dammed up Purgatory Creek. The water was rising to levels I'd never seen and, fearing Ma had fallen in, I eased my way through the slippery muck toward the creek. "Ma, Ma!" I cried out. "Where are you, Ma?"

It was then I lost my footing and tumbled into the rushing water, instantly stung by cold as it swirled about me. I managed to catch hold of a branch on the broken tree trunk and struggled to keep my head above water. But my weight was too much for the branch. It snapped free and all I could do was hold it tight as it swept me downstream. I fought against the current, but my young arms were no match for the force of water. I lost my grip and went under. As I fought to reach the surface, I instead took in water and went under a second time.

Suddenly, I felt someone grab hold of me, and the next thing I knew, I was lying safely on the bank, gasping for air. Ma appeared and scooped me up into her arms, and I coughed violently as water spewed from my lungs. I could breathe again at last. Using strength I didn't know she possessed, Ma fought through the mud, wind, and rain to carry me all the way back to the farmhouse, slamming the door against the elements. We clutched each other tightly, neither of us wanting to let go.

"Oh, Ma, I'm sorry," I cried. "I disobeyed you and fell into the crick, Ma, and I—I think I lost a shoe!"

"A shoe? Oh, Scrump, Scrump." She cradled me and wept, grateful that I had lost only a shoe and not my life. But I knew her tears weren't only for me. They were for Pa, for Duff, and for the hardships life was hurtling at us.

We clung to each other tightly, and when we finally parted, we went upstairs to change into dry clothes. We brought our wet ones to dry by the hearth, and after she added another log to the fire, we wrapped ourselves in warm woolen blankets and sat silently in the warmth of the crackling flames.

I was the first to speak. "Ma, what happened to you? I waited like you said, but you didn't come back."

"I slipped in the mud on the way to the coop, and then when I got there that ornery hen wouldn't let me grab hold of her. I had to finally give her up," she explained. "When I got back to the barn and you weren't there, I panicked. I saw the crick rising and made my way toward it."

"Lucky for me, you got there in time to pull me out, Ma."

She stared at me. "Scrump, I didn't pull you out."

"Yes, you did. I felt you grab me from behind."

"No. I found you in the mud above the crick."

"But...if it wasn't you, who was it?"

A furious thumping at the door startled us.

Ma jumped up, grabbing Duff's shotgun. "You stay put," she ordered as she moved to the door and called out. "Who's there?"

"We in trouble. Please help us," a man's voice moaned.

Ma opened the door to find a large man with muscular arms holding the small, lifeless body of another man.

"Oh, ma'am!" he cried as Ma let him inside. Water and tears streamed down his dark cheeks. "Can you help us, ma'am? A bunch of us was travelin' down crick when all hell broke loose. Oh, it was frightful! Crick rose so fast, it near swept us all away. Oh, you got to help us, ma'am. Please!"

Ma signaled toward the horsehair settee that sat before the hearth. The big man tenderly set down the soaked, trembling body. Then I saw who it was.

"Isaac!" I cried.

"We'll need to get him out of these wet clothes," said Ma. Turning to the man who had carried Isaac in, she said, "Undress him, will you? I'll get a blanket and something dry for him to put on."

Standing there wet and dripping, he just stared blankly at her.

"I said, undress him. Please!"

"But I—I can't ma'am. I just can't!"

"He'll catch his death, if you don't. Now hurry and take off his soaking wet clothes!"

"But ma'am...don't you know? Isaac be..." He looked helplessly to me, then back to Ma. "Isaac's a *lady*!"

Our mouths fell open.

"Merciful heavens," Ma said, putting a hand to her cheek. But there was no time to waste. She said to the big man, "Turn your back and keep it turned. You too, Scrump."

We faced to the fire as she removed the drenched, tattered clothes from Isaac's small frame, and then threw on a blanket for covering.

"You can turn around now," she said to us. "Scrump, run and fetch a flannel nightgown from my bureau, and the heavy quilt off my bed. And bring some of Pa's old clothes for this feller."

I returned with the things as quickly as I could, and she sent me and the big feller to wait in the kitchen.

He changed into Pa's clothes in the corner while I went to the larder and got out some biscuits for him, which he ate hungrily.

"I sure thought Isaac was a man." I told him. "I never met a lady called Isaac."

"Well, I ain't never met a boy, name of Scrump," he said with a grin.

But his look changed to worry and he peeked around the corner toward the parlor. Ma called us back in. Isaac had fallen asleep, curled up warm and dry on the settee.

"She okay?" he asked.

"She'll be fine, thank the Lord. What's your name?" she asked him.

"Samuel, ma'am."

"Well, Samuel, let's get you some food, and then you can tell us how you got here."

"Thank you, ma'am," said Samuel gratefully. "Isaac said you was good people."

When he'd finished eating, he started in telling us his tale.

"Isaac was leadin' the four of us, and we was runnin' hard on account o' hearin' dogs comin' up fast behind us. Finally, Isaac says to get in the water if we ever gonna lose 'em. But when we seen the lightnin' up ahead, we weren't eager to get into that crick."

I nodded in agreement.

"But Isaac yells, 'We got to get to the Armstrongs. They're good folks and they'll help us.' Well, 'round the time we get into the crick, the storm came up and rain starts a-fallin' like I never seen before! The crick started to rise mighty fast all 'round, and soon the water's so deep it's just pullin' us along!"

"I've never seen so much water in that crick before," said Ma.

"Now the others are so scared, they start tryin' to get out of the crick. Isaac's yellin', 'Stay calm, don't fight it, you're gonna be okay.' But they just keep slidin' right back in, and the water rises so high it starts sweepin' 'em away. We was tryin' to help 'em, Isaac and me both, when all a sudden Isaac sees your boy up ahead. Isaac left me so's to go help him. So you see, ma'am, it was Isaac who pulled him out of the water. Isaac's the one who saved your boy."

• • •

In the morning, a single ray of sunlight fell through my bedroom window and across my face. I awoke in my bed with Suzy snuggling against me. I barely remembered going to bed and wondered how I got there. Then the events of the night before came rushing back to me. I rose, dressed quickly, and went downstairs.

Sunshine filtered through the blue gingham curtains that covered the parlor window. I found Samuel and Ma sitting next to Isaac, who was still curled up asleep on the settee.

"Isaac? You awake?" said Samuel softly.

Isaac's eyes slowly opened and looked about the room. "Where am I?"

"You safe now, Isaac. I'm here with you," Samuel said.

"And the others? Joshua, Mike and Nettie?"

Samuel hesitated, then shook his head. "Lost 'em last night, Isaac. The water was so high, and the rain come down so fast, I couldn't see 'em no more. I don't know what became of 'em."

Tears flowed down her cheeks. Ma knelt down and sought to comfort her.

"You did the best you could. You got them this far, didn't you? Surely, you of all people, wouldn't think that God would just give up on them? You know as well as I do that they could have found shelter somewhere, perhaps at another farm. Don't give up hope."

"Thank you, ma'am. You're right," said Isaac as she brushed the tears away.

"But you're not going to be any good to them if you don't get your strength back."

Turning to me, she said, "Scrump, I put some barley soup on the stove. Bring a bowl of it in, with a spoon."

It was then that Isaac looked down and saw the nightgown, and then looked up at us, alarmed.

"It's alright, Isaac," Ma said gently. "We know your secret. And I don't know any other woman who coulda done all you've done."

She smiled weakly. Then she looked up and saw me holding out the bowl of hot soup.

"Oh, hello, boy."

"Hello," I replied. Ma nodded at me to continue. She didn't have to tell me what to say. "Thank you for pulling me from the crick last night, Isaac," I said, looking into her soft brown eyes.

Then Isaac's familiar smile returned. Ma and Samuel helped her sit upright. She took the soup from me and we all sat silently as she spooned it down.

When finished, she said, "Much obliged to you, ma'am."

The soup seemed to revive her, and as she finished and set the bowl aside, she announced, "Samuel, we got to be goin'."

Then she tried to lift herself from the settee, but didn't have the strength to stand.

"Isaac, it's too soon," Ma replied, helping her sit back down. "You're going to need more rest."

"Yes'm," she relented and leaned back, settling back onto the settee as Ma covered her with a quilt.

I sat down across from her. "You know, all this time, I was thinkin' you was a man."

"Fooled ya!" she chuckled.

"So how come you're pretendin' to be a feller?"

"Well, for one thing, it's a lot easier to run in britches than in a dress. But for some reason, I get more respect from my Passengers wearin' a man's hat than a bonnet. That's jus' the way it is, I guess."

"I can understand why you'd want to pass as a man," said Ma. "I imagine it's dangerous out there for a woman, all alone."

"Oh, I ain't never alone, ma'am. I got my friends, like Samuel here, and the good Lord who guides me."

"Amen," Samuel whispered.

Then curiosity got the best of me. and I blurted out the question that was nagging at me. "Isaac, are you still a slave?"

"Truman. Manners."

She smiled at me. "Oh, I don't mind, missus. No, boy. These days, I am a Conductor on the Underground Railroad and right proud of it. I ain't been a slave for some time. I'm a free woman and ain't no slave hunter ever gonna change that."

A shiver shot up my spine as I thought about the poster I'd taken from the Sheriff's Office.

Isaac continued. "See, I was born to slavery. They say my Mama got sold when I was 'bout three years old."

"Do you remember her?" I asked.

"No, not my mama. I remember Aunt Kizzy, who was my mammy, but I got no kin, so far as I know. I was raised on the plantation, but sold more than a few times before I was your age. I was always small, y'see, and I reckon they thought I couldn't do no big, really hard work. But every place I ended up, the massas or they wives always ended up picking on me. They got angry with me if I was too slow, or sometimes if I was fast. But most of the time, they just treated me like I wasn't even a human person.

"And God forbid ya getta massa who likes his drink," she continued, pointing to the scar on her forehead.

"A body can take so much, I found, and one day I jus' reached my limit! Without so much as thinking 'bout it. I walked right out the front door of the massa's great big house and kept on goin'. I ran through the yard and into the fields and everywhere beyond that. I hid in haystacks by day and ran through the cricks and gullies by night."

"Weren't you scared they'd come after you?" I asked.

"Oh, they tried to. And they're still tryin'. All I can say is, I may be little, but I'm fast. I outrun 'em *and* outsmart 'em all the time. Anyways, before I knew it, I ran all the way up into free territory. That's when I met up with some kindly Quaker folk. I never met no Quakers before, till they took me in and give me a bed and food. They tol' me they could get me all the way to Canada if'n I wanted, on accounta they got no slavery at all up there."

"Why didn't you go?"

"Cuz I had friends I left behind down South. So I told the Quakers that, and that's when they tol' me about this Underground Railroad. So I got the idea of goin' back. If'n I could escape the plantation, so could they, I figgered. That's how I come to be a Conductor. I lead my people out."

Now Ma had a question. "But do you still want us to call you Isaac? Surely you have another name?"

"Isaac is jus' fine, ma'am. That's what everyone calls me."

Then it was her turn to ask questions.

"I been wondering, Miz Armstrong? Where's your mister? Ain't seen him yet."

"My husband passed a few weeks back, Isaac. It's been hard for us, but it was peaceful at the end for him," said Ma simply.

"Oh, missus, my heart breaks for you. I only met Mr. Armstrong the one time, but I could tell he was kind and honest. You all are."

Then to me, she asked, "Say, where that good-lookin' big brother of yours?"

"Duff? He's not here. He...got in trouble for something. Only he didn't do it, and now there's going to be a trial. He'll be home after that, though."

"Lordy, no end o' troubles in this life," sighed Samuel.

"Duff's been falsely accused of murdering a young man he knew," Ma explained. "Even though he's innocent, he has to sit in jail for now. But the best lawyer in the country is a friend of mine and with his help, Duff'll be home soon."

"Why, sure he will. The Good Lord protects his own."

With that, Isaac tried rising again, but she was still too weak.

"That settles that," pronounced Ma. "You're going to need more rest and solid food before you can travel again."

"No, missus. We got to keep travelin'. The slave hunters are on our tail and they don't give up easy."

"So we'll keep you hidden in the barn just like before. You'll be perfectly safe. We hardly have any visitors since Duff got in trouble. So in a few days, when you're strong enough, you can be on your way."

Isaac shook her head, but Samuel took up the cause.

"Better listen to the missus, Isaac," added Samuel. "You too weak right now. And you need to be strong if we ever gonna find the others."

Isaac sighed. "Well, mebbe we could stay a day or two. But no more 'n that. God bless you for your kindness, Miz Armstrong."

Right after supper that evening, Ma excused herself and disappeared upstairs. Samuel helped me clear the dishes. Just as we'd finished, Ma returned, clutching something in her hand.

"Isaac, I'll give thanks every single day for you saving my boy. I don't know what I'd do if he ever... Well, anyway, I've given this some thought, and I want you to have this."

"Oh missus, you done plenty enough for me a'ready. It's the Lord who put me there in that crick for your boy. It's Him you should be thanking."

Ma opened her hand and there sat her beloved topaz brooch, her most prized possession. She pressed it into Isaac's palm.

"I want you to have this," she repeated.

"Oh, missus. It's so – so beautiful," she said as she smiled and gazed at it in her hand.

"But Ma!" I blurted. "Pa gave you that on your wedding day!"

"Scrump."

Isaac closed her hand around it and offered it back to Ma.

"Missus, I thank you, I truly do. But I can't take this, Miz Armstrong. It was a gift from your man. You need to hold onto it."

"Yes, but lately, every time I look at it, it reminds me of what I've lost and that I'm never getting that back. No, it's time to let go," she explained. "I want you to have it, and that's all there is to it. Besides, what you've given me is worth far more than that," she said, and put one arm gently over my shoulder.

Isaac continued to demur, but Ma's mind was made up, and in the end, got her way.

Fourteen

MATTHEW WELLMAN, WHO HAD FAITHFULLY tended the wheat crop in Duff's absence, rode out to the field to assess the storm damage. We were hoping for the best and we got it. The wheat had made it through with minimal harm. When Matthew came by the house to share this good news, he was surprised to see vestiges of the storm, the muddy yard and the fallen tree laying across the henhouse roof.

A few hours later, he rode back with Mr. Wellman, Luke, and a wagon full of lumber.

"Leftovers," Wellman called them, remnants of a barn repair he'd made the previous year. "Glad to be rid of it," said the old Quaker when Ma showered him with thanks.

Ma pulled him aside. "Thomas, Isaac's returned. She has another Passenger, named Samuel, with her. But during the storm, she got separated from three other Passengers." Ma explained. "They're hiding in the barn now. I keep telling her she's in no condition to go looking for them, but she's a very determined little lady."

Mr. Wellman looked at her quizzically. "Lady?"

"So you didn't know either. We found out last night," she whispered.

"Isaac is a woman," I interjected. "She says she pretends to be a feller so's she can throw off the law and slave hunters," I told him.

"Friend Hannah, this surprises me greatly. A woman, eh?" He chuckled. "Well, bless thee and thy son for offering them food and shelter. I'll slip in a visit with them shortly, as soon as we unload this lumber."

After the three of them emptied the wagon, Mr. Wellman headed to the barn and I followed along. Matthew and Luke, meantime, gathered limbs and branches from the fallen tree and began piling it onto the wagon bed to be hauled away.

Samuel was in the barn, brushing down Paintbox when I swung the door open for Mr. Wellman. Isaac was resting on a haybale, but at the sound of the door, the two of them had taken cover. The barn was silent and empty.

"It's okay. I brought Mr. Wellman to see you," I called out.

Isaac and Samuel slowly emerged from the shadows. After Wellman greeted them, they explained to him what had happened in the storm. Isaac, who was still wobbly on her feet, had in her mind to head out in search of them come nightfall.

"Now, now, Friend," he told her. "Thee must trust them to our Great Protector. If thee wish to travel on, then thee must rest for a night or more. I'll send word to the other Station Masters. Perhaps they will have news of the other Passengers."

"Yessir," she said softly.

"I'll return to see thee before I leave. My sons and I are going to repair Mrs. Armstrong's coop."

"Can I help, sir?" volunteered Samuel, eagerly. "My pappy taught me woodworkin' afore he was sold away."

"That's very kind of thee, Friend. But there is a risk of thee being seen in daylight."

"But Miz Armstrong done so much for us. I'd like to do this for her, if you'd allow it. Please, sir?"

Mr. Wellman considered it. "The work would go faster, I suppose, and your gratitude to Friend Hannah is commendable. Very well, Samuel. But you'll work from inside the coop itself, so you are not so easily seen. Isaac, you must remain hidden."

The men decided to patch the hole from inside the coop, so the Wellmans sawed the lumber and brought it to Samuel to nail in place.

As they worked, a rider unexpectedly appeared in the distance and trotted toward us. At the sight of the glinting silver spurs, my heart skipped a beat.

"See that feller? He's a slave hunter," I warned. "He came one night searching for a runaway. Pa didn't like him none at all." Wellman tossed a cautioning glance to the others and signaled for Samuel to remain hidden inside the coop.

"Afternoon, folks," yelled the slave hunter as he rode toward us. "Looks like you got some damage here."

"Yes, but we're managing it well, thank thee. Something we can do for thee, Friend?" Mr. Wellman asked.

The slave hunter studied Mr. Wellman and his sons, sizing them up before continuing.

"Lookin' for a slave runner who's been runnin' through these parts. I almost got 'em last night, but that damn storm set in."

"How inconvenient," Mr. Wellman commented slyly.

Big Jake removed a handbill from his pocket and when he handed it down to them, I saw it was like the one I'd removed from the Sheriff's Office. Mr. Wellman pretended to study it carefully as the boys looked over his shoulder. They all shook their heads and Mr. Wellman offered it back to him.

"You didn't show it to the boy," he said, nodding my way.

Mr. Wellman slowly lowered the handbill to me.

"Recognize him, Little Red?" asked Jake.

I shook my head.

"You sure?" the slave hunter asked me, and I nodded at him.

"Here thee are, Friend," said Mr. Wellman, politely returning the handbill.

"You boys all Quakers?"

"We are indeed, Friend. If thee would ever care to visit our little meeting house, we'd be more than happy to welcome thee."

The slave hunter smirked as he stuffed the handbill back in his pocket.

"If you see the runaway scum I'm lookin' for, you tell the sheriff and he'll get word to me. Understand?"

Then, without waiting for an answer, he turned his horse and galloped away.

"Does thee think he suspects, Father?" asked Matthew, watching after him.

"I don't know, but we can take no chances now. Samuel!" he called into the coop. "Back to the barn with thee," he ordered.

"Yessir." Samuel bolted from the coop and ran for the barn.

"I need to think," said Mr. Wellman, nervously stroking his beard.

Ma came out of the house toting a bucket of cool water and a sipping ladle.

"Thomas?" she said, looking after the rider who receded into the distance.

"Slave hunter," he said, with worry in his eyes. After he'd slaked his thirst with the cool water, he said, "Friend Hannah, we will have to finish up tomorrow. Right now, we must get our friends out of thy barn as quickly as we can. They're not safe here."

"You takin' them to your place?" I asked.

"Best not to say, young Friend. But I thank thee for all thee have done for them."

Matthew pulled his wagon up to the barn door while Ma packed up whatever grub she could find for them, along with Pa's old canteen filled with fresh well water.

When it was time, Samuel and Isaac slipped quietly from the barn and headed to the back of the wagon. That's when Ma noticed that Isaac had no shoes.

"Isaac, you're barefoot!" exclaimed Ma.

"Don't fret, Missus. The crick got my shoes, but runnin' barefoot ain't nothing new to me. I never had no shoes when I worked the fields."

"Wait!" I called, and sat myself on the ground where I speedily unlaced my own shoes. I pulled them off and offered them to her.

"These'll do you, I bet."

"Oh, sweet Scrump!" cried Isaac. "I can't take the shoes off'n your feet."

"Sure you can. Besides, I got another pair," which wasn't true, of course, because this was my other pair. Ma nodded her approval and Isaac gratefully accepted my offering.

"I do believe this is the nicest thing anyone ever done for me," she said, leaning down to thank me. "I can see you is the man of this house. You take real good care of your Ma now, little feller. And your brother."

As the Wellmans and their secret cargo rolled away down the muddy lane, Ma put an arm around me and I heard her sniffle.

"Ma? You cryin'?"

"Don't be silly," she insisted, brushing a tear from her eye. "Now make sure the chickens are secured inside the barn, then come on in. I'll get a start on supper for us."

When she got to the kitchen to begin supper, there, in her apron pocket, she found the brooch.

FIFTEEN

THAT NIGHT, AS I WAS setting the table and Ma was cooking, there was a sharp knock at the door. She froze.

"Think it's the slave hunter come back?" I whispered.

Still on edge from the afternoon, she grabbed the shotgun from the corner. "Stay here."

I peeked around the corner as she opened the door a crack.

"Abe!" she exclaimed with relief. "I didn't hear you ride up."

He took note of the gun in her hand. "You're smart not to take chances, seeing as it's just you and Truman here."

"Come right in. We were just sittin' down to supper and there's plenty. I hope you'll join us."

"Coming from the best cook New Salem ever had, that's an offer I'd be a fool to refuse," he said, deeply inhaling the aromas of her beef stew. "I've some important news. Can we talk over supper?"

As we ate, Mr. Lincoln explained. "The circuit judge, an old feller name James Harriot, arrived this morning and presided over Duff's arraignment. That means he's been formally charged with the murder. His trial is scheduled for later next week, on Thursday."

"Oh, I see." Ma's face blanketed instantly with worry.

"Judge Harriot's a fair man, so that's the good news. On the other hand, the State has assigned a prosecutor, Hubert Fullerton. I've encountered Mr. Fullerton on occasion before. He's smart, cagey, and politically ambitious. And as you know, the Metzkers are well-known far beyond this county. A conviction in this case would be quite a feather in his cap."

Seeing the worry lines etch deeper into Ma's face, Lincoln gently put his hand over hers.

"Hannah, I won't mislead you. This won't be easy. I've met again with Duff and he's still lacking in memory. A defense needs details, specifics, so I'll have to find 'em somewhere. But I've given you my promise, remember that. Your boy will come home."

Mr. Lincoln was the most entertaining supper guest I think we'd ever had. He told jokes, stories of his childhood home in Indiana, his journey to New Salem, the funny things his boys did to make him laugh, and how he came to be a lawyer. It was fascinating stuff, and it took our minds off Duff's trial.

Then I brought up my favorite story, the wrestling match with Pa. I reminded him he'd said he would tell me his own version.

"Ah, that. Well, back in those days I was a brash young man, very confident of my wrestling skills, so I didn't give a lick for your Pa. But in the week leading up to the match, more fellers came into the store, one after another, to tell me they wouldn't want to be in my shoes for all the money in the world. Considering all I owned was a pair of moccasins, not many folks would want to be in my shoes. But it did give me considerable pause when I found out the whole town was bettin' against me."

"Except for Ma."

"Yes, except for your Ma. So then I began asking around to find out how your father wrestled, to see if I could determine his weakness—if he had one. Folks generally agreed he was steady on his feet and exceedingly strong, but most of his matches were over in less than an hour. I figured if I could keep the match going longer than that, he'd eventually tire. Sure enough, he did. The moment I could see he was winded, I made my move! I threw him right to the ground and pinned him, whipping his ornery...backside.

"Well, his supporters, the Clary's Grove Boys, did not take kindly to this outcome, especially as they had placed their bets on him and stood to lose a substantial sum. But your father defended me in his defeat, and from then on, I was no longer the beanpole clerk, but one of the boys. Your Pa taught me a great lesson in leadership. He showed us that a man can lift people up even when he's down."

Afterward, Mr. Lincoln helped clear the table. He was drying dishes when Ma mentioned that, after seeing Duff tomorrow, she had an errand to run. "I want to take Scrump by the Mercantile," she continued. "I don't relish going in there, the way folks are behaving towards us, but he needs a new pair of shoes."

"Does he? Say, I have an idea. While you visit with Duff, why don't I take the lad to get his shoes? What do you say to that, Truman?"

"Sure!"

"That's sweet of you, Abe, but see that you put them on my bill. I don't want you paying for them."

"Whatever you say, Hannah."

We arranged to meet at the Sheriff's Office the next morning and by the time we arrived to Duff's cell, Lincoln was already interviewing him. The sheriff allowed us to listen in.

"What made you decide to go to this camp meeting?"

"Well, to be truthful, I didn't intend on goin' at all. Sorry, Ma."

"Go on."

"See, the whole thing was an excuse for me and my gal—Sarah May Metzker, I mean—to be alone. We was planning on being alone somewhere by ourselves. Anyway, when I got to the Metzker ranch, Sarah May was sick, her ma said, and couldn't go with me. 'Course I was disappointed, and figured I'd go on home. But Preston pressured me. In the end, I went on ahead with him and his buddies. Jim went with Preston in his buggy, me and Charlie went in our'n."

Duff put his hand to his head and strained to recall. "I remember getting there, and lots of preachin' and singin' and the like. But come nightfall, Preston got tired of it all. He wanted to leave. He said he knew a place."

"The whiskey camp? It was his idea, then?"

"Yeah, I never heard of it before."

"And after that?"

"After that, I can't remember."

"How well did you know this young man?"

"Preston? Well, we were friends, I guess. Though it was hard to tell with Preston. He was always goin' off on me. You know, makin' fun of me and the size of our farm. And I don't think he cared none for his sister bein' sweet on me. I'm pretty sure he thought I wasn't good enough for her."

"And what about Jim Norris and Charlie Allen? Did you know them already?"

"Not much, not before that day. I seen Charlie around, o' course, but we weren't what you'd call social."

Lincoln stood and rubbed his chin, lost in thought.

"Mr. Lincoln, you don't think they'll hang me, do you?"

"Don't even think like that, Duff. You just try to relax and let that memory of yours come roarin' back," he said. "We need to know what happened." Then he looked at me and noticed my stockinged feet.

"Truman, what do you say we leave your mother and Duff to visit while you and me go get you some new shoes?"

Duff pointed to my feet. "What happened to your shoes, little brother?"

Before I could answer, Ma made up an excuse about me growing so fast. She clearly didn't want me mentioning Isaac and the storm in front of Mr. Lincoln.

Leaving Ma behind with Duff, we headed out to Wilkins' Mercantile. It was a newer store, a sign of growth in Beardstown. Of course, we had the General Store, where we'd always shopped for staples, household goods, and hardware, and where we sometimes brought in eggs to barter for goods. But Mrs. Wilkins' Mercantile sold ready-made clothes, shoes, fancy things for ladies, and even toys and candy. I'd been there only once before with Pa, and I was looking forward to stepping inside again.

Seeing as he was a stranger in town, and somewhat of a giant, Mr. Lincoln turned heads when he walked into the store with me in tow. But he seemed oblivious to this. He went directly to the sales counter where he was greeted by Mrs. Wilkins, the shop's prim owner.

"Welcome, sir. How may I help you?"

"Thank you, ma'am. I'd like some shoes for this young feller here."

"What size?"

He looked at me. Having no idea, I shrugged.

"Wait here. I think I can find him something in back," she told us.

"Say, aren't you Abe Lincoln?" came a voice from behind us.

He turned, and one of the customers, a feller I didn't know, shook his hand.

"I voted for you in Congress back in '46," said the man, and from there the two lapsed into a conversation about politics.

When Mrs. Wilkins didn't return and Mr. Lincoln's political conversation droned on, I wandered to an aisle and ran into a friend of mine, Shorty Robinson. Shorty was anything but short. He was the same age as me, but he towered over most of us kids his age.

"Hey, Scrump!" he yelled.

"Oh hi, Shorty."

"I heared they locked your big brother up in the pokey," he taunted me.

I could feel my face redden, but whether it was anger or embarrassment, I wasn't sure.

"What of it?" I asked defensively.

"So they say he's gonna *hang*."

All of a sudden, I was like an Independence Day rocket going off. In a split second, I was all over Shorty. I pushed him to the floor and was about to pummel his pathetic puss when a big hand grabbed me from behind and yanked me off him.

"Here now! What's going on?"

Mr. Lincoln was mad! I'd never heard this tone of voice from him. Shoe box in hand, Mrs. Wilkins stood behind him.

"Good heavens! Sir, I will not tolerate fighting in my store," she scolded. "You and your son are welcome to leave!"

"Madam, I apologize," he said as he reached in and pulled some bills from his pocket. "We'll leave quietly. I hope three dollars will cover the shoes. Keep the change."

He snatched the shoes from her hand and marched me out.

When we were outside on the sidewalk, he looked down at me and I looked down at the sidewalk.

"I'm waiting," he said patiently.

"For what?"

"An explanation. Truman, that wasn't like you. Not at all."

"Well, I don't care! That big-mouth Shorty Robinson said Duff was gonna hang."

"Oh, I see." He looked around and spotted a nearby bench. "Come on, let's go over here and have us a chat."

We settled in on the bench and he knelt down before me, taking the shoes from their box.

"Hold out your foot, let's see if these fit," he said as he slipped one on and tied it up. "Perfect. Seems Mrs. Wilkins knows her business."

Then he slipped the other one on me, and began to lace as he continued, "Let me tell you a story, son. I once knew two brothers."

"What was their names?" I interrupted.

"Oh, let's call them James and John. Anyway, these two were tramping through the woods when they ran upon a ferocious, angry hog. Well, that old hog got it into his head to go after the brothers and they ran for dear life till James, to save himself, climbed lickety-split up a giant elm. So the old hog goes after John, looking to take a bite out of his trousers! But John ran 'round the tree so fast, he was able to grab the hog's tail! The hog still wouldn't give up so round and round they went."

"What happened?"

"Well, after they'd made a good many circles, John yelled up to his brother, 'Okay, James, you can come down any time and help me let go of this hog!'"

I laughed, and his grey eyes twinkled as he smiled at me, his anger completely gone.

"You see, Truman, you and your brother are a lot like James and John."

"How do you figure?"

"Duff's got himself up a tree just like James. And you, you're holdin' onto your anger and letting it pull you around like that old hog pulled John around. Truman, you're going to hear a lot of things said about your big brother during this trial. Folks are bound to say what they're going to say and think whatever they want to think. But *we* know the truth about Duff, so no sense gettin' riled up by somebody who doesn't. You can't fight the whole town."

"I reckon you're right," I admitted.

Back at the jail, Ma heartily approved of my new shoes. After saying good-bye to Abe and Duff, we headed back home in our rig. Along the way, she asked how I enjoyed my time with him. I told her it was tolerably good, but in truth it was unforgettable.

Sixteen

AS MR. LINCOLN HAD PREDICTED, Duff's trial was set to begin on Thursday, April 22, 1858. The previous night, no matter how hard I tried, I couldn't stop thinking of Duff. I wanted him free, I wanted him home, and I wanted this to be over. I tossed and turned, then turned and tossed, but sleep wouldn't come. Not till sunrise anyway.

"Scrump! Scrump, wake up! We don't want to be late!"

What time is it, I wondered? How could I oversleep on today of all days! I tumbled bleary-eyed from bed and scrambled into the clean clothes Ma had laid out for me. At breakfast, she tucked in my shirt and fussed with combing my hair.

"And Duff will have clean shirts every day," she announced, pointing to her ironing from the previous night. She had washed and ironed into the wee hours. "If the Armstrong boys are going to be gawked at by half this town, they'll be looking their best. I'll see to that, at least."

Ma had put on her black dress, as she was still mourning Pa. She carefully folded the freshly-pressed shirt for Duff and wrapped it in brown paper. Grabbing her purse, she took hold of my hand as we headed to the door, ready to brave the first day of the trial together.

As we stepped out, we were surprised to see Mr. Wellman pulling up in his buggy.

"Good morning, Friend Hannah," he greeted her, removing his broad-brimmed hat. "I hope I am not too bold, but I wish to escort thee to the trial. I feel called to stand by thee in thy hour of need. Friend Jack would have wanted it that way."

The relief on her face was plain to see.

"Thank you, Thomas. I'd like that *very* much. I don't mind telling you how nervous I am. I've never been in a courtroom before."

"Nor I, so we will face it together."

"I'm grateful," she told him. "And if you don't mind, I'd like to stop at the jail first. I have a clean shirt for Duff," she told him. We climbed into his buggy and set off.

It was a bright, humid morning. The wildflowers that had sprung up on either side of the lane risked being trampled by our wheels as we hurried along to our first day of the trial. For the most part, we didn't speak, I recall. We were all of us too nervous.

When we rolled into Beardstown, we were amazed to see an endless stream of wagons, riders, and pedestrians. The murder had been in all the papers, not to mention on everyone's lips, for weeks. Most folks felt as though they had a personal stake in it. Now they were all headed to the same place. The courthouse. As we passed by it on our way to the jail, we saw masses of people milling about outside, lining up at the door, waiting for their chance to get a seat at what the penny paper was calling "the trial of the century."

"Merciful heavens," Ma said quietly, as she craned her neck to take it all in.

When we arrived to Duff's cell, Mr. Lincoln was already there with him. Unlike the suits I'd seen him in so far, this one was brown and unrumpled. The frock coat hung loosely on his slender frame, and he wore a fresh white shirt topped with a smart black cravat. His boots were newly polished. His normally unruly brown hair was neatly combed and parted.

He greeted us with his big, friendly grin. "Ah, good morning, Hannah, Truman. Come in. I was just giving Duff some last minute instructions," he told us. He eyed Mr. Wellman. "I don't believe I've had the pleasure, sir. Abe Lincoln," he said, offering his hand.

"Thomas Wellman, Friend," came the reply as they shook hands. "I have shared a long friendship with Jack and Hannah, much like thee."

"You can speak freely in front of Thomas," Ma assured Lincoln. "He's offering some much-needed moral support today." She handed the package with the clean shirt to Duff, who changed into it as Mr. Lincoln continued.

"Very well. Now remember, Duff, when the judge asks you how you plead, you'll stand with me and simply say, 'not guilty.' The rest of the time, your only job is to sit attentively and listen to the testimony. That's all you have to do. And no outbursts. This includes the rest of the family as well," he said, glancing my way. "No matter what you hear, no matter what anyone on the witness stand says, whether it's true or not, you do not speak out in court."

"I understand, Mr. Lincoln," said Duff, as he buttoned up his clean shirt.

"Yes, Abe," nodded Ma, placing a hand on my shoulder. "We understand."

The sheriff arrived with his deputy. "Time to go, folks."

"Be strong, Duff. Remember. You're Jack Armstrong's son," said Mr. Lincoln.

"God be with thee both," added Mr. Wellman.

Mr. Lincoln stayed behind with Duff as the three of us made our way to the courthouse, the deputy escorting us all the way.

When we entered the courtroom, it was sticky with humidity and spilling over with humanity. Every seat appeared to have been taken by farmers who'd left their fields, womenfolk who'd put on their Sunday best, ranchers whose curiosity had gotten hold of them, and local merchants who'd shuttered their shops. They wouldn't have any business anyway today, thanks to the trial. The ladies fanned their faces to cool themselves and the menfolk had all opened their collars.

Mr. Lincoln had reserved the spectator bench directly behind the defense table just for us. Mr. Wellman ushered Ma and me through the crowd. A few men politely doffed their hats to Ma, but most of the women averted their eyes away. In our wake followed a buzz of whispers and critical comments about Duff. Apparently, most folks had already determined him to be guilty. He was the villain of the hour.

"I'm praying for your boy's miserable soul, ma'am," offered one man.

"Prayer won't help. He's guilty as sin," responded another.

Ma ignored them all and held her head high and proud. She took every step with confidence, displaying her absolute belief in my brother's innocence.

But right after we settled into our seats, a commotion erupted in the rear of the court. The Metzker family was arriving.

Mr. Metzker and his wife led the way. They were followed by their two surviving sons, as well as Sarah May. All five of them wore black mourning clothes. Some in the audience offered them effusive commiserations and warm condolences. Clearly, the crowd's sympathy lay with them.

As the Metzkers walked toward their seats behind the prosecutor's table, Ma unexpectedly rose and stepped into their path to greet them. Although they had shunned her at Preston's funeral, she was still determined to express her sympathy to them.

"Mr. and Mrs. Metzker," she said, "I want you to know how sincerely sorry I am for your loss and—"

Mr. Metzker stepped brusquely past her, pulling his wife along with him. But Mrs. Metzker resisted him and held back to speak to Ma.

"Thank you, Mrs. Armstrong. I hold no ill will for you. It's just...I'm so sorry for this whole thing. For Preston and..." A sob overwhelmed her.

Mr. Metzker pulled her to his side, while giving Ma a resentful look as he settled in with his family.

From my seat, I could see Sarah May. Her eyes were red, from weeping, I supposed. She glanced over at Duff until she saw I was watching her and averted her eyes from mine. As I studied the Metzkers, their sorrow was evident in their tired and weary faces. Right then, I realized that in my all-consuming concern for my brother, the Metzkers had lost a son and brother and we could lose Duff, too, if things didn't go our way. We were alike in many ways, all of us ensnared in a drama beyond our imagining and looking for a way out.

At precisely ten o'clock in the morning, the guards sealed the courtroom doors and the room quieted. A rear entry opened and the jury solemnly filed in, giving us our first look at the twelve men who held Duff's fate in their hands. They appeared to be mostly ranchers and farmers, and the two who wore suits with ties I assumed were local businessmen.

The jury was seated, and then a side door opened and in came Duff and Mr. Lincoln. Duff's blond hair glinted in the sun that streaked through a window. He looked back at Ma and me, and I saw the dark circles under his eyes, something I hadn't noticed before. Ma flashed an encouraging smile, and he returned it with a forced grin. He must have been terrified, but he never let on.

Hubert Fullerton, the State's prosecutor, entered from the other side of the court, followed by a young associate, and both took their places at their table. Mr. Fullerton's hair, black like his suit, was slicked and shiny, and a thin mustache perched under his angular nose. He greeted the Metzkers politely.

To one side of the judge's bench sat a little table where a wiry old feller with spectacles and wisps of grey hair was stationed. He had a generous supply of paper and pencils. Mr. Lincoln explained to us that he was the court reporter, who was in charge of taking notes for the trial.

Suddenly, the main courthouse door swung open and Mr. Walker of Walker & Mason burst in. But one of the guards held him back.

"It's all right, deputy. He's with the defense," said Lincoln. The guard released Walker, who went and settled into the seat at Duff's right.

"Sorry I'm late, Lincoln," he whispered.

Ma leaned in and tapped Lincoln's shoulder. "Abe? What's he doin' here?"

"Mr. Walker is my second chair."

"You didn't tell me that," she said with a frown.

"It'll be fine, Hannah. He's a good lawyer, and I can use his help."

"Oyez, Oyez. Court is now in session!" bellowed a bailiff. "The honorable Judge James Harriot presiding. All rise."

The entire room stood as the judge entered and took his seat.

It so happened, Lincoln had told us once, that he'd tried another murder case before this same judge. A woman had been accused of killing her abusive husband. Everyone in the town, including the lawmen, thought she had probably acted out of self-defense, for his violent nature was well documented through prior arrests. But the law being the law, they'd arrested her just the same.

On the day of her arraignment, Mr. Lincoln had pleaded with Judge Harriot to release her before trial on her own recognizance. Swayed by Lincoln's argument, the judge had allowed it. But when Lincoln next showed up to court, his client had gone missing. Judge Harriot was furious, demanding to know exactly what Lincoln had advised the woman.

Lincoln's simple explanation was that his client had said she was thirsty, and she'd asked him where to find a good drink of water. He'd told her that Tennessee was renowned for its drinking water, and that was the last anyone saw of her.

It had made Judge Harriot hopping mad at the time, but since then, he'd gotten over the effrontery. From then on, he certainly knew Lincoln would do anything to seek justice for his clients.

Judge Harriot settled himself into a high-backed chair behind a dark wooden podium. There was a silence as he scanned the room.

"Be seated," he ordered, and we all sat.

While it's true that Judge Harriot presided over the trial, I've long thought it would be more accurate to say that he *loomed* over it. His mere presence dominated. His snow-white hair hung over the collar of his flowing black robe, and his big mustache and fierce dark eyes highlighted his grim countenance. But Mr. Lincoln had said he was a fair judge, and I certainly hoped he was right.

"We are here in the matter of *The People v. Armstrong*," the judge announced. "Let me begin by saying I am fully aware of the intense interest this case has sparked in the community, and I welcome the quiet observation of peaceful citizens. But if there are demonstrations of emotion among spectators, if there are any outbursts, I will have this room cleared by the deputies, and anyone who resists will spend the night behind bars. Is that understood?"

The crowd sat quietly, many of them assenting to him with nods of their heads.

"Good. Then we're all agreed. Is the defendant present?"

"Yes, Your Honor," answered Lincoln, as he and Duff rose to face him.

"How does the defendant plead?"

Lincoln nudged Duff, who quickly spoke. "Not guilty, sir."

"Thank you. You may be seated. Mr. Fullerton, you are representing the State in this case?"

"I am, Your Honor."

"You may make your opening argument."

Ma took a deep breath and grabbed tightly onto my knee as Fullerton ran a hand over his sleek hair and stepped up to the jurors' box.

"Good morning, gentlemen, and thank you for your service. Murder cannot be tolerated in our civil society. This is a tragic case. A young man, James Preston Metzker, was struck down in the prime of his youth on the night of March 13, 1858. His family is heartbroken. His friends are devastated, his loss keenly felt by many in this county. The State offers its condolences. We intend to prove that this crime, this cold-blooded murder, was committed by this defendant, William Duff Armstrong. The facts are simple. On the night in question, James Preston Metzker was lured from a revival tent, a place where he'd gone to worship his Maker, and enticed by this defendant to accompany him to a godless 'whiskey camp.' There, they argued. And this defendant, in a drunken rage, viciously attacked James Preston Metzker with a wagon hammer, causing his death. You will hear eyewitness testimony to these facts, proving beyond any doubt that William Duff Armstrong is guilty of this brutal crime and, we will argue, should be punished to the full extent of the law – to be hung by the neck until dead. Justice demands it, James Preston Metzker's family demands it, and so must all of you demand it."

Angry murmurs rippled through the crowd as Fullerton returned to his seat. Duff's face went white. I looked anxiously to Ma who sat stone-faced and motionless. The judge banged his gavel and the crowd quieted.

The gangly Lincoln stood and walked to the jury. He studied their faces and offered them a friendly smile before speaking.

"Good morning, gentlemen. You've sacrificed a lot to be here today. Working in your fields, tending your stores, caring for kinfolk, or who knows what else. Thank you for your trouble, for taking time out of your lives in the cause of justice. I'm going to begin by making a startling admission. My client, Duff Armstrong, is no saint!"

He paused for effect. "But neither are any of us. Duff Armstrong is from fine stock, a descendant of one of the founding families in these parts. A loving son, a hard-working farmer, a respected member of the community. There is no conceivable way this boy is the cold-blooded murderer Mr. Fullerton would have you believe. He is merely a fun-loving youth who got in over his head one night when he stole away from a religious camp meeting. Why, I've snuck away from a few of those myself, as some of you may have, too."

Some members of the jury chuckled.

"So, I just want to ask a favor as we move along here. I seek your patience, your attention, your good will, and your readiness to do the right thing. And I believe that, in the end, you *will* do the right thing. Just remember, that the prosecution has to prove my client guilty beyond a reasonable doubt. But they can't, because as you will see, Duff Armstrong is innocent. Thank you."

With that, Mr. Lincoln sat back down. Ma again squeezed my hand and, for the first time that day, she smiled.

SEVENTEEN

"YOU MAY CALL YOUR FIRST witness, Mr. Fullerton."

"Thank you, Your Honor. The Prosecution calls Sheriff James Dick."

The sheriff took the stand and was sworn in by the bailiff. Once he settled into the witness chair, Fullerton approached to begin his examination.

"Tell us how you first learned of the murder of Preston Metzker, Sheriff."

"It was Sunday, March fourteenth, when Doc Parker came into my office around eleven o'clock and reported it. He said he examined the body and it looked like the boy had been bludgeoned in the head. Doc said he suspected foul play, and I should look into it straight away. So I rode out to the Metzker ranch."

"Go on."

"Well, Mr. Metzker and his whole family were in a state of shock, crying and all, 'cause the boy died a few hours before in his own bed. There was blood on his pillow. I took a look at the body and it was like Doc said. Struck on the right side of the head, just horrible. One of the sorrier sights I ever seen."

"Then what did you do?"

"Rode back to my office and started to fill out paperwork. You know, I had to open the case as a potential murder."

"That must require quite a bit of paperwork," said Fullerton. "Go on."

"Well, late that afternoon, I was still in the office when Charlie Allen and Jim Norris came in to see me. They said they just heard Preston died, so they thought they oughtta tell me they were there with Preston on Saturday night at the camp meeting and later at a whiskey camp further up Salt Creek. They said they seen who killed him."

"And who did they identify as the murderer?"

"Duff Armstrong." A murmur rustled through the crowd.

"And after they told you that, did you go to the Armstrong farm to make the arrest right away?"

"Oh no, sir."

"Why not?"

"Well, I wanted to take a look-see for myself. So, the next mornin', I had Jim and Charlie ride up with me to show me just where the whiskey camp was set up on the weekend. It was gone by then," said the sheriff. "Anyway, I told 'em to go over exactly what happened. They took me to the clearing, showed me where they said Duff and Preston fought."

"Did you find any evidence at the site?"

"Yes, sir. That's where I found the wagon hammer."

Fullerton crossed back to the prosecution table and retrieved something.

"Is this the same hammer, Sheriff?"

The sheriff studied it. "Yep, this is it. You can see it has blood on it right here."

"Your Honor, the State wishes to submit this wagon hammer as Exhibit A." He set it before the judge, who ordered it entered into evidence.

"So, after finding the murder weapon, what did you do next?" Fullerton continued.

"Well, there was folks that still needed talking to. I tracked down Mr. Randle, the preacher that set up the camp meeting, and old Mr. Watkins who ran the whiskey camp."

"And did the facts you gather bear out the report you received from Mr. Allen and Mr. Norris?"

"They did. Randle remembered seeing the boys leave the camp meeting, and Watkins said he remembered seeing someone arguing with Preston. That's when I went to the Armstrong farm and took Duff into custody."

"Did the defendant go along with you willingly?"

"Yes, sir."

Then came the most damning question of all, "Sheriff, have you ever heard the defendant make physical threats against Preston Metzker?"

The lawman shifted uneasily in the witness chair. "Well, yes, sir. I have."

Lincoln leaned forward intently.

"A few months back, Duff and Preston raced their rigs right into the center of town. Caused quite a commotion, so I spoke to 'em about it. I got the clear sense that there was bad blood between them."

"How so?"

"Well," the sheriff hesitated. "After I told Preston his recklessness was liable to get him killed, Duff said something about wantin' to kill Preston hisself."

The courtroom exploded. The judge vigorously banged his gavel and gave an angry look at the crowd. I looked at Ma, wide-eyed, and she covered her face with her hands.

"No further questions," said Mr. Fullerton, as he returned to his seat.

The room quieted when Mr. Lincoln rose and walked to the witness stand.

"Mornin', Sheriff."

"Mornin'."

"Tell me, you ever been mad at someone, maybe say you'd like to kill him, as a figure of speech?"

"Of course."

"Then couldn't that be the way Duff Armstrong said it on the day of that race through town?"

"That's how I took it at the time."

"And if you was a young feller about my client's age, never been in any trouble with the law before, and a sheriff like you came to your door to arrest you, what do you think you'd do?"

"Run like hell."

"Ah, but Duff Armstrong didn't run, did he?"

"No, sir."

"Why do you think that was?

Fullerton jumped up. "Objection, Your Honor. Calls for speculation on the part of the witness," said Mr. Fullerton.

"Sustained."

Lincoln lifted the hammer from where it sat on the judge's bench and studied it. "Now about this hammer. You say it was the weapon used to kill the decedent."

"Yes, because, like I said, there's dried blood on it."

"So I see, but something about it keeps nagging at me. Ever shoe a horse, Sheriff?"

"Can't say as I have."

Lincoln brought the hammer to the witness stand. "Well, Sheriff, I believe this is a farrier's hammer, the kind used to shoe horses."

"Looks like an ordinary wagon hammer to me."

Lincoln turned and scanned the spectators. He spotted someone he recognized among them.

"Your Honor, I see there's a smithy here from Mulgrave's Stable. Think we could ask him to take a look, get his opinion?"

"How about it, Mr. Fullerton? You want me to put him on the stand?" asked the judge.

"In the interest of time, Your Honor, we have no objection to him just looking at it without the formality of a swearing in."

The judge asked the blacksmith to step forward. He gave his name as Jasper Edwards.

"Thank you, Mr. Edwards," said Lincoln. "Take a look at this and tell us what you think. Is this a farrier's hammer?"

Mr. Lincoln handed it to Mr. Edwards, who turned it over once in his hands.

"Oh, it's a farrier's hammer, no doubt. They use 'em at the stable anytime there's a horse to shoe."

"And what about the blood? Do horses bleed when they're shod?"

"Not always, but I've seen it once in a while. Especially if the farrier trims the hoof too close or hits a bone spur."

With a nod from Lincoln, the judge told Mr. Edwards he could return to his seat.

Mr. Fullerton rose irritably. "Your Honor, the State is all too happy to concede the point Mr. Lincoln is trying to make. But it makes no difference to us what kind of hammer it is. We still contend that it is the murder weapon." With that, he sat back down.

"Noted," said the judge.

Lincoln turned his attention back to Sheriff Dick on the stand. "Tell me, Sheriff. You say you rode out to see the Metzker family. Did you learn anything you didn't expect from them?"

"Not much. Just that when Preston left home that day he was fine, and when he returned early next morning he had a head wound. He had already expired before I got there."

"And did the family mention anything else to you? Anything at all?"

"As a matter of fact, they did. They mentioned a money clip that was missing. A gold one. I rode all the way back up to the whiskey camp to look around for it, but never found it."

"Did you find it in Duff Armstrong's possession?"

"No. I assume it was lost before the fight."

"You assumed it was lost, but not stolen? Why in the world?"

"Well, I've known Duff Armstrong for years. He comes from good people. That boy ain't no thief."

"That's quite a character reference, Sheriff. Thank you for your testimony," said Mr. Lincoln, as he returned to his seat.

The next witness to be called by the prosecution was Dr. Eli Parker. Ma had been through so much with him over the years. I knew it would be hard for her to hear his testimony against Duff. But, of course, he had no choice, and she understood that.

"Dr. Parker, you were called to the Metzker ranch in the early morning hours of Sunday, March 14, 1858, correct?"

"That's right, Mr. Fullerton. I was."

"And at the time you examined Preston Metzker, how would you describe his medical condition?"

"He had a wound to the right temple, and he had lapsed into unconsciousness. I administered morphine to ease whatever pain he might've had. He expired shortly after that."

"What was the official cause of death?"

"Cerebral hemorrhaging on the right side. Should have been tended to immediately, but even then, it might not have saved him."

"Did he have any other injuries?"

"Yes, he had a split lip. It appeared as though he'd been punched in the mouth."

"But despite the injuries, he was still able to get himself home in his buggy?"

"As I understand it, yes. I was surprised he could have done that."

"Could his stallion have pulled the buggy home without guidance?"

"Well, I've known it to happen."

Then Mr. Fullerton picked up the hammer from the judge's desk. "In your medical opinion, is this the weapon that killed Preston Metzker?" he asked.

"I believe so, yes. After the sheriff asked me to compare it to the head wound, I went back to the Metzker ranch with it. The family graciously allowed me to come back in for that purpose. As far as I could tell, the head of that hammer matched up to the size of the blow on the head."

"I see. One more thing, doctor. You're the defendant's family physician, are you not?"

"Yes. And Preston's family, too, for that matter. Watched both those boys growing up. Never thought I'd see something like this."

"And what do you think of Duff Armstrong?"

"He's always been a fine young man, as far as I know."

"Were you aware the defendant was courting the victim's sister?"

"Objection!" Mr. Lincoln called out. "Relevance, Your Honor."

"Sustained."

"Thank you, doctor. No further questions."

Fullerton sat and Mr. Lincoln approached the witness stand.

"Hello, doctor."

Doc Parker nodded.

"You say you like my client, do you?"

"Yes, sir. Whenever I've been out to the Armstrong farm, I've observed Duff to be hardworking and good to his family."

"Glad to hear it."

Lincoln reached up to the judge's bench and once again retrieved the hammer.

"So, if I understand correctly, it's your contention that this is the very hammer used to kill the murder victim."

"Yes, sir."

"But wouldn't a similar hammer, an identical one, match up to the wound the way this one did?

"Well, yes. But you can see there's blood on this one."

"Is there any way to tell if it's the Metzker boy's blood or, say, the blood of a horse?"

"Well, no."

"Now, he was wounded on the right side of the head. Would that indicate to you that the victim was struck by someone who is left-handed?"

He scratched his chin. "Yes, I suppose it does."

"An experiment, Your Honor?" asked Lincoln, but before the judge could respond, he'd flung the hammer over to Duff, who caught it in his right hand.

"For the record, Your Honor, my client is right-handed."

The spectators murmured, and the judge looked angry as he rapped his gavel.

"Your Honor, I object!" fumed Fullerton, springing to his feet.

"Mr. Lincoln, you know better than to pull a stunt like that in my court!" scolded the judge. "Don't try me. I won't warn you again."

"Yes, Your Honor," said Lincoln innocently. "No further questions."

Mr. Wellman leaned over to Ma and whispered, "Thee have found thyself an impressive lawyer."

But as the doctor stood to leave, Mr. Fullerton rose again. "Redirect, Your Honor."

"Very well. Doctor, would you sit back down, please?"

Mr. Fullerton went to the bench and picked up the hammer. "Doctor, you say a wound to the right side probably indicates a left-handed attacker. Is it possible that the assailant had already knocked his victim to the ground before wielding the hammer? Or that the attacker approached the victim from behind?"

"I was not there to see it, but I suppose anything is possible."

Fullerton excused the doctor, who was finally allowed to step down. It was now well past noon, and the judge adjourned the court till two o'clock. Mr. Lincoln nodded to us as he and Mr. Walker left with Duff, in the custody of a deputy.

Then Mr. Wellman told us he had brought along a food hamper packed by his wife, so we headed out to his buggy to eat. But as I stepped out the door, someone called to me.

"Psst! Scrump! Scrump, over here."

I turned to look, and there, peering around a corner of the courthouse, was Sarah May Metzker. She motioned me over, pulling me around the corner, so we wouldn't be seen.

"Scrump, I need a big favor. I need you to give this to your brother," she said as she handed me an envelope. "But no one, and I mean no one, can know about it. Not your mother, not my folks, and none of the lawyers. No one! Promise me?"

"Okay. I promise." I said, stuffing the envelope quickly into my pocket. She pecked me on the cheek and ran off.

EIGHTEEN

COURT RECONVENED AFTER THE NOONTIME recess, and Mr. Fullerton put up his next witness. When the name was called, a pall of silence covered the room. John Joseph Metzker, Preston's father, took the stand and placed his hand on the Bible while the bailiff swore him in.

Everyone in the courtroom, if not the entire town, knew that Mr. Metzker was the county's most successful rancher. He looked it, too, in his black frock coat and snakeskin boots. Upon his swearing in, he answered with a sonorous but melancholy, "I do."

Mr. Fullerton began by expressing personal sympathy for his loss and promising to be as brief as possible. "Perhaps we could begin by your telling us how your son happened to be going to the camp meeting on the day in question?"

"Yes, sir." He wiped his brow with a handkerchief before speaking. "Well, there's too much sinning in the world, but my wife and I trust in the good Lord. We want our children to believe the same. So, I thought the camp meeting could help the cause. When the reverend came to me for a donation, I was glad to oblige."

"The reverend?"

"Reverend Randle. He comes through these parts to put on camp meetings. I gave him money to help with expenses. Done that a couple years now."

"I applaud your benevolence. Please go on."

"Anyway, as the date for the meeting got closer, and since the reverend wanted to reach young people in particular, we were hoping our own children would attend. But only one was really eager to go. That was Sarah May, our daughter over there." He pointed her out and continued. "My two oldest boys were out of town on ranch business. And Preston, well...he loved Our Lord too, but he was shy about attending. I told him he should take some friends and enjoy himself. So he finally agreed, like the good son he was."

Mr. Metzker paused to compose himself. "And he *was* a good son. Polite to his ma and me, a hard worker, always there to help anybody..." His voice trailed off as he choked back tears and brushed his handkerchief across his eyes.

"Were you aware that the defendant was one of the young people planning to go to the tent meeting?"

"Yes, I knew that. Sarah May told me."

"Did she tell you she'd be accompanying the defendant?"

"Yes. They were courting."

"How did you feel about that?"

"Well, any father wants the best for his daughter. Duff comes from a fine family. I knew his father some. They're hardworking, honest people. But, truth be told, we were hoping Sarah May might end up with someone a little more established. You know, someone who has property of his own and can support her in the way she's been raised."

"And in what way was that?"

"Well, we always provided nice things for our children. They each had a real fine horse, and Sarah May liked to ride out in our buggy with Preston..."

Mr. Metzker seemed near tears again.

"I know this is painful, sir. But please, tell the jury what happened on your son's last night."

"Well, sir, it was nigh onto two o'clock in the morning when we heard Preston come in. We were used to him coming home late and bumping into things on his way up to his room. But on this particular night, he yelled up to me, 'Papa,' which was unusual. I got out of bed, lit a lantern, and hurried downstairs. He was staggering, and as I stepped closer, I knew something was wrong."

"And then what happened?"

"He looked at me, took a step, and then just...fell to the floor. That's when I saw the blood trickling all down the right side of his head. I called to my wife, and together we managed to get him into his bed. Then I roused one of my hired hands to fetch Doc Parker."

"And how long between the time he came home and the time he...expired?"

"No more than four hours. He left us to join the Lord at about six o'clock." Mr. Metzker sighed deeply and dabbed his eyes with his handkerchief.

Silence filled the crowd. The only sound we heard was Mrs. Metzker's soft sobs. Fullerton thanked him and he quietly returned to his seat at the prosecutor's table.

Mr. Lincoln took a breath, pushed his chair back, and started to rise. But Mr. Walker pulled him back, vigorously shaking his head at him.

"A moment, Your Honor?"

The judge nodded, and the two spoke in hushed tones.

"What is it, Walker?"

"Lincoln, you can't question him."

"Why on earth not?"

"Look at that jury," Walker said in a hushed voice. "They're practically crying along with Mrs. Metzker. How's it going to sit with them when you, Mr. Big City Lawyer, go after a grieving father—*and* the town's most prominent citizen?"

"What do you think we should do?"

"Let *me* question him! I knew Preston and believe you me, he was no little tin Jesus like they're making him out to be. I know this town. Trust me, if I do the questioning, they'll take it a lot better than they would from you."

Lincoln looked back at the sad-faced jury, then nodded his assent.

Mr. Walker stood and readied himself. He brushed his coat lapels and politely stepped up to the witness box. The judge raised a bemused brow and settled back to watch from his perch.

Like Mr. Fullerton before him, Walker offered condolences, which Mr. Metzker accepted with a curt nod of his head.

"I was just wondering, sir. You say you were used to your son coming home late at night. Could you elaborate on what you mean by that?"

"Well, sometimes we would hear him come home after midnight. He was young."

"And on those nights, would you say he'd been out enjoying himself by, maybe, tipping a few back?"

"I'm not naïve, sir. Preston was a young man. Young men like to sow their wild oats."

"Then you were aware that he drank liquor?"

Mr. Metzker sat in stone silence. Mr. Walker looked to the judge, who in turn leaned over and politely instructed him to answer the question.

"He never did it in front of me or his mother," he finally replied. "Never."

"So, when he would come home late at night and make noises, as you say, he most likely had been drinking?"

"I just said so, didn't I?" Metzker retorted with an edge in his voice.

"Were these nighttime arrivals common? Or just a now-and-then thing?"

Mr. Metzker sighed. "Well, I'd say no more than two or three times a week. I spoke to him about it, we both did."

Having made this point, and gauging the mood of the witness, Walker tactfully moved on. "Now, you say your son was bleeding when you came downstairs and saw him?"

"Yes, bleeding from the right side of his head."

"Did you see any other visible wounds?"

"Well, his lip was bloodied."

I looked over at Mr. Lincoln. He was leaning forward on his elbows, intently tracking every word.

"So, in addition to the head wound he already had, might there have been a second injury that compounded his condition?"

"Objection. The witness is not a doctor."

"Sustained, Mr. Fullerton."

Walker smiled. "You've been very patient, Mr. Metzker. Just one more thing, sir. The sheriff mentioned a missing money clip."

"Yes, a gold one that had belonged to my father. We gave it to Preston because they both had the same initials, JPM. My father had them engraved on the clip. But to be fair, we don't know for sure if Preston had it with him when he left for the camp meeting."

"You haven't found it yet, it sounds like."

"We're hoping it'll turn up."

Walker indicated his cross examination was concluded, and Mr. Metzker was excused. Out of the jury's view, Mr. Walker gave Lincoln a toothy grin before he sat, and Lincoln patted him gratefully on the arm.

Mr. Fullerton's next witness was the Reverend Frank Randle, an itinerant minister who described himself as a "country parson." No preacher I'd ever seen in those parts had ever dressed so fine. He sported glossy black boots, a blue twill coat, and a flashy red string tie with a matching pocket-handkerchief. He not only put his hand on the Bible and agreed to the oath, but he kissed the Good Book for good measure.

Settling in, he adjusted his gold-rimmed spectacles as Mr. Fullerton approached him.

Fullerton asked him to describe his ministry. The parson said he moved from town to town throughout Illinois, holding camp meetings to save "the lost and degenerate." He boasted that his ministry was supported through donations harvested from a handful of "the faithful." He decided to come back to Beardstown, he testified, after he had passed through a few months back and noticed the opening of a new saloon.

"Alcohol is the devil's elixir," he announced, flicking a speck of lint from the sleeve of his well-pressed coat.

In response to Mr. Fullerton's questioning, he told the jury that on the night of the murder, he'd hosted over two hundred "souls" at his camp meeting near Salt Creek.

"And was Preston Metzker among the attendees that night?"

"He was indeed. I knew him to be John Metzker's son, and I noticed him sitting in the rear with several other young men. Those boys looked to be a bad influence on him, I'm afraid."

"How so?"

"Very rowdy. Especially during the preaching. One of them actually heckled me!"

"How do you mean?"

"Shouting rude comments, telling me to 'shut my pearly gates.'"

"Tell me, Reverend. Was Duff Armstrong among the group that heckled you?"

"He was. I saw him in the torchlight next to young Metzker. I recall the floppy hair. He and his friends were a distraction to the other worshippers. I'm sad to say so, but I wasn't sorry when I saw them leave. I do regret them spiriting young Metzker away with them, but you have to give the Devil his due."

"Objection! My client is not the Devil," shouted Mr. Lincoln, and the judge quickly sustained.

"So Preston Metzker left that evening with Duff Armstrong?"

"Yes, at 9:20 p.m. exactly. I remember checking my pocket watch at the time in anticipation of my 9:30 altar call. So that's when they left, right at 9:20."

"Thank you, Reverend. Your witness, Mr. Lincoln."

The preacher fidgeted with the bow at his collar as Lincoln approached.

"Now Reverend Randle. How is it you recognized Preston Metzker that evening? Had you met him before?"

"Yes, I stopped by the Metzker ranch a few weeks before the camp meeting. These events are costly, you know. I have to pay men to set up the tent, print handbills and such. I solicited a donation from Mr. Metzker since he'd helped in the past. On my way out, I met and personally invited Preston. Nice looking young feller. Such a shame."

"And how did he react to this invitation of yours?"

"He was, shall we say, reluctant? Didn't seem much interested. So, you can imagine how pleasantly surprised I was to see him that night, especially since his father was one of the evening's largest benefactors."

"I see," continued Lincoln. "And did you ever stop by the Armstrong farm to ask them to donate to your ministry?"

"I didn't know the Armstrongs at the time."

"But you were soliciting donations."

"I rely on a group of generous donors with a history of giving. I did not preclude the Armstrongs. Anyone can make a donation."

"I'm sure, but my point is, you had met the decedent. But you've never met the accused, have you? He's right over there. You sure you recognize him from that night?"

The Reverend adjusted his glasses and peered at Duff.

"Yes, I think he was among the rowdy ones in the rear."

"You think? You just testified you didn't know my client previously. How can you be absolutely sure it was him? He was sitting at a distance from you, in the rear of the tent. Reverend, a man's life is at stake. Having sworn on the Holy Bible, are you one hundred percent certain this is the young man you saw?"

He furrowed his brow and glanced over at the Bible sitting on the corner of the judge's bench, then back to Duff. He fiddled with his eyeglasses.

"Well…the hair is certainly similar."

"Similar? I notice you keep adjusting your spectacles, sir. Is it possible that you could be mistaken?"

Randle nervously smoothed his lapel and tipped his chin down to look at Duff over the top of his glasses. "Well…I suppose it's possible."

I saw Mr. Fullerton grimace.

"Thank you, Reverend. That's all for now."

The Prosecutor next called the proprietor of the whiskey camp where Preston Metzker had been attacked. Nelson Watkins was unshaven. He wore tattered overalls, a dirty shirt, and a cranky scowl. He clearly didn't want to be here.

The bailiff came over with the Bible and Watkins placed a shaky hand on it. Instead of responding to the oath with the customary "I do," he irritably replied, "Why the hell wouldn't I?"

Mr. Watkins reeked of tobacco and cheap alcohol. The judge barked at him, "Sir, are you sober?"

"Only till I get out of this damn courtroom."

Some men in the crowd sniggered as Fullerton approached the witness and began his interview. In short order, the jury learned that, yes, he was selling whiskey at a camp near Salt Creek that night, that he remembered Duff because he was a new customer, and that he'd heard Preston arguing with someone in the clearing. When urged to provide specifics on this last point, however, he pushed the court's patience to the limit with his answer.

"Hell, if I investigated every dang fight that broke out in the camp, I wouldn't have time to sell my goddam whiskey!"

This brought another snicker from the gallery.

"Mr. Watkins, you will watch your language out of respect for this court and the ladies present."

"Sorry, Judge."

Since Fullerton had successfully established Duff's presence at the murder scene, he retreated with relief from his own witness, handing him off to Mr. Lincoln.

"So, Mr. Watkins. You were selling whiskey to a lot of fellers at the camp that night. How many customers did you have?"

"I don't count 'em. I just pour 'em. They come at me all higgledy-piggledy."

"Could you make a guess?"

"Oh, I'd reckon thirty, mebbe more."

"And of those thirty or more, you know specifically that the defendant was there that night?"

"Him and his floppy hair? Sure do. Kept pushing it from his eyes like a goddam girl. Besides, I allus try to make new customers happy, and I remember givin' him an extra pour on the house."

"And you say he was with Preston Metzker?"

"He was, and they was downin' their fair share, I can tell ya."

"My client is not wealthy. Who was paying for all these drinks?"

"Well, 'cept for the one on the house, the Metzker kid paid. He had a wad of cash big as your fist, all folded up in a gold money clip."

"You saw him with the money clip?"

"He done showed it to me hisself. Pure gold, he bragged. Had his initials carved right into it. JPM, it was. Said his real name was James, but ever'body called him Preston. Oh, he was a real showboat, that one was."

"How much cash would you say he had on him?"

"Musta been near a hundred, I bet."

"That's quite a lot of money for a young man. Do you remember him talking with anyone else besides my client that night?"

"Well, they was together quite a bit, those two, and there was fellers comin' and goin' all the time. But come to think, there was another feller talkin' to the Metzker boy for some time."

Lincoln glanced around at Duff, hoping for a look of confirmation, something to indicate he remembered this new feller, but my brother just shrugged.

Turning back to Watkins and clearly intrigued, Lincoln pursued this line of questioning. He asked if he could identify this stranger.

Watkins' memory was utterly disappointing. He'd seen the feller before but he didn't know his name.

"All I know is he was a big feller and he wore a beat-up cowboy hat like half the sumbitches who come 'round. Guess he mighta had a mustache…I just can't recall right this minute. Maybe when I get a drink or two in me, it'll come back."

We heard a chortle from the men in the courtroom.

"Anything else you can remember about this stranger and young Mr. Metzker?"

"Well, after a time, they had some kinda disagreement. Metzker was a-wavin' his hands around, and slammin' his glass down on the barrel. But I ain't got no idea what they was goin' on about."

"And where was Duff Armstrong while the decedent and this man were arguing?"

He hesitated. "Well, I dunno as I should say, seein' as the judge here is concerned for the ladies in the room."

Judge Harriot intervened. "Perhaps you could just tell me." He leaned over to allow Watkins to whisper to him, trying to hide his displeasure at the old timer's pungent odor. Then the judge announced, "Let the record show that the witness saw the defendant go into the woods to relieve himself."

I could see Duff's ears blush bright red as laughter rose from the gallery.

The judge gave one knock with his gavel. Lincoln smiled and moved on.

"Did you see Preston Metzker go toward the clearing in the woods?"

He rubbed his whiskers as he considered. "I mighta, but I know fer sure I hear'd a loud argument in the woods."

"But if they were a ways off, how can you be sure it was those two you heard arguing in the clearing?"

"That's what they told me."

"Who told you?"

"Charlie Allen and Jim Norris. They told me it was Metzker arguin' in the clearing with the Armstrong boy."

"So, what you're saying is, you never actually saw Duff Armstrong argue with Preston Metzker in the clearing? You just *thought* they were the two young men arguing because Mr. Norris and Mr. Allen told you so?"

"Well, I reckon that'd be fair to say," he replied with a satisfied look.

At that moment, you could almost hear the prosecutor's jaw drop on the floor. Lincoln had just scored a heavy blow against the State's case, but it was far from a knockout. There were still two eyewitnesses to contend with.

Lincoln addressed the judge. "Your Honor. I'm done questioning this man for now, but I reserve the right to call him to the stand as a hostile witness."

"Hostile? Who's you callin' hostile?"

The judge ignored the question and dismissed Watkins, advising him to not leave town in the event he was recalled to the witness stand. The old feller grumbled as he shuffled out the door. Then the judge adjourned us for the day.

• • •

As the room emptied, Mr. Wellman stepped up to the railing and shook Mr. Lincoln's hand. Ma reached over and squeezed Duff on the shoulder, giving him an encouraging look before he was led back to jail.

"Won't we be goin' back to the jail with him?" I asked.

"Abe will be with him," said Ma. "But we'll see him in the morning first thing. Right now, we need to get on home. It's been a long day."

Mr. Wellman drove us back to our farm. Ma fixed supper, then insisted we turn in early.

"We need to rest up for tomorrow," she told me.

But that night, as it had the night before, sleep eluded me.

"Ma? Ma, are you awake?" I whispered as I tapped lightly on her bedroom door.

"Come in. What is it, Scrump? You're not sick, are you?"

"I can't sleep."

"Want to stay in here tonight?" she asked, and when I hesitated, she added, "It's alright. I can't sleep either."

She threw back the covers invitingly, so I crawled into Pa's empty side of the bed.

"My, how you've grown," she said, tucking the patchwork quilt over my shoulders.

"Everything's going to be fine, Scrump," she murmured reassuringly as I settled into the comfort of her goose down mattress. "Mind if I tell you a story like I used to when you were little? Only this one's true. It's about me and Abe."

I nodded, yawning wide.

"When your Pa and me lived in New Salem, I sewed Abe a new suit. He needed something to wear for his lawyer's exam and I knew he'd never find long pants and a frock coat his size in any country store. My, but he loved that suit! Once he slipped it on, we rarely saw him without it. Well, one day he was riding along and heard a loud squawk from a tree as he trotted by. He got off his horse, and there on the ground he found two little birds that had tumbled right out of their nest! Now most folks would've just rode on. But not Abe, oh no. He scooped up those tiny birds in his big hands, put 'em in his pocket. Then he climbed up that tree and put 'em right back in their nest with their mama!

"Wouldn't you know, on the way down, he ripped a hole in his britches. When he brought 'em back to me for mending, he told me the story. 'Abe Lincoln,' I said, 'What were you thinking, climbing a tree like a schoolboy at your age?' And he says, 'Hannah, you may laugh at me, but I knew I wouldn't sleep a wink that night had I not saved those two baby birds. Their mama's cry would have rung in my ears all night long.'

"So, I think that's how it is with us, Scrump. Mr. Lincoln won't rest till he gets us all back together. Why, I bet he's awake this very minute, just like we are."

"I reckon."

As I finally fell asleep, I stopped worrying about all our problems. Instead, I dreamt of Mr. Lincoln climbing a tree and returning those babies to their mama's nest.

Nineteen

IT WAS THE SECOND DAY of trial, the day Jim Norris and Charlie Allen were slated to testify against Duff, and everyone in town, it seemed, wanted a seat in the courtroom. We saw the line snaking out the courthouse door and down the block as we passed by in Mr. Wellman's buggy on our way to the jail to deliver Duff a freshly pressed white shirt. Some in the crowd were reading the penny papers and we couldn't help but see the big headline:

MURDER WITNESSES TO TESTIFY TODAY!

"A man looks more respectable in a clean shirt," Ma told Duff, handing him the brown paper package. "And keep the hair out of your eyes. People need to see how handsome and honest you look. Did you get a good breakfast?"

"Yes, Ma. They fed me fine," he replied as he unwrapped the package. That's when he found what I'd slipped inside the pocket before Ma wrapped up the shirt. Sarah May's note. I raised a finger to my lips, and he kept silent about it as he turned his back and slid it under his pillow.

After he'd put the shirt on, Ma continued to fuss, fastening his collar button, pushing the hair back off his forehead. Then Mr. Lincoln arrived with Mr. Walker, so we left them alone and walked over to the courthouse.

When we got inside with the help of the deputy, the room was already brimming with people. Crowds of onlookers lingered anxiously out front, hoping someone inside might give up their seat.

When the doors finally closed, the court was called to order. The prosecution entered, as did Duff and his lawyers, and they all took their places. Prior to the judge's appearance, however, Duff signaled me over to him. He leaned over the railing that separated us and I stood so he could whisper in my ear.

"Tell Sarah May it's okay to come see me. But tell her not to tell nobody."

Before I sat down, the bailiff cried, "All rise!"

Ma looked at me quizzically as she stood, wondering what Duff had whispered to me.

Judge Harriot entered and scanned the packed courtroom. His brow furrowed.

"Before we begin the day's proceedings, I will remind our spectators that you are here to do just that—spectate. Please sit silently and let the lawyers do their jobs. The court will not tolerate unwarranted commotion," he said sternly. "Very well, then, Mr. Fullerton, call your next witness."

"Thank you, judge. The State calls Mr. Charles Allen."

All eyes on him, Charlie stepped forward to the witness stand. He raised his hand, swore an oath to the truth, and settled himself into the witness chair. Ma grabbed hold of my hand and didn't let go all the time he was up there.

"Mr. Allen, please tell us how you knew the decedent, Preston Metzker."

"We was drinking buddies," began Charlie. "Got together a few nights a week."

"And what prompted you to go to the camp meeting with him on the night of March thirteenth?"

"I'm not much on religion, but Pres said he hadda go 'cause his dad give the preacher some money. I tagged along jus' for fun, wantin' to see what goes on at somethin' like that."

"Had you met the defendant before this day?"

"We seen each other around town every now and then, and I seen him when he brought a horse into the stable."

"The stable?"

"Mulgrave's. I shoe horses for 'em."

"When did you first see the defendant that day?"

"About six o'clock or so, out at the Metzker place. He stopped by to pick up Pres's sister, but Mrs. Metzker told us Sarah May was sick in bed and couldn't go."

"What was his reaction to that?"

"He took it kinda bad. We all knew him and Sarah May was pretty sweet on each other lately. He wanted to jus' head back home, but Pres talked him into goin' along with us."

"How did he do that, talk the defendant into going?"

"Pres told him Sarah May would wanna see him go. I dunno if that was true, though."

"Did the four of you travel there in the same rig?"

"No. Duff wanted to drive his own buggy. I climbed in with him, and Jim went in Pres's buggy."

Fullerton asked about the evening at Salt Creek. Charlie said it was crowded with folks socializing, gals and fellers spooning, and all of them waiting for the preacher's sermon.

"How would you say the accused and the decedent were getting along?"

"Well, once we all got to Salt Creek, Pres started in on him."

"Started in on him? What do you mean by that?"

"He called him 'farmer boy,' made fun of his work boots, and the way his hair kept fallin' over his eyes. Pres had a way of needling him that really got under Duff's skin."

"How would you say the defendant handled it?"

"Didn't like it at all. Oh, he tried not to show it, but he got all steamed up and red in the face, so you could see it was gettin' to him. I think Pres knew it, too. It was kinda funny at first, but then it got ugly. He started tellin' Duff how Sarah May had eyes for other fellers."

"What was his reaction to that?"

"I noticed he clenched his fists at his sides. I dunno if Pres saw that or not. But I got the feelin' Duff was gonna slug him."

"What do you think held him back?"

"Objection," interjected Lincoln.

"Sustained."

"Was there anything else that stands out in your mind from that evening?"

"Yeah, when Pres told Duff that Sarah May would never marry him 'cause he's too poor. I think Duff was mad 'cause he's afraid it's true."

Lincoln shot up. "Objection, Your Honor. Speculation."

"Your Honor," responded Fullerton, "unfortunately, Mr. Metzker can't speak for himself. But his friend here can. It goes to the crux of the relationship between young Mr. Metzker and the defendant. We need this witness's testimony to establish that."

"I'll allow it. Overruled."

"You were saying about the defendant and Miss Metzker?"

"Ever since they started keeping company, Pres kept puttin' Duff down. He thought Sarah May could do a whole lot better."

"Your Honor, sir," Lincoln interjected. "The defense concedes that enmity existed between Duff and the decedent, but I see no earthly reason to drag the relationship between this young woman and my client any further into the public record."

Judge Harriot nodded. "I think you've made your point, Mr. Fullerton. Move on."

Fullerton led Charlie through a description of events inside the tent. The witness confirmed that the four of them sat in the back, which he said was Duff's idea, so he could sneak out early.

At this point, I saw Duff lean over and whisper something to Mr. Lincoln.

"What happened next?"

"By this time we all had enough preachin' to last us a long while. Then Duff said he'd heard they was pourin' whiskey up the crick aways, and wanted to see if he could find the spot."

"So it was the defendant's idea to head to this whiskey camp?"

"Yessir."

"How did you all go up there?"

"The same way we got to the camp meeting. Two buggies. Jim and Pres in his fancy one and I rode with Duff in his."

"What happened once you arrived?"

"Well, we found the whiskey wagon bein' run by this old feller, Mr. Watkins, who asked us for money upfront. Pres said he'd pay for us all, so we started into drinkin'. After a while, we were feelin' pretty good, and me and Jim went to hang 'round with some other fellers. You know, just bein' friendly."

"I see," said Fullerton. "So the defendant had several whiskies while you were with him at the wagon?"

He nodded. "I seen him knock a few back. After we left them, I dunno what he drank. To be honest, for a time we lost all track of him and Pres. It warn't till we heard Duff yellin' like a madman that we went back to find 'em. We found 'em in a grove, just as Armstrong took his first swing at Pres."

"And about what time would you say this was?"

"Eleven thirty, maybe midnight."

"Did you try breaking them up?"

"Wished I had. But I just figured Pres could hold his own."

"At what distance were you watching them, would you say?"

"Well, they kept moving about. but I'd say between ten and twenty yards."

"Was Preston at a great disadvantage? Was he holding his own?"

He was till Duff reached into his boot for somethin' – then bam! He slammed Pres in the head and he fell to the ground."

"Did you see the weapon you say he hit him with?"

"Objection. It's already been determined it was a farrier's hammer."

"Sustained."

The prosecutor retrieved the hammer from the judge's bench. "Is this the same hammer?"

"Looks like it, yes."

"So you saw the defendant, Duff Armstrong, administer the blow that killed Preston Metzker with this hammer?"

"Yessir. Plain as day I seen it."

"Did you hear what the two were arguing about?"

"No, sir. But whatever it was, Duff sure wanted him dead."

"Objection!" bellowed Lincoln.

"Sustained."

"Tell the jury what happened next."

"Well, me 'n Jim headed over to break things up, but Duff ran away from us, hopped in his buggy and sped off."

"And the decedent? What about him?"

"I went over to him and saw blood tricklin' down the side of his head. We helped him up and we warn't sure what to do next, but Pres said he could get on home by hisself, so we got him into his buggy."

"Why didn't you see him home yourself?"

"Well, he said he was fine, and I guess I believed 'im. That was the last time I seen 'im..."

His voice trailed off, leaving a silence that hung over the room, as though it were a moment of respect for the victim's life.

"Your witness, Mr. Lincoln," Fullerton said quietly and returned to his seat.

Lincoln rose. Slowly but deliberately, he removed his long coat and hung it carefully over the back of his chair. Then he loosened his cravat and ambled casually to Charlie.

"Morning, Mr. Allen. Quite a story you told there."

"Ain't a story. It's the truth," he replied defensively.

"Yes." He paused. "You sure you got all the details right?"

"Yessir."

"Let's go over 'em one more time. Now why do you suppose the decedent was so eager to have the accused go along to the camp meeting?"

"He said he promised his old man he'd get as many fellers to go as he could."

"I see. So later, after the camp meeting, you boys were enjoying your whiskies until you and Jim got up to join some other fellers. Where were they, these fellers?"

"Just a ways from the wagon. There was a campfire and fellers were laughing and drinking around it. I usually like to join in with 'em."

"Usually? So you'd been there before?

"Well, not at that exact spot. Mr. Watkins moves his wagon from place to place, but he's always pourin' somewhere Saturday night. Somehow word always gets around to his customers."

"Very enterprising. Tell me, did you ever see my client drink anything before that night?"

"No. But we don't generally run together."

"You ran with Preston, though. You ever know him to drink too much before this?"

"I can't rightly say."

"But you just testified that you were drinking buddies. I imagine you knew all the local watering holes."

"We got around."

"So you had whiskies. Were you drunk when you witnessed this fight?"

"Even if I was, I know what I seen."

"So you *were* drunk that night." Lincoln hurried on. "Now, we've been told by a prior witness that Preston Metzker had quite a bit of cash on him the night he was killed. Do you recall that?"

"Preston always had cash on him."

"Funny how all that money disappeared, though."

"I reckon he spent it all on drinks. I said he was buyin'."

"You a church going man, Mr. Allen?"

"Not regular, no."

"How about the decedent?"

"I wouldn't know."

"You said he took you to the camp meeting only to please his father."

"That's how he told it."

"Doesn't it seem likely he'd want to stay for Reverend Randle's whole sermon?"

Charlie shrugged. "All I know is it was Duff's idea to leave."

"Mr. Watkins, who poured the drinks that night, testified that he saw the decedent arguing with a gentleman in a cowboy hat. Did you hear or see him speaking with anyone else that night?"

Charlie paused. "Not so's I can recall."

"Let's talk about this fight. You say you heard the decedent and the accused arguing."

"Like I said."

"And you got there just in time to see Duff Armstrong throw the first punch."

"That's right."

"And you saw my client wield a hammer and strike Preston Metzker in the head?"

"Like I said."

"And you say you saw all this plain as...how did you put it?"

"Plain as day."

"Only it wasn't *day*, Mr. Allen. It was almost midnight, according to you. Were there any torches or lamps in that clearing?"

"No."

"So it was dark, yet you saw everything plain as day from what you previously said was a distance of ten to twenty yards. Yet, you saw it so clearly and remember every detail. Who was up, who was down. Why, you can even identify this very hammer. That's some eyesight you've got there, Mr. Allen."

Charlie took a moment to answer. "That's 'cause the moon was full that night. And I seen everything just like I said I did."

"The moon must have been mighty bright to light a clearing in the woods." Lincoln paused. "Since you saw so much, did you happen to notice if my client was carrying a farrier's hammer?"

"Not that I could see."

"But you'd recognize one if you saw it, wouldn't you?"

"'Course I would. I work at Mulgrave's."

"That's right. What is it you do there again?"

Charlie glared at him. "I'm a farrier."

"Really?" Lincoln said with a look of feigned surprise. "Then don't you find it strange that my client, who is a farmer, had a farrier's hammer with him that night? It's a tool of *your* trade, after all."

"Objection, Your Honor. Mr. Allen is not on trial here," called out Fullerton.

"I withdraw the question," said Lincoln and went on. "So Preston Metzker went home in his buggy, and Duff Armstrong had already left in his. How did you and Mr. Norris get home?"

Charlie hesitated, then answered, "We hitched a ride back to town with one o' the other fellers. We spent the night at the stable."

"What was the name of this feller who gave you the ride back to town?"

"I don't recall his name just now. Russel, maybe? He was a friend of Jim's."

"One last question, Mr. Allen. Are you right-handed?"

"Yes."

"Thank you."

Charlie stepped down.

Just then, Sheriff Dick entered the courtroom through the rear and made a beeline to the prosecutor's table. He conferred quietly with Mr. Fullerton, and Judge Harriot impatiently checked his pocket watch.

"Next witness, Mr. Fullerton."

"Your Honor, the State had planned on calling Jim Norris today. But, um, we seem to be having trouble finding him. The State would like to request more time, sir."

"How much time?"

"A day. Maybe two, according to the sheriff. The State does not object to Mr. Lincoln proceeding with his defense until our witness is located."

"Mr. Lincoln?"

"We have no objection to the State taking all the time it needs to find its wandering witness. We will defer our defense until then."

The judge drummed his fingers on the desk. "Very well. We'll recess until Monday morning, nine o'clock sharp. Mr. Fullerton, the clock is ticking. Your witness had better be here."

"Yes, Your Honor. Thank you, Your Honor."

• • •

Amid the clamor of court-watchers filing out, Sarah May caught my eye. Slipping away from Ma, I squeezed through the crowd and we met up as we had before, at a side of the building where no one would see us.

"Did you give Duff my note?"

"Yeah. He says he wants to see you, but you shouldn't tell nobody."

She bit her lip, and suddenly Ma rounded the corner.

"Scrump! Where have you—oh! Sarah May," she said, stepping between us.

"Mrs. Armstrong! I…I…"

"It's all right, dear," said Ma gently. "You don't have to say anything. I'm sorry for your loss and, well, I'm trusting in God that this will all work out somehow. I hope you are, too."

"Yes, ma'am. I'm sorry for your loss, too. Thank you," she answered nervously. "I better go now."

We watched as she hurried off, then Ma turned to me. "What was she saying to you?"

"Nothin'. Just wondered how we all was is all."

"Well, hurry along. I want to see Duff before we head home."

Duff and the lawyers were already deep in conversation by the time we arrived, so we sat and listened.

"Duff, do you have anything you're not telling us?" Lincoln asked.

"No, sir."

"Because if you do, now's the time to speak up. We're your lawyers and anything you tell us is strictly confidential. We won't repeat it."

"I wish I had something to tell you, Mr. Lincoln. It's just that...I got no memory." He sat on his bunk, punching an angry fist into his open palm.

Lincoln studied him, and then glanced at Walker before placing a reassuring hand on Duff's shoulder.

"Son, we're heading into the homestretch. If I'm gonna save your life, it would help me to know how you got to that clearing and fought with Preston Metzker. You must try to remember. Do you have any idea what started the fight? Or any memory of another feller arguing with Preston?"

"No. But I would never attack nobody with no hammer. Somebody else must've done that."

"You think it was Charlie?"

"Coulda been. I don't know." He pushed the hair from his eyes and rose anxiously.

Lincoln pressed on.

"Let's go over what you do recall. You remember leaving the farm and going to the Metzker home?"

"Yes, sir. Sarah May's Ma said she was sick. I wanted to go home, but Preston said that Sarah May wanted me to go to the camp meetin'. I don't know why I ever listened to him. Somehow they talked me into goin' with him and Charlie and Jim."

"Did you know Jim and Charlie?"

"I knew Charlie some. I never met Jim before that."

"I see," said Lincoln, who was still gathering all the facts he could. "And was it really Preston's idea to go on up to that whiskey camp?"

"'Course it was."

"All right. So you went to the camp and had a few drinks."

"Yes."

"And then you and Preston separated from the others."

"I guess."

"And we know you went to a clearing and got into an argument."

"I…I don't remember that."

Lincoln paused, then asked, "Duff, the witnesses all say Preston said some pretty mean things about you and your gal. You don't suppose by any chance you two were arguing about Sarah May?"

"No!!"

Duff's tone was so adamant that Lincoln was taken aback.

"For a feller with no memory, you seem awful sure of yourself about that."

Mr. Walker, who had been listening carefully, finally spoke up. "I don't know, Duff. If I was on the jury, what you're saying is just not believable. You remember everything except what happened in that clearing. You're not holding back on us, are you?"

"No, sir."

"Duff, you need to think carefully about what I'm about to say," said Lincoln. "The only thing we got working for us now is the absence of Jim Norris. Without his testimony, it's your word against Charlie Allen's. And if the sheriff can't find Jim, the best way, perhaps the only way to save your neck, is for you to take the stand and tell your story."

"But I can't! I…I got nothin' to say."

"I tell you what. We've got a couple days till we go back into court. You take the time to go over things in your mind, see if you can't recall something. Anything. It'll come to you, I'm sure," encouraged Lincoln, as he rose to leave.

"Mr. Lincoln? About Sarah May. Please. Can we keep her out of this?"

"I'll do my best, Duff. I give you my word."

The meeting ended, so Ma kissed him goodbye and promised we'd visit before Monday.

The two lawyers walked ahead of me and Ma. The sheriff escorted us from the cell, and I heard Mr. Walker whisper, "You know what I think, Lincoln? I think he's protecting someone."

"Perhaps," replied Lincoln. "But who would be worth risking his neck for? That's what I want to know."

TWENTY

THE NEXT DAY WAS SATURDAY and the sky had turned grey and drizzly. I hadn't been sleeping well, if at all, these days. But this particular morning, I only woke when Suzy's cold nose roused me. Pulling myself from under the covers, I made my way to the kitchen where Ma had breakfast waiting for me. I yawned and rubbed my eyes as I entered.

"There you are, sleepyhead! Thought you was going to sleep all day. I fed the chickens for you," she said, setting a plate of eggs with bacon before me. I picked up the bacon with my fingers and took a huge bite.

"Thanks, Ma," I mumbled, as I chewed.

"Scrump, don't talk with your mouth full. And don't eat with your fingers!"

"Good morning," we heard a voice call. It was Matthew Wellman, poking his head through the door.

"Hello, Matthew. Come in out of the weather and dry yourself. Care for some coffee?"

"No thank thee, ma'am. I never partake," he said shaking the water from his hat before stepping in.

"Oh, forgive me, I forgot. Water, then? Or I could rustle you up some eggs."

"Water would be much appreciated."

Ma poured him a cup from the pitcher on the table.

"I thank thee, Missus. I was checking thy winter wheat crop when the rain started."

"And how are things looking?"

"Quite good. I think it will be a banner year for thee. But when I checked in the barn I noticed thee are low on feed for the chickens."

"Yes, I nearly used the last of it this morning."

"I can get more for thee. I'm headed to the Feed Store presently."

"Much obliged, but we're going in to see Duff, anyway."

"Then let me drive thee! Father would certainly wish it so. Our buggy's isinglass curtains will keep thee dry."

"You do so much already," said Ma. "But all right, Matthew. I'll take you up on that. Scrump, finish up your breakfast. I'll get my raincoat."

"Yes, Ma."

The rain kept falling all morning. It was gentle, but continuous. Matthew determined he would pick up our feed for us while we visited with Duff. Ma thanked him and, as she darted through the rain to the jail, she commented how glad she was she'd worn her hooded raincoat.

We carried in sandwiches and apple pie to Duff and watched as he eagerly ate them up.

"Any memories come back to you yet?"

"Nope," he told her matter-of-factly as he dug into a pie slice.

"Well, whether they do or not, you need to consider what Abe says. Speak for yourself, I mean. Just get up in that box and tell folks the way it happened. They'll believe you. I know they will."

"I can't, Ma. I don't remember nothin'."

"But Duff—" Ma began.

Just then the deputy arrived and interrupted. "Excuse me, Miz Armstrong. There's a Matthew Wellman in the office asking for you. Says he wants to see you right away."

The deputy opened the cell and led Ma and me to the office to speak with him. As it turns out, the Feed Store wouldn't let Matthew put the cost of the chicken feed on our account without speaking to Ma first.

She sighed. "Scrump, you stay with Duff. I'll be back shortly."

"Sure, Ma."

She left with Matthew and I turned to go back to Duff's cell.

"Oh, no you don't," said the deputy, blocking my way. "Minors ain't allowed alone with prisoners."

"Yeah, but…"

"Rules is rules. Either sit down or wait outside."

I chose to step outside. The rain had stopped, and I watched any number of rigs going past me. Before long, however, I noticed a woman lingering at a store window just down the sidewalk from me. She wore a raincoat with a hood, much like Ma's, and it hid her face. To my surprise, she hurried toward me.

"Psst! Scrump! Psst, it's me," she whispered.

"Sarah May?"

"Shh. I been trying to get my nerve up all morning. I want to go in and see Duff, but if anyone sees me, there'll be no end of trouble."

Suddenly, a plan hit me.

"I got an idea. Follow me, and just don't show your face."

I opened the door to go inside, but she held back.

"C'mon!" I whispered.

She pulled her hood over her head and followed me back inside where the deputy was tacking up new 'Wanted' posters on the wall.

"'Scuse me, Mister Deputy? Can we see my brother now?"

He turned to me as my heart pounded. But because her raincoat was similar to Ma's and her face was hidden, he led us right down the hall and into Duff's cell. Before Duff could speak, I put my finger to my lips, and he kept quiet. Once we were alone, she lowered the hood.

Duff had to keep himself from shouting for joy. "Sarah May? Is it really you?" he said as quietly as possible. "I can't hardly believe you really came."

"Of course I came," she said softly, falling into his arms. "How could I not?"

He held her, and she nestled her head on his shoulder. Then he raised her chin and kissed her on the lips. It was the first time I'd seen such a tender kiss. When their lips parted, he told her, "Sarah May, I didn't kill Preston. I swear to you I didn't."

"I believe you, Duff."

"Only...only why did you tell him? I told you it was a secret."

"What...what are you talking about?"

"Preston. About the runaways hiding on our farm. He said you told him everything and he threatened to turn us in."

"Oh, Duff, I never meant to tell him. He came to me and said he knew the Wellmans were part of the Underground Railroad, and he demanded to know if your family was involved, too. He grabbed my arm and forced it out of me. I'm so sorry, Duff."

"I forgive you, Sarah May. But there's more. Oh, how do I tell you this?" We waited for him to compose himself before he continued. "When we were alone in the clearing that night, Preston told me he was part of a secret group. The White Vigilantes, he called them. They go after runaways and lynch them. He even bragged about chasing a feller to our farm and lynching him right on our land."

Sarah May's eyes opened wide. I could see she was horrified. She put her hand to her mouth as Duff continued.

"I begged him not to tell anyone, but he just laughed. He said we were no good dirt farmers, called my Ma and Pa terrible names. That's when I punched him. He went down but he wouldn't stay down. He got up and came right back at me. I hit him again, and I mighta give him a bloody lip, but I swear that's all. I wasn't the one who used that hammer. I'd never think of doing somethin' like that."

Sarah May buried her face in her hands.

"Please don't cry, Sarah May. I don't lay any blame on you," he said, as he again took her in his arms.

I couldn't believe what I was hearing, and couldn't hold my tongue any longer. The suspense was killing me. "Then what happened, Duff?"

"After we fought, I hopped in our buggy and headed straight home," he said. "But it weren't long till I heard hoofbeats comin' up behind me, and someone—I don't know who—ran me off the road."

"Oh, Duff!" Sarah May said breathlessly.

"I hit my head pretty bad. Next thing I remember, I was home in bed."

"But Duff," I interjected, "it was me and the Wellmans that found you and brung you home. But I thought you didn't remember anything from that night."

"It came back in flashes here and there, till I finally recollected it and put it all together. I remember most everything up until I hit my head in the ravine."

"So...you been lyin' to Mr. Lincoln about not rememberin' a thing?"

"Don't you see, little brother? I had to. If they found out what happened between Pres and me, they'd just say I killed him to shut him up. And they'd still take the farm from us. Maybe even the Wellmans' farm, too."

"Duff, you have to tell your lawyers. We can't let you get hung!" cried Sarah May.

"Sarah May, my family ain't like yours. Our little farm is all we got in this world. If it gets taken away from us, what will happen to my Ma and Scrump?"

"But Duff, surely—"

"Sarah May, I'm begging you, please promise not to tell a soul. Just do this one thing for me. Please!"

"All right, Duff, I promise I won't tell a soul. You have my word."

"You too, Scrump. Promise on Pa's grave that you won't say nothin'."

"But Duff!"

"Promise me, dammit!"

"Okay, Duff. I promise. On Pa's grave."

Just then, we heard Ma's voice as she came down the hall with the deputy.

"Sarah May! What are you doing here?" she demanded, then turned to scowl at the deputy.

"I—I thought it was you comin' in, ma'am!" he mumbled, red-faced and fumbling to open the cell.

"Merciful heavens, does she even look like me?"

"No, ma'am."

Ma entered the cell. "Sarah May, it's a very bad idea you being here. I think you should leave. Now, please."

"But I only wanted to—"

"Now."

"All right, I'll go." She kissed Duff softly on the cheek. "Goodbye, Duff."

Ma waited till she was gone before she spoke. She frowned at me and asked, "Did you have something to do with this?"

"Don't be mad at him, Ma," said Duff. "It was my idea."

"Well, you should both know better. Her folks would be furious. We got to get back home now. Matthew is waiting to drive us. I'll be back tomorrow with Abe, so you rack that brain o' yours till you remember something, anything, Duff. I mean it."

"Okay, Ma. Whatever you say." He looked at me. "Remember what we talked about, Scrump."

"Okay, Duff. Don't worry 'bout me."

Sunday morning, Ma insisted on going to church before seeing Duff.

"We need to check in with the Lord," she told me when I said I'd rather sleep in. "We don't want Him to think we've forgotten Him," she explained.

So I dressed, hitched Paintbox to the wagon, and we headed off.

When we entered the little white church, Mrs. Hoffman was furiously pumping the pedals of the reed organ, from which a hymn wheezed forth. We settled ourselves into a pew just as the service began. It included the usual hymns, Bible readings, and one overly long sermon, which I had come to expect. Afterwards, folks continued to ignore us and flocked around the Metzkers. Sarah May looked over at me with a sad expression.

But it wasn't so much the folks avoiding us that bothered me that day. It was something the parson had said in his sermon, and I asked Ma about it as we set out to the jail.

"Ma, what did the parson mean when he said we got to 'pay our vow'?"

"Oh, he was preaching on Ecclesiastes. It means if you promise to do something, you must keep your word. Your Pa always said, a man's word is his bond."

"So then, a vow is a promise?"

"It is."

"And is it a sin to break your promise?"

"I suppose the Lord might consider it so. My, you certainly listened to that sermon today. I'm glad. It's a sign you're growing up."

When we finally arrived to the cell, Mr. Lincoln was with Duff.

"So nothing's come back to you? Nothing at all?"

Duff lowered his eye as he spoke. "No, sir. Nothin'."

We watched as Mr. Lincoln silently mulled this over.

"Mr. Lincoln?" I blurted out.

"Yes, son?"

Duff glared at me, knowing I was that close to spilling the beans.

"Oh, never mind," I said.

Just then, Mr. Walker arrived to the cell, followed by the deputy.

"Lincoln! Lincoln, I got news. I found him! I found Jim Norris."

"What? How?"

"I got to thinking how people gossip in this town. So last night I headed to the saloon and hung around to see what I could learn. Well, there was an old feller knocking back a drink at the end of the bar and yappin' about a poker game being run out of a hotel up in Rushville, over in Schuyler County. So I sidled closer and asked how he knew about it. And he says he learned it from a feller, name of Norris, who said he was headin' there."

"Did you tell the sheriff this?"

"Just now. He's ridin' over to Rushville to pick him up," he proudly concluded.

"What's this mean for Duff, Abe?" asked Ma.

"Well, it might buy him another day to regain some memory," he said, looking at Duff. "But it also puts more pressure on you to testify on your own behalf, Duff. I can try to discredit him when he's on the stand, of course. A witness who suddenly leaves town is obviously hiding something. But after all's said and done, it may yet come down to you. You need to give this some serious thought."

Later that day I went by myself to sit by Pa's grave, and I asked him what in the world I could do to save Duff. I listened closely, but never got an answer.

TWENTY-ONE

BY THE TIME THE COURT reconvened Monday morning, news that the second eyewitness had been found spread like wildfire and pulled in as many people as Charlie Allen's testimony had, or maybe even more. Curiosity seekers were lined up all along the walls. The humidity that plagued us still hung in the air, but now it was even stickier after the rain.

"The State calls Jim Norris," announced Mr. Fullerton after the judge was seated.

Norris approached the stand and took the oath. He wore tatty buckskin trousers, worn moccasins, and a threadbare shirt. His weathered face was unshaven, and his tangled brown hair looked like it had never met a comb.

The prosecution zeroed in on the night in question, and Jim's testimony tracked Charlie Allen's almost exactly.

"And after you and Mr. Allen saw the defendant attack Mr. Metzker with a hammer, what did you do then?"

"Well, Charlie tended to Pres and I ran after Duff."

"Why?"

"To try to stop him. But he got to his buggy and hauled his sorry ass out of there."

The judge frowned, and cleared his throat.

"Sorry, Your Honor."

"He left in a hurry then?"

"Yeah. He knew he done wrong."

"Objection," said Lincoln. "Conjecture, Your Honor."

"Sustained."

All in all, it was a damning corroboration of Charlie's testimony, and we all knew it by the end of Fullerton's probe. Things looked even bleaker for Duff now.

But it was Mr. Lincoln's turn.

"So, Mr. Norris, Mr. Allen testified that you and he left Mr. Armstrong and Mr. Metzker alone and wandered off to be with some other fellers. I'm just curious. What attracted you away to other fellers, other than the drinking, I mean?"

He hesitated. "Do I have to say?" he asked the judge.

"You do."

"They was rolling dice. You know, playing craps."

Lincoln's piercing eyes settled accusingly on the witness. "Mr. Norris, why'd you leave town even though you were set to testify?"

"I ain't under arrest. I just wanted to go somewheres and relax. All this court stuff makes a body weary. I got my dates mixed up is all."

"Where'd you go?"

"On up to Rushville."

"For what reason?"

"Well, I heard tell about a big money game goin' on at the hotel up there."

Mr. Fullerton stood. "Objection. Relevance."

"Mr. Lincoln, where is this going?" the judge asked.

"To the character of the witness, Your Honor. He was called to testify and left town to gamble."

"Noted. Now let's get back to the crime at hand," said the judge.

"Yes, Your Honor," said Lincoln and returned his attention to the witness. "Mr. Norris, whose idea was it to leave the camp meeting and head out to this whiskey camp?"

"Duff Armstrong's."

"And after a time, you say you and Mr. Allen went off to roll dice?"

"That's right."

"Was Mr. Allen at the craps game? He didn't mention that in his testimony."

"Yeah, he was with me alright."

"I see. And what did the two of you do next?"

"Well, we left the game when we heard Pres arguin' with Duff."

"And prior to this, had you seen the decedent arguing with anyone else?"

"No, sir," Norris said emphatically.

"So you heard someone arguing in the woods?"

"That's right. Pres sounded like he was in trouble, so we ran toward the clearing."

"And after you reached the clearing, what did you see?"

"It's just like I told Mr. Fullerton," he began, clearly annoyed with Lincoln's continued probing of his story. "Pres and Duff was rollin' on the ground, fightin'. We went to break it up, but before we could get to them, Duff ran. He took off in his buggy. When I got back to check on Preston, there was blood tricklin' down the side of his head, but it didn't seem that serious. Charlie and I offered to take him home, but he said no, he'd be fine. So, we got him to his buggy, and he drove hisself off. Never saw him no more after that. That's exactly what happened."

"You saw quite a bit, it seems to me. But how, I wonder? Being past midnight, without torches or lanterns, it was certainly pitch black in that clearing."

"Uh...the moon was full, so I could see plenty good. And I seen Duff Armstrong hit Preston Metzker with a hammer, and it don't make no lick of difference how many times you ask, *that's what I saw*."

Undaunted, Lincoln pursed his lips and kept going at him.

"You say my client left in a hurry, and Mr. Metzker insisted on returning home in his own buggy."

"That's right."

"But why didn't you two go with him? You knew he was wounded."

"His little buggy woulda never fit the three of us. 'Sides, I told ya he said he warn't feelin' too bad at the time."

"So when and how did you and Mr. Allen leave the whisky camp?"

"A while after Pres left, we hitched a ride back to town."

"With whom?"

"I dunno. Some feller from the whiskey camp. Didn't catch his name."

"But Charlie Allen testified he was a friend of yours."

"No, I'd only met him that night."

"So, this complete stranger, this good Samaritan, took you all the way into town and never once mentioned his name to you?"

"If he did, I forgot it."

"A convenient lapse of memory," noted Lincoln. "Especially since you recall everything else in such detail."

This brought an immediate objection from the prosecutor, followed by a reprimand from the judge.

Lincoln pressed on. "One last question. Are you by any chance left-handed?"

"What of it?"

"Just answer the question, sir," instructed the judge.

"No, I ain't."

"No further questions."

Norris left the stand after two hours of testimony and Mr. Fullerton rose to address the court. "Your Honor, the State rests."

The judge nodded. "Mr. Lincoln, you ready to begin your defense this afternoon?"

Lincoln creased his brow and considered. "If Your Honor would allow it, the defense prefers to wait till morning."

"He's had plenty of time to prepare, Your Honor," Mr. Fullerton complained, pressing his advantage.

"I was generous giving you time to locate your witness, Mr. Fullerton," said the judge. "I'll extend the same courtesy to Mr. Lincoln. Besides, the court has other matters on the docket. So, let's say we resume this Wednesday morning at nine o'clock. Does that suit you, Mr. Lincoln?"

"Thank you, Your Honor," nodded Lincoln, and Fullerton assented as well.

A short while later, the lawyers and Ma huddled with Duff back in his cell. Mr. Wellman and I sat and waited in the front office, as the sheriff worked silently at his desk. After a spell, Mr. Walker came out, explaining they had finished up and he had another client to meet up with.

"How do thee think it looks for Duff, Friend Walker?"

"Not too good, sir," he said as he hurried out.

Lincoln escorted Ma from the cell, and concern was written all over their faces.

"But if he simply refuses to take the stand," Ma was saying, "what's to happen to him, Abe?"

"I don't know, Hannah. We can't force him. But it just don't add up."

Right then, the deputy rushed into the door and spoke privately with Sheriff Dick in hushed tones. The sheriff rose and spoke to Lincoln.

"I'm afraid we got bad news for you, counselor."

Glancing over at Ma, he hesitated.

"Go on, Sheriff. What's happened?"

"Nelson Watkins has been murdered. According to my deputy here, a farmer found his old nag wandering along the road and discovered his body in a grove near Eagle's Rock. The deputy checked it out and says Watkins took a bullet straight through the gut, and at pretty close range, too. He bled out pretty quick."

"Good Lord," said Mr. Wellman.

"Why would someone shoot him in cold blood?" asked Ma.

"Hard to know, ma'am," answered the sheriff. "I imagine he'd made a few enemies at that whiskey camp of his."

"When I got to the scene," the deputy said, "I rolled Watkins over and checked his pockets. He had a wad of money on him, so it weren't a robbery. When I hoisted the body up to the horse, I noticed he done scratched something in the mud before he died. Kind of a hook and loop," explained the deputy.

"Can you take me there? I'd like a look of my own."

"Sorry, Mr. Lincoln," replied the sheriff. "Deputy's got to stay here and watch the prisoner while I got to report this to the judge and Mr. Fullerton."

"I know where Eagle's Rock is," I volunteered, jumping to my feet.

"Hannah, you mind if the young'un takes me out there to have a look? I'll bring him home in one piece, I promise."

"Well…just be careful, the both of you."

Mr. Lincoln and I went straight out. He hoisted me up onto Old Bob and then hopped on behind me and we rode off.

Eagle's Rock was nearly two miles away. The road there was winding and furrowed with wagon ruts from the recent rain. We approached a rock formation that towered overhead, and I pointed to it.

Time and weather had etched the stone in such a way that it looked like the wingspan of an eagle. Lincoln pulled on the reins and Old Bob halted. We hopped off and he went to the side of the road to look about. We soon found what we were looking for.

"I reckon this is the spot where he died," said Lincoln.

There was still some blood in the mud, and it did indeed look like a hook and loop had been scratched out by the dying man.

"I wonder what it means," he said, wiping the perspiration from his brow.

From my angle I saw it clearly. "That ain't just a hook and a loop," I said. "That's a J and a P."

Lincoln kneeled for a closer look. "I think you're right, son. It's a J and a P."

"What do you reckon he was trying to tell us?"

"Well, we know Preston's initials were JPM. Maybe he was trying to signal that the shooter had something to do with Preston, which means he must have seen his shooter. He rose and scanned the area.

It was then I noticed the glint of a shiny bullet casing a few yards away. I ran and brought it over to Mr. Lincoln.

"Well done, young man! A forty-five, it looks like. I'll deliver this to the sheriff, but right now, we better get you home to your Ma."

Riding toward home, I asked him something that had been on my mind for weeks.

"Mr. Lincoln? How long do you think I'm going to keep missing Pa?"

"All your life, I'm afraid, Truman. We never stop missing the people we love."

"Oh."

"You know, Truman, you and I are a lot alike."

"How do you figure?"

"Well, my own mother died just two years after our family moved to Indiana. I was nine years old at the time, same as you. So, I know something of how a feller your age feels about those things. My, I thought my world had come to an end."

"What was she like, your Ma?"

"Oh, she was very gentle and gracious. Her name was Nancy. Nancy Hanks. Her people were farmers from

Virginia, and she met my father in a little village where she was workin' as a seamstress like your ma. She was very soft-spoken, gentle. She loved singin' at church. My father always said I got my grey eyes and love of books from her."

"You still miss her?"

"Oh my, yes. The years don't take that away. But our parents live on in us, Truman, and will always be with us."

I took comfort in that.

Arriving home, I ran directly in to tell Ma all about the initials in the dirt and the bullet cartridge I'd found.

"You're quite the sleuth, young man."

"He is indeed," agreed Mr. Lincoln, and he thanked me as he made for the door.

"Abe, aren't you staying for supper?"

"I'd love to, but I got to bring this bullet shell to the sheriff right now. It could be important."

Later that night, I stood outside Ma's bedroom and listened to the sound of her weeping softly through the closed door. It made my heart ache. I had to find a way to help my brother. I just had to.

Twenty-Two

THERE'S SOMETHING ABOUT A GOOD night's sleep that helps us see the world differently, for I awoke at sunrise the next morning certain of what I must do. Tiptoeing from the house so as not to rouse Ma, I hurried to saddle up Paintbox, and galloped off as dawn broke on the horizon.

I got to Beardstown before any establishment had opened, and it looked like a ghost town. No one was on the sidewalks or streets. A lone cat skittered by as I trotted through town.

Arriving to my destination, I saw a curtain drawn across every window. Most likely, everyone was still asleep inside, but there was no turning back now. Tying up my filly, I slowly climbed the wooden steps and knocked at the front door of Jenkins' Boarding House.

A moment passed before I heard a stirring inside. Footsteps. When the door opened, it was Mrs. Jenkins, the usually affable landlady of the boarding house, clutching her dressing robe about her and scowling down at me.

"Land sakes alive! What's anyone doing here at this hour? Why, you're the little Armstrong boy, aren't you?"

"Yes'm."

"Well, you're waking the whole house!"

"Sorry, ma'am. But I need to see Mr. Lincoln. It's important!"

"At this hour? Oh, very well," she sighed. "Come in, come in."

She led me up the creaky staircase and down the hall, all the while continuing to grumble.

"It's too early for these shenanigans. I hope you have a good reason for this. I don't like waking my guests without a good reason."

We reached the door at the end of the hallway and she rapped softly so as not to disturb the rest of the house.

"Mr. Lincoln?" she said softly, then rapped some more.

When his door eventually opened, Lincoln stood barefoot before us. His feet were the biggest I'd ever seen on a feller. A long, striped nightshirt fell all the way to his ankles. His hair was mussed, and he yawned at us.

"What is it, Mrs. Jenkins?"

"I apologize for waking you, sir, but the little Armstrong boy here come to my door and insisted on seeing you," she said, stepping aside so I could step in.

She padded away down the hall, still muttering about the inconvenience I inflicted on her and her houseguests.

Mr. Lincoln invited me in and sat himself on the edge of his bed. He motioned to a nearby wing chair with flowered upholstery and I sat.

"I'm guessing your Ma doesn't know you're here."

"No, sir. I left before she was awake."

"Then suppose you tell me what's so urgent."

I bit my lip, carefully considering my words.

"Well… I think I gotta tell some stuff to someone and I'm thinkin' it should be you."

"Stuff? What kind of stuff?"

"Only…I kind of gave my word I wouldn't tell nobody."

"I see. Well, a feller's word is his bond, that's for sure," he replied.

"Yeah, that's what Pa always said. You think it's a sin for a feller to break his word?"

"A sin? Well, I reckon that would depend on exactly what was promised."

"Oh. Well, remember what you told Duff the other day? That you bein' his lawyer and all, anything he told you was confluential?"

"I believe you mean *confidential*. Yes, that means I can't repeat anything he tells me."

"Is you my lawyer, too?"

"No. I only represent Duff."

"But say I was to hire you. You couldn't tell nobody nothin' I say, could you?"

"I suppose not."

I reached in my pocket and took out Pa's nickel, the very one Mr. Lincoln had given me at the gravesite. "Is this enough to hire you?"

"That would more than cover my services," he told me, taking the nickel. "Now then, young man. Seeing as how I'm your lawyer, you'd better tell me what's eating at you."

So I did. I told him how I found the black feller hanging in the tree. I told him how, at Mr. Wellman's urging, my family had become part of the Underground Railroad, and how we'd hidden runaways in our barn. I even told him about the storm and how Isaac saved me from drowning in the creek.

When I was finished, he stared at me for an exceedingly long moment and then leaned forward, putting his elbows on his knees.

"Truman, is what you're telling me the truth? This isn't some kind of fabulation?"

"Huh?"

"A story. You're not making up a story, are you? I've known your Ma and Pa for years, and I find what you're saying to be…."

"You think I'm lyin'?"

"No, no! But why are you telling me this now?"

"On account of Duff."

"Duff? Does this have something to do with the trial?"

"Yes, sir."

"I don't follow."

"Gee, I don't know if I can tell you this next part or not. I swore to Duff *on Pa's grave* that I wouldn't say a word!"

"Truman, I knew your Pa pretty well. If there's something that I ought to know, something that'll help Duff, he would *want* you to tell me. And I assure you, it won't be a sin to do so."

So, I finally unburdened myself of Duff's whole story. By the time I got it all out, his jaw was agape. He stood and his long nightshirt billowed as he paced barefoot on the cold wooden floor. He ran a hand through his already mussed hair before turning back to me.

"You know, for a such a little feller, you certainly harbor a lot of big secrets. I mean, how long have you known all this?"

"Just a couple days. I learnt it when I snuck Sarah May in to see Duff."

"You did what?"

Then I confessed that to him as well.

"You know, I think I better take you home and have a serious talk with your Ma."

Just the thought of that filled me with fright! I had broken her confidence too, after all, and I protested mightily.

"Now, now. I'm your lawyer, remember? I wouldn't be much good to you if I couldn't present your case without getting you in trouble, would I? Now you run downstairs to the parlor and wait while I get into my duds. If you see Mrs. Jenkins, tell her I said to give you a hot breakfast, along with a plate for me, too."

When he came down, I was at the dining table enjoying a huge helping of Mrs. Jenkins' johnnycakes with honey. He smiled as he sat in the chair next to mine, and as soon as we'd had our fill, we rode away together toward home.

It was still early morning when we arrived to the farm. But I recognized Mr. Wellman's buggy sitting in front of the house. My heart jumped.

"Uh oh! Mr. Wellman's here."

"Good. I want to talk to him, too."

He got off his horse and started to the door, but then stopped when he realized I was holding back.

"Truman, it's going to be all right." He pointed to himself. "Lawyer, remember? You just keep still and let me do all the talking," he instructed, and marched us through the door.

Ma was in the parlor with Mr. Wellman when we entered. They both stood.

"Scrump!" she cried out. "Where've you been? You had me worried sick. Matthew and Luke are out looking for you now. Abe, how did you find him?"

"The boy came to see me at the boarding house this morning, Hannah," said Mr. Lincoln as he removed his hat and stepped into the parlor. "Good morning, Friend Wellman. I'm glad you're here. What do you say the four of us sit and have a little chat?"

Puzzled, they sat and waited for him to speak. Abe joined Ma on the settee and set his hat on a table.

"It's like this, Hannah. Truman here has hired me as his lawyer. At a very early hour, I might add."

"What? Scrump, why would you do that?" she asked me.

I stood mute.

"As his lawyer, I have advised him not to speak."

"His lawyer? Abe, what on earth is this about?"

He took a deep breath. "Well, I have it on Truman's word that your two families have been active with the Underground Railroad. Is this true?"

"Truman Joshua!" exclaimed Ma, her face flushing red with anger. Whenever she called me by my first two names, I knew I was in big trouble.

Mr. Wellman rocked back and cried, "Oh, calamity, calamity!"

"Well, that answers that," concluded Lincoln. "Then the two of you were…are abolitionists?"

"Abolitionists," repeated Ma, softly. "We never called ourselves that. Jack and me was both raised where there wasn't slavery. We never knew anyone who even owned a slave. But the more we heard about lynchings going on right here in Cass County, the more concerned we were. Then Scrump finding that poor soul hanging in our tree, well, that changed everything. It was as if evil itself had come knocking at our door. We may be simple folk, Abe, but we knew we couldn't look away any longer. So yes, I suppose we *are* abolitionists."

"You realize, of course, the penalties for assisting runaway slaves are severe. The law in Illinois is very clear about that."

"Bah! The law is unjust, ungodly," scoffed Mr. Wellman.

"What about Duff? Did he know about this?"

"Well, we couldn't help runaways without telling the boys. Why? What's this got to do with Duff?"

"Hannah, Duff told Truman that Preston Metzker had found you folks out, which is why Duff fought with him that night. Preston was threatening to turn you all over to the law."

"Merciful heavens..."

"That's why Duff refuses to take the stand. If any of this came out at trial, I'm afraid they would not only convict him, but go after the two of you as well. You could lose everything. So you see, Duff's protecting *you*, Hannah, even if it means he has to hang for it."

"Oh, that poor lad," lamented Mr. Wellman. "This is all my fault. I never should have gotten thee and thy family involved, Friend Hannah! What have I done?"

"Now, Thomas," consoled Ma, rising to pat his shoulder. "We knew what we were getting into. You can't blame yourself."

Lincoln smiled at them.

"You have bravely stuck to your own convictions. Acting on your conscience is a noble thing, which is certainly rare in these times, and I admire you both for it. I assure you, Friend, you may depend on my complete confidence." He leaned back on the settee and casually crossed one leg over the other. "The question now is, how do we get Duff out of this without revealing your secret?"

"What can we do, Abe?"

"I don't rightly know, Hannah. But I'll have to think of something without putting Duff on the stand. I may have been foolhardy to promise I'd get him home," he admitted. "I never expected to run into a situation like this."

"Jack believed in you, Abe. So do I. Just do your best."

After he had said goodbye to Ma and Mr. Wellman, I walked him back to his horse.

"You were right to come to me, son. Thank you for trusting me."

I stopped as we reached Old Bob. "Mr. Lincoln," I said, "you think Duff is gonna hang?"

"Now don't you worry about that. That's my job. You just be good to your Ma," he advised as he reached for the saddle horn. "None of this is easy for her."

"Yes, sir. I will."

After he rode away, Mr. Wellman told me he thought I had done a very wise thing in going to see Mr. Lincoln.

"The truth shall make thee free," he quoted.

While it was comforting to hear, it didn't make me worry any less about Duff's fate.

TWENTY-THREE

AFTER MR. LINCOLN'S DEPARTURE, WE said goodbye to Mr. Wellman. He'd promised to pick us up for trial early the next morning. But we had no sooner returned to the house when I coughed. Not softly, but painfully. This triggered Ma's maternal instincts.

"I hope you didn't take a cold being out so early this morning," she said.

"You mad at me, Ma?"

"No, Scrump. You did what needed to be done and I'm proud of you," she admitted as she caressed my cheek. "My, you feel warm! And your face is flushed, too. Maybe you should head back to bed for a while."

"Aw, Ma."

"Don't argue. March, young man!"

After I'd been sleeping for nearly an hour, she came in to check on me. I was still warm. If I hoped to be there when Mr. Lincoln started Duff's defense, she warned, I had to stay down. Thus, my confinement continued the rest of the day. Come evening, I was bored something awful. At times like that, imagination is a child's best friend and, in this instance, a fateful friend at that. With scraps of paper, I fashioned myself little soldiers to travel across my bedding in pursuit of an unnamed enemy. From under my blanket, my knees created mountains which mysteriously rose to block the pursuing forces. The same mountains just as mysteriously disappeared, and the fleeing army had to turn and fight. My men fought valiantly, falling one by one till only generals were left and resorted to hand-to-hand combat. The last man standing was hailed by a cheering throng of one, namely, me.

But now I was weary of battle and sought some other kind of activity.

The Old Farmer's Almanac for 1858. I'd hardly picked it up since this whole nightmare began.

I leaned over to retrieve it from my side table and opened it to a page I'd never paid much attention to before, a page that listed Indian customs and words. I can't explain it, but just then I heard my father's voice, as plain as if he was in the room with me.

"Study up, old man. One day something will pop out of those pages that will change your life."

It was the first time I'd heard Pa's voice since he had passed away. I looked around, but he wasn't there, of course. I stared at the page and saw a listing of Indian moons, a romantic notion which sparked my imagination, so I decided to study them. I memorized as many as I could, until the significance of what I was seeing finally hit me. I couldn't believe my eyes. It could mean the difference between life and death for Duff.

Though I was excited, I somehow drifted off to sleep. I awoke the next morning to Ma sitting on the bed to gauge my temperature. She pronounced me "well enough" and got me ready for the trial. I strongly suspected she wanted me with her as Duff's defense began. Besides, with no one to watch me at home, it was just as easy to bring me along so she could keep an eye on me, especially after my recent exploits.

After breakfast, Mr. Wellman arrived as usual to drive us to town.

When he saw me clutching the almanac he smiled. "Expecting to do a little reading, are thee?"

"Yes, sir." I wasn't sure if I should say any more, but I decided it would be better to talk with Mr. Lincoln first. Best not to get their hopes up, I thought, although mine were soaring.

After bringing yet another clean shirt to Duff, we left for court. The courtroom was once again overflowing with onlookers and the humidity was worse than ever for that time of year.

"He ain't got a prayer," I overheard a feller saying as we passed to our seat.

"Even if he does," answered the other, "that's about *all* he's got."

Soon as Mr. Lincoln entered with Duff and took his place at the defense table, I leaned over the railing and tapped his shoulder.

"Yes, Truman? What is it?"

"I gotta show you somethin'! It's in here, in my almanac."

As I held the little book out to him, he fumbled for his glasses, slipped them on, and studied the page I indicated. Then he showed it to Mr. Walker.

"Well, whaddya know," whispered Walker. "How you going to get this in the record?"

Lincoln lifted a sly eyebrow. "I've got an idea."

"All rise!"

We all stood for the judge and watched as he settled back onto his chair before the rest of us were seated.

"Good morning, all. Mr. Lincoln, are you ready to present your defense?"

"I am, Your Honor. But, er, something came up just before you got here. If it please the court, I need one very short moment before we begin."

"Very well, I'll grant you five minutes."

Lincoln conferred briefly with Mr. Walker, and then stood to consult quietly to me and Ma.

"Hannah, Truman just gave me something crucial to the case. It needs to go into the court record, but I need witness testimony to get it in. Would you allow me to put Truman on the stand?"

She looked at him, clearly taken aback, but he didn't wait for her answer.

"Hannah, you need to trust me on this. Truman, would you be willing to go up there and answer a couple of questions for me? It'll help Duff."

Glancing up at Ma, who gave me a slight nod, I answered, "You bet."

"Good boy. But only answer what I ask you, understood? Don't say anything else," he instructed.

"Okay."

Mr. Lincoln turned to the judge. "Ready, Your Honor."

"Call your first witness."

"The defense calls Truman Armstrong to the stand."

A soft babble echoed through the crowd. Duff's eyes grew wide. Mr. Walker, smiling, sat back to watch while Mr. Fullerton leaned over and whispered to his paper-shuffling associate. Mr. Lincoln signaled me with a nod of his head, so I stood and moved slowly toward the witness box like a man condemned.

The judge encouraged me. "Step up, son. Don't be nervous. We're all friends here. You're not scared of me, are you?"

"Well, a little," I said.

Most folks in the courtroom chuckled, and I felt my face flush.

"I've got grandchildren your age, and they're not scared of me. Step on up here, young feller," he coaxed.

I stepped up into the box and sat on the chair, my feet dangling above the floor. The bailiff approached with the Bible.

"I'll handle this, Silas," said the judge, shooing him away. He leaned over to me. "Now, Truman. You know the difference between the truth and a lie, don't you?"

"Yessir."

"Well, what's important up here is that you tell *only* the truth. Is that clear?"

"Yes, sir."

"Good man! Your witness, Lincoln."

Mr. Lincoln's grey eyes smiled at me, putting me more at ease.

"Why don't we begin by having you state your full name and age for the record?"

"My name's Truman Joshua Armstrong, but everybody calls me Scrump," I began.

The spectators tittered again.

"And how old are you, Truman?"

"Almost ten."

"Now as court began this morning, you handed me something. Will you tell everyone what that was? And speak loudly so everyone, including Mr. Fullerton, can hear you."

"*The Old Farmer's Almanac for 1858.*"

"And is this it?" he asked.

"Your Honor, really!" bellowed Mr. Fullerton, his voice dripping with sarcasm. "Would the defense care to introduce us to *McGuffey's Reader* as well?"

"Is that an Objection?" admonished the judge.

Mr. Fullerton shook his head with chagrin and sat down again.

"Let the record show that Mr. Fullerton had no objection."

Mr. Lincoln handed me the book. "Truman, tell the court what you showed me in the almanac this morning."

"Oh. Well, there's a part about Indian names for full moons. It has all the dates for the year. September's the Full Corn Moon, on account o' that's when corn is ready for harvest. October's the Hunter's Moon because it's good to hunt by. November's the Frost Moon, 'cause that's when winter comes on."

"Judge, must we endure a lunar lesson?" Fullerton piped up.

"I want to see where this is going. Out of order," said the judge, and the prosecutor sat. "Tell me, young man, what does all this moon business have to do with this case?"

"Well, sir, the almanac says the Crow Moon is in March."

"And what day of the month did the full Crow Moon appear in March, Truman?" prompted Lincoln.

"Not till the twenty-ninth."

"The twenty-ninth—a full two weeks *after* the murder. And on the thirteenth, the day of the murder, what kind of moon was there that night?"

"Oh, there wasn't no moon at all that night. On account of it was a New Moon."

"No moon at all on the thirteenth, the very night of the murder."

Then Lincoln turned and addressed the jury. "Both of the State's eyewitnesses have testified to seeing the murder by the light of a full moon. Yet, according to the almanac, there was no full moon that night, so it would have been impossible to see anything in the pitch darkness."

The court broke into an uproar.

"Order! Order!" the judge shouted, banging down his gavel.

Mr. Fullerton jumped to his feet. "Your Honor, I object!"

"What's the objection?"

"How do we even know that the almanac is accurate? Granted, it's a charming compendium of folk sayings, old wives' tales, humorous anecdotes, and questionable weather predictions. But it's certainly not a scientifically authenticated text," he argued.

The judge ordered Mr. Fullerton to sit. "Go on, Mr. Lincoln."

"I can assure you, Mr. Fullerton, that no one disputes the veracity of the almanac when it comes to the phases of the moon. It's a scientific fact that the moon cycle repeats approximately every twenty-nine days. I wonder how many folks here consider this cycle before planting their crops?"

He had intended it as a rhetorical question, of course, but the courtroom spectators didn't take it that way. One by one, they raised their hands in assent until at least half the people—including some in the jurors' box—attested to the fact.

Mr. Fullerton surveyed the roomful of hands and his face fell.

Lincoln smiled. "Thank you, Truman," he said, concluding his examination of me.

"Mr. Fullerton, do you have any questions for the boy?"

"No, Your Honor," he sighed. "None."

"In that case, you may step down...Scrump. You did just fine."

Mr. Lincoln smiled at me as I passed, and then turned to the judge. "Your Honor, at this time I ask that this almanac be placed into evidence."

"Objection."

"On what grounds?"

"Your Honor," said Mr. Fullerton. "According to Rules of Evidence in the State of Illinois, 'only facts *from eyewitness testimony* are admissible at trial.' That would certainly preclude any other source, such as an almanac. While I commend the boy's reading prowess, I insist that *The Farmer's Almanac* is not admissible as evidence. The State vigorously objects to Mr. Lincoln's motion, and urges you to strike young Mr. Armstrong's testimony from the record, and instruct the jury to disregard any reference to the almanac."

Lincoln exploded. "Tarnation, Fullerton! There was no moon that night! The facts are clear!"

"The state of Illinois judicial rules are clear as well, Mr. Lincoln," retorted Fullerton, "and they're the same for all trials, including this one. The court's highest duty is to assure that the judicial rules are followed and not bent to your will or that of any one individual."

"Mr. Fullerton," interjected the judge sternly, "Do not presume to speak for this court. I am well aware of the judicial rules and how to apply them."

"I meant no disrespect, Your Honor."

"Well, Mr. Lincoln? Mr. Fullerton raises a good point. Our judicial rules, the rules that determine how we conduct trials, clearly say that evidence may only be entered through eyewitness testimony. Our young friend Truman obviously loves his brother very much, but he was not an eyewitness to any events relating to the crime. I am inclined to sustain Mr. Fullerton's objection unless you have an argument to convince me otherwise."

"But the almanac, Your Honor! The information on the moon phases is indisputable."

"Yes, the almanac. Unfortunately, the rules don't allow content from *any* outside sources to be admitted into evidence—in any trial. It's as simple as that."

While I was trying to follow the legal intricacies, the stricken look on Ma's face and Mr. Wellman's closed eyes told me all I needed to know. Duff's defense was in serious jeopardy.

Lincoln ran a hand through his bushy brown hair, and I could see he was scouring his brain for something, anything to counter Fullerton's argument.

Then his eyebrows shot up and I knew he had it.

"Your Honor! I invoke... judicial notice. Yes," he said as though to solidify this thought, "judicial notice!"

"What!?" spat Fullerton.

"Your Honor, if I'm not mistaken," continued Lincoln, "according to the State's own rules, which Mr. Fullerton so greatly admires, a fact may be introduced into evidence if the truth of that fact is so notorious, so well known, so authoritatively attested to, that it cannot be reasonably doubted. Agreed?"

The judge leaned into his bench and rested on his elbows. "I'm interested to see where you're headed with this, Lincoln. Continue."

"Your Honor, I submit that the facts about the lunar cycle *are* provided by an authority, as the rules require. That authority being *The Old Farmer's Almanac for 1858*. Why, the wide use of the almanac in this community alone attests to its authority. The almanac meets the Rules of Evidence because it presents facts that cannot be reasonably doubted. I implore you, Your Honor. You must enter the almanac into evidence so it may be considered by the jury. Fairness demands it, justice demands it."

Fullerton rushed to the bench. "Your Honor, what Mr. Lincoln suggests is entirely without precedent. You yourself just said that the Rules of Evidence are perfectly clear."

"Yes, I said that," agreed Judge Harriot, which brought a look of relief to Fullerton's flushed face.

"But Mr. Lincoln raises a novel yet persuasive argument. It seems to me—that is, to this court—that if any evidence, such as a scientific fact, sheds light at trial, it need not come *only* from the mouth of an eyewitness but, as the rules themselves stipulate, 'from any credible and authoritative source.' Since nearly every farmer in this country relies on *The Old Farmer's Almanac*, this court deems it to be a credible and indisputable authority. Mr. Fullerton, I am sustaining your objection, but only part of it. The lad's testimony will be stricken from the record. However, I am overruling you regarding the almanac.

"Mr. Lincoln, your motion is granted. *The Old Farmer's Almanac for 1858* shall be entered into evidence. So ordered!" He rapped his gavel with a bang so loud it startled Ma and seemed to echo in my ears.

"What just happened?" I asked Ma.

"I'm not sure, but I think Abe just turned the tables," Ma said.

Following the admission of the almanac as evidence, Mr. Lincoln recalled Charlie Allen and, in turn, Jim Norris to the stand and asked if they wished to "reconsider" their testimony. Confronted with the new evidence, they conceded that maybe they'd been "mistaken" about the full moon, but it was the only point of their stories they would alter. They still maintained that, moon or no moon, my brother had killed Preston Metzker.

Soon it would be up to the jury to decide.

Twenty-Four

THE JUDGE SCHEDULED CLOSING ARGUMENTS to follow the lunch break.

"Your boy will be free by sundown," Lincoln assured Ma, as court went into recess. He had always tried to offer hope, but now he spoke with sure confidence, as if the conclusion were inevitable. He was on the cusp of victory, but he had one last hurdle to surmount – his final summation to the jury. And as had been demonstrated in the morning session, anything could yet happen.

As court reconvened in the afternoon, all eyes were upon the twelve men in the jurors' box. They had been there through every moment of the proceedings and their faces reflected the weight of the responsibility they had accepted. They gave the lawyers their full attention.

Mr. Fullerton was the first to address them. His manner was composed and confident.

"Gentlemen of the jury, good afternoon. You have sat here patiently for a good many days, and now it is almost time for us to hand this case over to you for your best judgment. Let's review the standings.

"The defense will no doubt tell you that the State's eyewitnesses are not to be believed because there was no moon that night. But the absence of a moon changes nothing about this crime. You don't need the light of the moon. You only need the facts. Sheriff Dick testified that Duff Armstrong had threatened Preston Metzker's life. And if that's not enough, we know Mr. Metzker ridiculed the defendant in front of others for not being good enough for his sister, accusing him of only courting her for her family's money. Cruel, perhaps, but proof of the animosity and anger that Mr. Armstrong felt toward Mr. Metzker.

"And then we have the night of the murder. The defendant goes to a camp meeting and lures the victim to a whiskey camp. There was an argument, so loud that the eyewitnesses identified the voices as Preston Metzker's and Duff Armstrong's. Investigating, they stood in close proximity as the two fought. When one of them fell to the ground, bloodied and beaten, they rushed to his aid. And what did Duff Armstrong do? He ran. Jim Norris chased after him, but the defendant continued to run. Why? Because he knew he'd done something wrong. He knew the victim was wounded, and still he fled the scene which in itself is evidence of guilt. Gentlemen, to see your way to the truth in this case, you need only look at the totality of the evidence, which points to only one person, William Duff Armstrong. So, take your time, consider carefully, and I am certain that in the end, you will return a verdict of guilty."

His summation now complete, Fullerton confidently returned to his chair.

The judge nodded to Lincoln, who rose slowly, approached the jury, and began with simple eloquence.

"Gentlemen of the jury, the law clearly says that a crime can be proven by one credible witness. The state says they have two such witnesses, but that's up to you to decide. Are the State's witnesses credible? One of them went missing at a key point in this trial. He fessed up to gambling the night of the crime, but only after admonished by the court to do so. Both witnesses testified that they were under the influence of alcohol that night and watched from a distance. And both say they saw my client fight with Preston Metzker. And they say they saw this by the light of the moon. They say they saw my client strike Mr. Metzker with a hammer blow to the head, by the light of the moon. They say they saw Duff Armstrong flee, also by the light of the moon. But as we now know, there was no moon that night. It was black as pitch in that clearing, and Charlie Allen and Jim Norris could not possibly have seen what they claim they saw—especially not from ten or twenty yards away. Yet, they came before you, swore to tell the truth before God, and testified that Mr. Armstrong committed this heinous crime—by the light of the moon! Heaven only knows their motivation. But whatever it is, it's a great injustice not only to Mr. Armstrong and his family, but to the Metzker family as well. Preston Metzker's father and mother, sister and brothers, have had to endure his untimely and tragic death, and they deserve the truth.

"Today, gentlemen of the jury, you cannot bring justice to Preston Metzker's murderer, who remains at large. Nor can you bring justice to his family, who seeks answers amidst their terrible grief. But today, you can bring justice to Duff Armstrong, who has been wrongly accused of this crime.

"So, I ask each of you to review the testimony and weigh the facts honestly, and to determine whether these eyewitnesses are credible. If you are honest with yourselves, you will agree that no one saw Duff Armstrong kill Preston Metzker—because Duff Armstrong did not kill Preston Metzker. So now, it is incumbent upon you, a jury of his peers, to set the record straight and restore his good name.

"You can do this by returning him to the arms of his widowed mother and his young fatherless brother whom you met this morning. You can do this by returning him to this community, where he is loved and respected. But you can only do this by first deciding that the accused is innocent. For the sake of justice, I ask you to return a verdict of not guilty!"

The courtroom was silent as Mr. Lincoln returned to his seat, and then the judge asked Mr. Fullerton, "Does the State wish to exercise its right of rebuttal?"

"We do, Your Honor."

Mr. Fullerton rose and returned to the jurors for a second bite at the apple.

"Gentlemen, Mr. Lincoln is correct in one thing and one thing only. All you need is a credible witness to prove this crime. Fortunately for you, and for the Metzkers, there is not just one eyewitness, there are two. Two witnesses who saw the crime and tended to the victim, who were as close to him as I am to you. Closer, perhaps. Two witnesses who told us what happened, each corroborating the other's testimony. Forget the moon.

Because in the cold light of day, the facts are clear. The defendant committed this crime. I trust you to return a verdict of guilty."

The judge gave the members of the jury their final instructions and dismissed them before adjourning the court. But it was still early in the afternoon, so most folks remained in their seats to wait out the deliberation. Lincoln told us a rapid verdict would indicate good news, but a longer deliberation meant there was disagreement amongst the jurors. My palms were sweaty, and my brow dripped with perspiration. I chalked it up to nervous anticipation and silently struggled to swallow against my increasingly sore throat.

In less than an hour the judge reappeared and called us to order. The jury had reached a decision.

Mr. Walker looked to Lincoln and, with a twinkle in his eye, mouthed, "Quick verdict!"

We watched the jury re-enter. My head began to ache, and I coughed mightily. Ma was so focused on the jury and the verdict that for once she didn't stop everything to look at me. I fought to focus my attention as the judge faced the jury foreman.

"Gentlemen of the jury, have you reached a verdict?"

"We have, Your Honor."

The bailiff carried the written verdict from the foreman to the judge, who read it and sent it back.

"The defendant will rise."

Mr. Walker and Mr. Lincoln stood alongside Duff, with Lincoln placing a fatherly arm around his shoulder.

"How say you, gentleman of the jury," Judge Harriot intoned, "in the matter of *The People v. Armstrong*?"

"Your Honor, we, the jury, find the defendant *not guilty*."

I could tell Duff had been holding his breath and I saw him exhale with relief. Mr. Lincoln embraced him. Several spectators broke into applause and some swarmed around me and Ma with good wishes and congratulations. Duff broke away from Lincoln and bounded for Ma's arms, then reached down to hug me.

"I owe you one, little brother!" he told me. But then my knees went wobbly, and as I looked up into his joyful eyes, my world went black. I fell to the floor.

Ma screamed, and Duff lifted me from the courtroom floor to lay me on the bench where I'd been sitting. The crowd squeezed in, but the bailiff ordered everyone back. Ma brushed my hair back and Mr. Lincoln even slapped my cheek to revive me.

The judge sent the bailiff to fetch Doc Parker, who arrived quickly. He only had to touch my brow to know it was serious.

"This child has a raging fever!"

He ordered me removed immediately, but judged I was too ill to make the journey back to our farm. Mr. Lincoln volunteered his room at Mrs. Jenkins' boarding house. After carrying me there in Mr. Wellman's buggy, Mr. Lincoln scooped me up in his strong arms, carried me up the stairs, and laid me in his own bed. He stood with Ma and watched as the doctor continued his examination.

"Has he been ill lately?"

"A low fever yesterday. I kept him in bed, but he seemed fine this morning. He told me his throat was sore this afternoon. I thought it was just a cold."

Doc took my pulse, put his stethoscope to my chest to listen to my lungs and heart, and slipped a thermometer under my tongue.

"What's wrong with him, Doctor? What is it?"

"There's a fancy medical term for it, but I believe it's what we call 'walking pneumonia.' It starts with mild symptoms like a cold, but it can be ferocious if not caught early."

"How serious is it?"

He removed the thermometer.

"His temperature's almost one-oh-five. That's far too high for a child this age."

"What should we do?"

"This is the time of day temperatures soar, Hannah. Use a cool cloth on his forehead. and try to get water down him. The best you can do right now is keep him comfortable, while he sweats this out, and hope for the best."

"He'll…he'll recover, won't he, Doc?" Ma asked.

The doctor hesitated. "We'll know by morning. It's all up to your boy. Now, now," he consoled her when he saw how his words had landed on her heart. "He's a little fighter, this one. You just keep him comfortable. I'll be back first thing in the morning."

As I laid on the cool white sheets, fighting the ache in my bones, I struggled to make sense of what little I heard. My fevered brain was giving way to delirium and I soon drifted from consciousness.

I awoke to find myself in a lonely forest full of tall trees towering high above me. An eerie wind rattled through the treetops, and I glimpsed someone climbing above me in the high branches.

I squinted against the sun's gleam to see the climber, a feller who turned back to me and released something from his great hand. Two small yellow finches. They flew down and playfully encircled me. Soon, I was chasing behind them, running along the soft forest floor in the dappled sunlight.

Onward I ran until the birds rounded a bend and vanished. They had led me to a dark, shadowy glen where the air was cool and the sky was black. Then I saw a gentle flicker and turned to discover a campfire.

The heat of the fire's dancing flames slowly warmed my face, causing beads of sweat to flow down my cheeks like tears.

"Hello there, son! I been waiting for you. What took you so long?"

"Pa!"

It was my father. Alive and real as life, and he was sitting before the fire, wearing his old overalls and his favorite red flannel shirt. His eyes gleamed in the firelight.

I ran to him and he folded his big arms about me. I nestled my head against the soft flannel shirt.

"Pa! Pa, I miss you so much. I thought I'd never see you again."

"Why on earth would you think that, old man? Why, I been with you every single day."

Patting my tears with his bandana, he invited me to sit.

"We been havin' some real tough times, Pa."

He nodded. "Yes, but you'll get through it. Your Ma and Duff, they're counting on you. You know, in a way, I envy you. Your life is so rich and full. You have a lot to go back to."

"Go back? But I want to stay here with you."

A voice echoed from the woods.

"*Fight as hard as you can, Truman. I'm right here with you.*"

"You hear that, Pa? Someone's calling to me."

"Yep. That'd be your Ma," he said. He poked a branch into the campfire. "Looks like the fire's almost out. You got to go now, son. It's time."

"But I don't want to."

"Sure you do! You just do what Abe says, understand? Be sure to read your books. You get to readin'."

"What books, Pa? Pa!" I shouted as he faded into darkness.

My eyes opened slowly. I looked about the pleasant room where morning sunbeams danced on flowered wallpaper. Mr. Lincoln leaned over me and wiped my brow with a cool cloth.

"Where am I?" I asked weakly. "Where's Pa?"

"Hannah, he's awake!" Placing a hand on my brow, the familiar grey eyes looked down on me and smiled. "You're fine, son. We're all here with you."

Ma hurried to my bedside and knelt down, lifting a cup of cool water to my lips.

"Scrump, honey? I'm right here," she said, tenderly stroking my damp hair.

"What happened to me?"

"A fever. But you're going to be okay now."

I sipped again as Duff stepped into view, the sight of his grin as welcome as the soothing water on my parched throat. His pesky hair fell forward as he gazed down on me.

"Hey there. Boy, you had me plenty scared, little brother."

"Duff, you're free!"

"He surely is, son," Lincoln reported happily. His sparkling eyes were edged with dark circles from lack of sleep. I later learned that he had stayed with me throughout my night of crisis, never leaving my side. He hadn't even given a thought to contagion, though he himself was on the verge of collapse from sleeplessness and stress.

"Then it's just like in the story," I said with wonder.

"What story's that, Scrump?"

"The story about Mr. Lincoln, Ma. He did just like you said. He put the two little birds back in their nest."

"Yes, Scrump, he did. He certainly did!"

My strength returned and the next day I was able to go home, where Ma made good on her promise. She took the brass key from her apron pocket and wound the grandfather clock. Its ticking greeted us like a long-lost friend, and soon we heard its sonorous chime heralding the hour and Duff's return home.

Twenty-Five

THREE DAYS LATER, IT WAS my tenth birthday, and after we'd had our dinner, we had a celebration. Mr. Lincoln was there, and all of the Wellmans, and of course, Ma and Duff.

Soon we all squeezed around our little table for birthday cake. Everyone sang loudly and off-key, and Ma held up a candle for me to blow out, for fear of spreading any lingering germs on Mrs. Wellman's famous chocolate confection. Then I opened my presents. Rebecca had drawn me a picture of Suzy and Marianne, and Duff gave me a new pair of stockings.

"To go with them new shoes," he boasted.

But my eyes popped when Mr. Lincoln presented two packages to me wrapped in brown paper.

"Since you share my love of books, I am giving you two of my favorites. Open this one first," he said, handing me the smaller of the two packages, which I immediately tore into.

It was a copy of *Robinson Crusoe*.

"I've read it myself many times. It's a wonderful adventure story. I think you'll like it," he explained. Then he handed me the second package.

I unwrapped it. Its cover was rich, glossy brown leather, its pages edged in shiny gold. I had never seen such a fine book as this. On the spine was the title *Kent's Commentaries*.

"I know it's over your head, but just hold onto it. Justice James Kent wrote his commentaries on American law some thirty years ago. Whenever you feel ready to read it, maybe you'll see why it's my favorite law book. I first read it when I was nineteen."

I stared blankly at Mr. Lincoln's eyes as I tried to figure out what this had to do with me.

"Truman, I see in you a good mind and character. You are bright and curious, you have an affinity for the written word, and you certainly retain your facts. Don't get me wrong. Farming is a fine livelihood, and I admire it greatly. I come from farm people myself. But I've been thinking that as you grow and begin to consider your life's vocation, you may wish to give some thought to becoming a lawyer."

"A lawyer? Me?"

"He's sure got the mouth for it," offered Duff and everyone howled, but no one louder than Mr. Lincoln.

"You really think I could be a lawyer someday?"

"Well, you keep this book for a spell. When the day comes, crack it open and, well, I think you'll find your answer."

Not long after the last cake crumb was consumed, Mr. Lincoln rose and announced it was time for him to leave. He told us he was eager to get home to his family, and who could blame him after the weeks he'd so unselfishly given to mine? Still, my heart dipped when I realized I might never see him again.

Ma hugged him tightly as she thanked him again, and we all followed as the two of them walked out the door arm in arm.

"Tell me, Friend, where will thee go next? What will thee do?" inquired Mr. Wellman.

"Well, Friend, from here I'll go pack up my things and settle up with Mrs. Jenkins at the Boarding House, then head directly back to Springfield. I'll kiss my wife and play with my three sons. I promised I'd take the boys fishin' when I get home. I'm not too fond of fishin', actually. I might have to keep the boys waiting. There are some fellers who want me to make a run for the Senate, and there's work to do if that's to happen. A lot of work. Come to think of it, I'd rather be fishin'."

"Well, fishing is fine, but we need men like thee in government, Friend Lincoln. Honest men who will speak out for what is right and just, men who will bring us together."

Lincoln rubbed his chin thoughtfully. "I think you're right. As it says in the book of Mark, 'If a house be divided against itself, that house cannot stand.'"

Mr. Wellman's mouth dropped open. "Imagine that. A lawyer who knows the Bible. If that doesn't put the fear of God into Satan, I don't know what will."

"Friend Wellman, I'm going to miss you," laughed Lincoln, shaking the old Quaker's hand.

Next, he shook Duff's hand, clapping him on the shoulder. "Duff, you're a good man like your father. But a word of advice? I'd stay away from whiskey camps if I were you!"

"Mr. Lincoln, I got no words for what you done for me. I'm just ever grateful to you, sir! I'll never forget it. Never."

Then Abe turned to Ma and their eyes met. "Oh Abe, how will I ever thank…" but then her voice cracked with emotion. She covered her mouth to stifle it. He took her hand in his and comforted her.

"Hannah, it was a privilege to help yours and Jack's family. You have some fine sons. But this isn't good-bye. We'll meet again."

Then he smiled and recited,

> *"Near twenty years have passed away*
> *Since here I bid farewell*
> *To woods and fields and scenes of play*
> *And playmates loved so well."*

"That's lovely, Abe. Who wrote it?"

"I did. I'll send you the whole thing when I get home."

"God bless you, Abe Lincoln."

Finally, he turned to me. Just like he had at our first meeting, he stooped down, and leaned his elbows on his knees to meet my eye. He grinned at me, but before he could speak, I had grabbed his neck and hugged him as if he were my own father. His arms slowly wrapped about me and he held me close.

"You live up to that name of yours, Truman. Grow up to become a true man."

He finally stood, and we watched as his long stride propelled him across the yard to his waiting horse. Once atop his chestnut steed, he raised his hand in farewell before trotting Old Bob away down the lane.

"There goes a good man," said Mr. Wellman, almost like a benediction.

It was a good hour later that the adults had gone back in the house, leaving Rebecca and me outside. The two of us were playing a round of ring toss in front of the house, as I recall. That's when I found a familiar-looking pair of spectacles on the ground. I figured they had to have tumbled from Mr. Lincoln's side pocket when he hopped on his horse to leave. I ran them in to Ma.

She decided that Duff should head out to catch up with Mr. Lincoln before he got too far along the road to Springfield.

"Can I go along, too? Please?" I pleaded of her.

Before answering, however, she eyed me closely, putting her hand to my forehead. It had only been a few days since I'd been in bed with fever. Although both my appetite and energy had returned, I could tell from the worry lines in her face that she was against it. Luckily, Mr. Wellman spoke up before she did.

"Oh, let him go, Friend Hannah. Fresh air will do the boy good," he said, and Mrs. Wellman agreed with him.

Minutes later, it was like old times. Duff was galloping off with Paintbox while I sat just behind him, hugging into him. He yelled and pushed the filly to make time against a headwind that had suddenly sprung up. I held on tight as the wind rushed past me, whipping my hair every which way. It was heaven.

"We're not going near fast enough," I yelled, and Duff took the bait.

"Okay, little brother. Hold on!" he ordered, and gave Paintbox a lively heel kick to her sides. Her speed picked up, and I was sure we'd catch up with Mr. Lincoln on the road before he passed through Beardstown on his way home. But we didn't.

We stopped by his boarding house only to be told by Mrs. Jenkins that he'd already checked out.

Duff figured we'd best stop by the Walker & Mason law office, in case Lincoln had made one last stop there. But according to Mr. Walker, he'd cleaned out his desk and said his goodbyes the day before. He hadn't seen him since.

So we trotted apace down Main Street, our necks craning for any sight of him.

"Look!" I shouted. "It's Old Bob up ahead at Mulgrave's Stable!"

We arrived just as Mr. Edwards, the smithy, walked Old Bob to a water trough out front. Edwards explained that the animal had thrown a shoe on Mr. Lincoln's way out of town, and he had just replaced it. He then pointed inside, where he said we'd find Mr. Lincoln.

Entering the stable, we followed the sounds of raucous laughter, and found him surrounded by a group of townsmen who were eager to hear from the famous Abe Lincoln after Duff's acquittal. Ever the storyteller, Lincoln was spinning them one of his colorful yarns when he caught sight of us approaching.

"Ah, the men of the hour! Duff, Truman! Come on over here and say hello to the fellers!"

Soon they were crowding around Duff to shake his hand in congratulations. They pretty much ignored me. Lincoln must have noticed, for he stepped up to me, "Didn't expect to see you so soon, Truman. What brings you boys here?"

I pulled his spectacles from my pocket and held them up to him. He hadn't yet missed them, and was glad we'd saved him the worry over losing them.

Duff was still the focus of everyone's attention, and Mr. Lincoln turned back to the crowd to join in their conversation. That's when I wiggled through the crowd and finally stepped away from them. I decided I'd just wait in peace till Duff's moment in the sun was over.

But then I glimpsed a figure furtively slipping in through a side entrance. I recognized him immediately from the trial. Jim Norris. I watched, as he slinked along the stalls, glancing back over his shoulder, looking this way and that, like someone who was not wanting to be seen.

My curiosity piqued, I decided to trail him. I hugged the shadows so he couldn't see me in case he looked back my way.

Jim found his way to a stall where Charlie Allen was grooming his palomino with long brush strokes. But when he saw Jim, he pulled him quickly inside the stall, pushing the door to the stable closed. I crouched down, listening as they spoke in hushed tones.

"What are you doing here? You know it ain't safe to be seen together," Charlie began.

"I'm worried, Charlie. Worried that they'll get us for lying in court like we done."

"Relax. Nobody's going to get us, you fool. Look here. The cowboy came by a few minutes ago and paid up. Look. Five hundred cash. That's two-fifty for each of us.

"Only two-fifty? After what we all done? Well, you tell him if he wants to keep me quiet, it's gonna cost him plenty more. Two-fifty is just a start."

"All right, I'll talk to him. But you should take your share now and go off somewheres. Wait a few weeks until things quiet down."

At that moment, an old tabby slinked by, raised its ratty back, and scratched at me. As I hit back at it, the stable door I hid behind swung open.

"Well, well. Look what we got here," Charlie smirked as he grabbed my collar and yanked me to my feet. "Looks like we caught us a little rat. Okay, what did you hear, you little snoop?"

When I stood mute, he shook me.

"C'mon, tell me before I smack it out of you."

"N-nothin'! Nothin', honest!"

"Don't trust him. He's lyin'," said Jim. "We gotta get rid of him."

"Let go of me!"

I hollered and kicked at them, but when Jim pulled out his Bowie knife and put it to my throat, I fell silent.

"Quiet down," he ordered, holding the knife below my chin.

"What are you doing?" demanded Charlie.

"We got to get him out of here. Are you with me or not?"

Charlie nodded.

"Good. Now this is what's going to happen," Jim said to me. We're moving you to my rig out back. You're going to get into it nice and quiet when we get there—or else I skin me a rat, got it?

I nodded silently, and was led to a rear door where Jim's old buckboard was standing. But when Charlie reached to lift me into the back of the wagon where a rope was waiting, I sank my teeth into his hand.

"Ouch! Damn you, you little—"

Charlie raised his fist and was about to strike me when Duff appeared. With angry force, he pulled Charlie away from me, and then landed a fierce blow to Jim's jaw. Charlie fought back, jumping Duff from behind and they scuffled in the dirt until Mr. Lincoln and a stable hand arrived to break up the fight.

"What's going on here?" demanded Lincoln.

"They was taking me away!" I cried out. "They was gonna kill me!"

"Aw, Scrump. We was just havin' some fun," began Charlie.

"No, you wasn't!" I pointed to Jim. "He put his knife to my throat, and they was trying to put me in the buckboard!"

This set Duff off again and he went for Jim a second time, but Lincoln held him back.

"Okay, Duff, that's enough now," he ordered. "What do you say we continue this discussion at the Sheriff's Office?"

The stable hand helped us get Charlie and Jim to the sheriff's. The two of them were cussing and struggling so much, the sheriff had to put them in hand irons and lock them in a cell till he could get to the bottom of things.

"Truman, would you tell Sheriff Dick what you told me on the way here?" prompted Lincoln.

So I repeated to him exactly what I'd overheard.

"Lying at trial is serious," said the sheriff, "but who's this 'cowboy' that paid 'em to do it? That's what I want to know. Do you have any idea who it was?" the sheriff asked me.

I shook my head.

"I have a thought on who he might be," said Lincoln. "I suspect he is the murderer of Preston Metzker. And old Mr. Watkins too. Only we'll need proof. Sheriff, I have an idea that may just lead us to this feller. Are you willing to trust me in this?"

"After the way you saved Duff's neck, I'd be a fool not to! What's your idea?"

Lincoln told him his plan, so the sheriff dispatched his deputy to set things in motion. Mr. Lincoln entertained us with stories as we waited anxiously, and a while later, the deputy returned.

"Found him, Sheriff. Told him just what you said, and he came right along."

Spurs jangling, Big Jake Perry, the slave hunter, strutted into the little office. "Afternoon, Sheriff. Deputy here says you got some reward money for me."

"We'll get to that, Big Jake. First, I got something I need to discuss with you."

"Ain't got time for no chit chat. Just gimme my money."

"What's the hurry, Mr. Perry?" interjected Lincoln.

Big Jake eyed him suspiciously. "Don't believe we've met, stranger."

"Name's Lincoln. Abe Lincoln. I was the defense attorney for Duff Armstrong here."

"Sheriff, what the hell's going on here?" demanded Perry.

"We're about to find out," said the lawman, ordering the deputy to bring in Charlie and Jim. At the sight of them, Big Jake froze. He turned to make a hasty retreat out the door, but Duff and the deputy blocked him.

"Hold on now, Big Jake. Let's just see what Mr. Lincoln has to say before you go on your way," said the sheriff.

"How about it, boys?" asked Lincoln of Charlie and Jim. "You want me to tell it? You can talk now or hang later. It's up to you."

The pressure was too much for Norris, who began to break. "Charlie! This warn't s'posed to happen like this!"

"Shut up, Jim."

"But I ain't gonna hang for somethin' I didn't do!"

"I said shut up!"

"Sheriff, I don't know what you're trying to pull," said Big Jake. "But I can tell you, I never seen these two before in my life."

"Lincoln?"

"Sheriff, the way I see it is this," he began. "Thanks to the testimony of Mr. Watkins who ran the whiskey camp, we know young Metzker argued that night with someone other than Duff Armstrong. A stranger. And now I know who that was. Guess I owe that as much to Truman as I do to Old Bob."

"Who?" asked the sheriff.

"Old Bob. It's his horse," I said.

"That's right," Mr. Lincoln went on to explain. "Old Bob threw a shoe right outside Mulgrave's Stable on my way into town. Good thing, too, as I was planning to be on my way to Springfield today. While I was waiting outside for Old Bob's shoeing, just resting my eyes, a jingling sound caught my attention. It was you, Big Jake. 'Course, I might not have remembered you at all if it weren't for those fancy silver spurs of yours. Truman pointed 'em out to me a while back. Well, I got curious, so I followed you on your way to see Charlie Allen. In fact, I watched you pay him out a large roll of cash."

"No law against payin' my debts, is there? I owed him fer shoein' my horse," shrugged Big Jake. "That's his job, ain't it?"

"I thought you said you'd never seen him before?"

The slave hunter said nothing.

"Keep goin', Lincoln. I'm listenin'," said Sheriff Dick.

"You see, Sheriff, Preston was capturing and lynching runaways that passed through the county. He admitted as much to Duff the night he was killed, so that much I knew. But what I didn't know was, who was the stranger Mr. Watkins had seen arguing with Preston at the whiskey camp? I believe it was that argument that led to Preston's death. And the feller he was arguing with was you, Big Jake."

"You're plum crazy," scoffed the slave hunter. "I never went to no whiskey camp and I sure as hell don't know what you're babblin' on about."

Mr. Lincoln continued. "To men like you, runaway Negroes are a commodity, a means to fill your purse—your bread and butter, so to speak. But you have to bring them in alive, and Preston was cutting into your territory."

"What I do is legal," insisted Perry.

"Unfortunately, it is. But Preston was lynching runaways and that was reducing your opportunities. You wanted him to stop. In his view, Negroes were a blight on the country, a pestilence to be eradicated. He'd rather see them hang than turn them in alive, and did his part to make that happen. I suspect you tried to strike a deal with him, offered to cut him in, something like that. But he was a wealthy and arrogant young buck who liked his own game too much to share in yours, so he turned you down cold, didn't he? That's when you decided he had to go. So, sometime after Duff had fought with him, you went after him yourself, going to the clearing and striking his head with Charlie's farrier hammer.

"My guess is, you thought you'd finished him off. He was probably unconscious when the three of you loaded him into his buggy and kicked his steed, sending his rig homeward. A clever way to dispose of a body, all nice and neat, I must say.

"But now, of course, you needed a story and someone to pin the attack on. Duff was the obvious choice. He'd already fought with Preston, after all, and everyone knew there was bad blood between them. So the three of you rode out after his buggy and ran him off the road into a ravine. You heard it crash, and thought he was dead. Then you paid these two to tell the sheriff that Duff attacked Preston and fled the scene. Only thing is, nothing works out quite like you planned. For one thing, Preston made it home and made it inside. Lucky for you, he passed out before he could tell his story. As for Duff, he fooled you, too. He survived the buggy crash, which was terribly inconvenient.

"It meant a trial, evidence, witnesses. But of course, these two were already in cahoots with you, so you continued paying them to perjure themselves in court and keep your name out of it."

Lincoln turned to Charlie and Jim. "I hope he paid you boys plenty. If you're going to hang with him, it should at least be worth your while."

"No! I ain't no murderer, I tell you, I ain't!" yelled Norris. "Tell him, Charlie. Tell him I ain't a murderer!"

"Of course you're not, Mr. Norris. Anyone with eyes can see you're just a snivelin' coward. And like a coward, you got cold feet and had to be dragged in to testify.

"And another thing," added Lincoln, turning to Big Jake. "You also shot Mr. Watkins. He was the only one who could place you at the camp that night, and you couldn't risk him coming out of his alcoholic stupor and remember that you were the stranger who had been arguing with Preston. But he still managed to scrawl your initials JP in the dust before he died.

"I'll wager if you look at his gun, Sheriff, you'll find it's a forty-five, the same caliber used to kill Watkins."

"Think you're damn smart, don't you, mister?" sneered Perry. "Well, all you got is a theory with no proof. And 'less he has that, Sheriff, you got to let us all go."

"You're right. I don't have proof," announced Lincoln coolly, taking everyone by surprise. Then he smiled and added, "But you do, Big Jake. It's in his pocket, Sheriff. I saw him take it out when he paid off Charlie at the stable. A gold money clip, the same one he stole off Preston Metzker's body right after he attacked him."

While the deputy held the slave hunter's hands behind his back, the sheriff searched Big Jake's left pocket and, just as Lincoln had said, there was the gold money clip engraved with the initials JPM.

Sheriff Dick arrested the three of them for murder right on the spot.

TWENTY-SIX

FOR THE SECOND TIME IN two days, I bade farewell to Abraham Lincoln. Only this time it was for the last time. He returned home to his family and his constituents. We exchanged a few letters before we lost contact with him entirely.

I held out hope that Isaac would return one day. But then tensions between the North and the South escalated into war and we never saw or heard from Isaac again.

My brother Duff, finally acquitted of the murder, married Sarah May. But two years later, when war came, he enlisted in the 85th Illinois Volunteers to fight for the Union. He served until 1863, when he became very ill in Louisville. At Ma's personal request, Mr. Lincoln arranged for his honorable discharge. He was brought home to our farm where Ma and Sarah May nursed him back to health.

When they got over the hurt of losing Preston, Sarah May's father and brothers welcomed Duff into their cattle business, and their sons are still farming and ranching in Cass County to this day."

As for the three murderers, they stood trial and were found guilty in the fall of 1858. Jim Norris, who agreed to testify against his buddies in exchange for a lighter sentence, got twenty-five years in prison for his trouble. Charlie Allen was sentenced to life without parole for his part in the murder, but Big Jake Perry was hung. It was a fitting end, I thought, for the ruthless slave hunter who had sold so many innocent souls back into slavery.

One evening, shortly after Mr. Lincoln had left Cass County for good, I was alone in the parlor with Ma when Duff called insistently for me to come upstairs. I found him leaning on the windowsill in our room, staring dreamily into the night. He pointed to a silvery full moon hanging low in the sky. Bathed in its cool pale glow, I joined him at the window and he comfortably slipped an arm over my shoulder.

"What's the Indian name for this moon, Scrump?"

"I don't quite remember," I said after thinking for a bit. "But I know what I'm gonna call it."

"What's that, little brother?"

"The Lincoln Moon."

Epilogue

IN APRIL 1900, WE WERE at the dawn of a new century and the country looked to its future. But we couldn't entirely escape our past, for the year also marked the thirty-fifth anniversary of the Union's victory over slavery.

Hannah, my beloved mother, had died peacefully the year before. But in her last precious hours, she spoke again of Isaac, recalling the debt she still felt to her for saving my life. When asked why she brought this up now, Ma told me that she still wished for her wedding brooch to go to Isaac.

"By rights it *should* be hers," she insisted. "I gave it to her once before, remember?"

To be honest, I hadn't thought of Isaac for years. We hadn't seen her since the day she left our farm, just before Duff's trial began. Over the years, we'd sometimes wondered what had become of her. We hoped she had survived the war, but eventually we ceased to mention her at all.

Now, I gently told Ma that I might never be able to find Isaac again, but she was undaunted. "There'll come a day," she predicted. "Hold onto it till then. I'm depending on you, Truman."

A few days later, Ma passed peacefully, with all of us Armstrongs at her side. After the funeral, I remembered her last request of me, so I found the little brooch in its box and resolved then and there to find Isaac.

Writing to courthouses all over the South, I sought any help they might offer. But the confusion of war and the tumult of Reconstruction had left few, if any, public records regarding slaves, freed or otherwise, and the answer was always the same: *We're sorry to inform you…*

I refused to give up on my mission. I was reduced to scanning random obituaries and assorted periodicals for any mention of a former slave named Isaac. But nothing ever turned up, until one day when I stopped to browse at a favorite news stall near my office. It seemed that every newspaper or magazine I picked up back then focused on either where the 1900s were headed, or on what the last one hundred years had wrought. Somehow the April issue of *Harper's Weekly* caught my eye, and as I flipped through the pages, one particular headline jumped out at me, *The Lady Conductor of the Underground Railroad.*

I quickly plunked my nickel down and hurried to the nearest park bench, where I sat and read with fingers crossed. The article was about a woman in Canada named Winnie Sinclair. Mrs. Sinclair, formerly enslaved in Kentucky, was sold at least four times before she escaped, traveling on the Underground Railroad," said the article. "Soon she became a 'Conductor,' disguising herself in men's clothing and returning South at great personal risk to guide others out of bondage. By following creeks and rivers through the free states of Illinois, Indiana, and

Michigan—sometimes pursued by slave hunters—she safely delivered dozens of 'Passengers' to freedom."

My heart leapt, as I kept reading. "Today, at the age of seventy, Mrs. Sinclair lives quietly in Emeryville, Ontario, where she enjoys gardening, quilting, and hosting friends for tea."

The writer never mentioned the woman traveling under an alias, but the more I thought about it, the more I became convinced that this had to be our Isaac. The facts matched up too perfectly to be a coincidence. Or so I hoped.

One week later, I stepped off a train in Emeryville, a small town in Western Ontario. Unlike the depot in Chicago, there was just one platform. There were no passengers scurrying like ants to their various tracks of departure. Nor were there any porters scrambling about and offering to carry my luggage. Evidently, in Emeryville, you carried your own bag. There were no cabbies either, so I took it as an opportunity to stretch my legs after my long ride. Receiving directions from the ticket clerk, I set out along a lane lined with green maples, which eventually led me to a bustling town square.

From there, it was pure good fortune, or maybe the hand of Providence, that the first person I came upon was an elderly Negro gentleman who was tying his mule to a hitching post. He looked at me warily as I approached him, but when I asked if he could help me find Winnie Sinclair, his face brightened instantly.

"Miz Winnie? Why, sure! Everybody in Emeryville knows Miz Winnie," he said. "You know her, do you?"

"Yes, we were friends a long time ago, back on my family's farm in Illinois."

"Well, then, she'll be right glad to see ya. She lives just off the square," he said, pointing the way for me. "Turn right at the corner, then keep an eye out for a blue cottage with a picket fence. It'll be on your left. That's where you'll find her, all right. And you tell her old Daniel sends his regards, won't you, sir?"

We shook hands and I headed off, following his directions. I easily found the blue house he'd described. Its fence was ramshackle, but the front yard was planted with gay flowers bursting with the colors of spring. I was about to pass through the gate when I spied a slight black woman in a yellow dress and wide-brimmed hat. She was stooped over a hoe and vigorously churning the dark earth along a row of vegetables in the side yard.

"Excuse me? I'm looking for Winnie Sinclair?"

She stopped hoeing, rose up, and turned to me. When she took off her hat to get a better look, I recognized her at once. Her hair was now streaked with white, but other than that, she was just as I remembered her. Isaac.

"I'm Miz Sinclair," she said with a familiar gravelly tone. "Who might you be, young man?"

I removed my hat and smoothed my red hair, which these days was increasingly flecked with grey. Now in middle age, I sported a handlebar mustache and was just two inches shy of my father's six-foot-two height. In other words, I was a far cry from the small boy she had known all those years ago.

"My name is Armstrong, Truman Armstrong. You used to visit our farm along Purgatory Creek in Illinois."

She gave me a quizzical look.

"Folks used to call me Scrump," I prompted.

"Well, Lordy be! You're not that sweet little white boy who gave up his shoes for me?"

"Yes, ma'am. You remember?"

She broke into a generous smile and her eyes twinkled as she looked me over from head to toe. "Now how could I be forgettin'? Those shoes stayed on my feet for years. Such a generous thing you done back then."

"You saved my life," I reminded her. "I wouldn't be here if not for you. It's so good to finally to see you again."

"And a downright pleasure to see *you* again. But what you doin' around these parts? You a long way from Illinois."

"Actually, I came here just to see you."

"You don't say." She brushed dirt from her hands and said, "Well, you sure found me, then. Come on inside with old Winnie. I got some tasty vittles and I reckon you're hungry for a meal after your journey."

I followed her up the creaking front steps and into her little home. It felt warm and inviting. A faded red braid rug covered the wood floor, and two patchwork quilts graced the backs of twin wooden rockers. Between the chairs, a lush green fern flourished in a chipped ceramic pot, and the nearby window was covered with indigo curtains. On the wall hung a framed portrait with another familiar face, President Lincoln.

Off to the left was a little kitchen with a wood burning stove and a small table covered by a dainty lace cloth. Two slat-backed chairs were on either side, and she invited me to sit. "You like tea, Scrump? Mind if I still call you that?"

"Yes, I like tea, and no, I don't mind if you call me Scrump. It reminds me of my childhood. So many memories, and mostly good ones."

She lit the stove and placed a tea kettle on it, then sat and shook her head in wonder. "My, my. How in the world did you find me?"

"Well, I read about you in a magazine. I never knew your real name, but when the article said you guided runaways dressed as a man, I was pretty sure it was you."

"And you found me jus' like that? You always was bright, Scrump. Nothin' ever fooled you—'cept maybe me," she said with a wink. Then she got up to prepare a pot of tea.

She returned with two steaming cups, along with fresh bread and homemade jam for us to share. As she sat back down she said, "You folks were so kind whenever I brought Passengers through."

"We were all happy to have you."

"What about that big brother of yours? I seem to recollect he was in some trouble."

"Well, he was wrongly accused in a murder. After spending weeks in jail, the case went to trial and he was found not guilty."

Then I told her about our time with Abraham Lincoln, and how he'd won Duff's freedom. The mere mention of Mr. Lincoln astonished her. She revered him and had never known anyone who had met him face to face.

When I'd finished the story, she was quiet for a moment, and then she shared a wise insight.

"So, he set your brother free, too. Just like for my people."

I had never thought of it that way.

"So what's he done with his freedom, your brother?"

"Well, after the trial, he came home and eventually he and Sarah May were wed and started a family. Later, he joined the Union army in its fight to abolish slavery. He told me he thought of you whenever they faced battle. He survived, but he became ill in 1863 and, at Ma's request, he was discharged by President Lincoln himself."

Then I told her of Ma's passing. Her dark eyes moistened and she took my hand gently in hers. "I'm so sorry to hear that, Scrump. She took care of me like I was one of her own. Not a lot of white ladies in those days woulda done that. I liked her, I liked her a lot, Scrump."

She released my hand and then filled our cups. As she poured, I removed the small black jewel box from my pocket and set it on the table before her.

"Oh son, you didn't need to do this, I—"

She fell silent when she saw the contents: Ma's treasured topaz brooch. It caught the sun's afternoon rays which showered golden sparkles across the room.

Then I admitted why I was really here. "Truthfully, the main reason I came was to bring it to you. I promised her that I'd look for you, and if I ever found you, I'd make sure it would be yours. She never forgot how you pulled me from the creek that night. She tried to give it to you then, but you left it behind."

I could tell she was pleased by the way she smiled at it. But she hesitated before she said, "Oh, I can't accept this. A good lookin' feller like you surely has a gal of his own to give his mama's treasures to. You need to give this to her, son."

"I've been married to my gal for some years now and, believe me, she has all the jewelry she could ever want," I insisted. She picked the brooch up admiringly and fastened it onto her yellow dress, her face beaming bright like the Canadian sun.

The remainder of our time together was punctuated with lively stories and happy laughter. We feasted on friendship, memories, and a delicious meal of fried chicken, biscuits, and greens from her garden. I learned that during the war she had helped guide Union troops deep into southern territory. And I told her that Ma had continued to take in Passengers after the trial and right up until the war began.

Over a generous slice of apple pie, she told me of her life after the war, how she had married a Canadian man and moved to Emeryville. She said with a sigh that he had died three years earlier.

"Elias was quite a feller, that's for sure. How I wish you two coulda met. He woulda liked you so much."

When the sun started to dip low in the sky I knew it was time for us to part. She rose to fetch my hat from her little parlor. "I'm right pleased you came to visit, Scrump, 'specially after all these years," she said with a smile as she dropped her chin to glance admiringly at her new brooch.

"Isaac...Winnie. If there's ever anything I can do for you..."

"I'll let you know. I promise."

I left her that day with a bounce in my step and a feeling that something had been lifted from me. Perhaps it was the weight of the past, but whatever it was, the visit had buoyed me. I walked briskly through Emeryville, admiring its peaceful streets as I hurried back to the station where I hoped to catch the evening train. I was eager to return to Chicago, to my work, but mostly to my lovely wife.

I reached the station just when the conductor was finishing his final boarding call. The train lurched forward as I stowed my grip overhead and settled into my window seat for the journey home.

Emeryville faded fast behind as the train rumbled away under the setting sun. Lulled by the gentle rocking and the rhythm of the wheels on the rails, I soon nodded off.

I don't know what time it was when I awoke, but from my window, I beheld a magnificent milky moon hanging just above the tree line.

I once read about an illusion that occurs when the moon hangs low like this on the horizon. It appears much larger than it really is. On that night, it occurred to me that this is a lot like Abraham Lincoln. He appeared larger than life on our horizon and drew all of us—my family, our town, and eventually our nation—along in his awesome tide.

Right after Mr. Lincoln's death, when fear gripped the nation and we were all heartsick with grief, I sought consolation from the book Mr. Lincoln had given me for my tenth birthday, James Kent's *Commentaries on American Law*. It was layered with dust, and the cover let out a creak as I opened it. There, on the frontispiece, I found an inscription in his own hand:

For Truman. Best wishes for all the years to come. Stay grounded in the law, but always reach for the moon.

A. Lincoln

Thus began my love affair with Lady Justice, which continues to this day. She has taken a backseat only to my childhood sweetheart, my lovely wife with the cornflower blue eyes, Rebecca Wellman Armstrong.

From the Author

In the spring of 2007, I read presidential historian Doris Kearns Goodwin's book, *Team of Rivals*. Her portrayal of our 16th President was so vivid that it left me with a thirst to know more about him. In the weeks that followed, I read eight biographies and fell in love with his humanity, his humbleness, and his mind. A number of the books I read mentioned *The People v. Armstrong*, one of his most celebrated cases, and it occurred to me that it might be an interesting story for a novel.

My story is highly fictionalized, but adheres to some basic facts of the actual story. Lincoln really did wrestle and defeat Jack Armstrong in New Salem and, in typical Lincoln fashion, made a friend of his competitor. Jack and Hannah took Abe into their home when he was a young man and treated him like family. Years later, when Duff was accused of murder, he took the case *pro bono* and won his acquittal.

The details of Preston's death follow the broad outlines of the murder. He had been at a whiskey camp after slipping away from a tent revival. There was an altercation among Preston, Duff and another man. Preston suffered a head wound and drove himself home and died the next morning. Duff was charged with the murder after eyewitnesses said they saw him do it by the light of the moon.

Lincoln eventually discredited the eyewitness by introducing the moon phases from the almanac. Beyond exonerating Duff, the victory was even more significant because Lincoln cleverly persuaded a court to admit evidence at trial that came from an "outside authoritative source." This was something new, and it eventually gave rise to expert and scientific testimony, which has become a standard tool in the arsenal of criminal defense lawyers and prosecutors. It was a change that eminently served the cause of Justice.

Although many of the characters are based on actual participants, the Armstrong family's involvement with the Underground Railroad is a fiction, as is the subplot with Wellman and Isaac. Scrump, too, is fiction. I decided early on that I wanted to portray his growing awareness of the racist society around him, a social system that condoned the enslavement of African-Americans. His question to his father inquiring after the 'n-word' echoes a conversation with my own father, Lee Nelson, when I was a boy and asked the same question. His response was much the same as Scrump's father. So I wanted to include that incident here, because I felt it demonstrated how Scrump was taught prejudice by the society's language and norms, and how his father sought to counter that in his upbringing.

Michael Price Nelson
Long Beach, California
September 2020

Acknowledgements

This book has been a long journey for me, and I sincerely thank all those who read, advised, encouraged, and supported me along the way. Of special mention is Janet Dulin Jones who cheered me on early in my process and offered brilliant plot notes. Paul Dinas was my editor and guiding light. He helped me refine the tone, tempo and realism of the story and I felt like I got a masterclass in writing from him. Kristi N. Gibson, my line editor, was diligent and helped sharpen the story's action. Rad Gaines, Esq., offered technical advice on trial law, courtroom procedure and decorum, and I am grateful for his input. Lisa Paden Gaines is a treasured friend who happily read a number of drafts, and her thoughts and support were invaluable to me.

For kindnesses great and small: Jeff Jones, for the solitude of his home in the California desert where I finished my first draft; Joel Bute, for editorial advice; Vicki Pearlson, Gina Gollop and Pamela Nelson, for comments and encouragement; Tina Ireland, for proofreading multiple drafts; author Claire Hoffman, for her publishing advice; Neal Luebke, my teacher and creative mentor, for his friendship and encouragement through the years.

Most importantly, I thank my spouse, Dale Von Seggern, who encourages me to write and supports me every step of the way.

About the Author

Michael Price Nelson lives and writes in Long Beach, California. He has written for magazines, radio, television, and stage. *The Lincoln Moon* is his first novel. If you would care to post a review of this book, or learn more about *The Lincoln Moon* and Michael's upcoming projects, please visit www.michaelpricenelson.com.

Made in the USA
Las Vegas, NV
12 November 2023